GODS OF GOLD

GODS OF GOLD

An Inspector Tom Harper Novel

Chris Nickson

This first world edition published 2014
in Great Britain and the USA by
SEVERN HOUSE PUBLISHERS LTD of
19 Cedar Road, Sutton, Surrey, England, SM2 5DA.
Trade paperback edition first published
in Great Britain and the USA 2015 by
SEVERN HOUSE PUBLISHERS LTD.

British Library Cataloguing in Publication Data

Nickson, Chris author.
  Gods of gold.
  1. Missing children–Fiction. 2. Murder–Investigation–
  Fiction. 3. Strikes and lockouts–Gas industry–England–
  Leeds–Fiction. 4. Great Britain–Social conditions–
  19th century–Fiction. 5. Detective and mystery stories.
  I. Title
  823.9'2-dc23

ISBN-13: 978-0-7278-8428-2 (cased)
ISBN-13: 978-1-84751-537-7 (trade paper)
ISBN-13: 978-1-78010-582-6 (ebook)

All Severn House titles are printed on acid-free paper.

Severn House Publishers support the Forest Stewardship Council™ [FSC™],
the leading international forest certification organisation. All our titles that
are printed on FSC certified paper carry the FSC logo.

Typeset by Palimpsest Book Production Ltd.,
Falkirk, Stirlingshire, Scotland.
Printed and bound in Great Britain by
TJ International, Padstow, Cornwall.

To Leeds. It's good to be home.

Sing a song of England,
Shuddering with cold,
Doomed to slow starvation,
By the gods of gold,
See her famished children,
Hunger-marked, and mean,
Isn't that a dainty dish,
To lay before the Queen?

Mammon in the counting house,
Counting out the money,
His lady in the parlour,
Eating bread and honey.
The worker on the highway,
Short of food and clothes –
God bless happy England!
And save her from her foes.

From, *A New Nursery Rhyme*, by Tom Maguire
Published in *The Labour Champion*,
November 11, 1893

And all the Arts of Life they changed into the Arts of Death
in Albion

William Blake, *Jerusalem*, Chapter 3

LEEDS, JUNE 1890

ONE

Tom Harper pounded down Briggate, the hobnails from his boots scattering sparks behind him. He pushed between people, not even hearing their complaints as he ran on, eyes fixed on the man he was pursuing, leaping over a small dog that tried to snap at his ankles.

'Police!' he yelled. 'Stop him!'

They didn't, of course they didn't, but at least they parted to let him through. At Duncan Street, under the Yorkshire Relish sign, he slid between a cart and a tram that was turning the corner. His foot slipped on a pile of horse dung and he drew in his breath sharply, the moment hanging. The sole gripped and he was running again.

Harper ducked in front of a hackney carriage, steadying himself with a hand on the horse's neck. He felt its breath hot against his cheek for a second, then plunged on. He was fast but the man in front was even faster, stretching the distance between them.

His lungs were burning. Without even thinking, he glanced across at the clock on the Ball-Dyson building. Half past eleven. He forced his feet down harder, arms pumping like a harrier.

As they reached Leeds Bridge the man leapt into the road, weaving between the traffic. Harper followed him, squeezing sideways between a pair of omnibuses, seeing the passengers stare down at him in astonishment through the window. Then he was free again, rushing past the row of small shops and watching the man disappear round the corner on to Dock Street.

By the time he arrived the street was empty. He stood, panting heavily, holding on to the gas lamp on the corner, unable to believe his eyes. The man had simply vanished. There was nothing, not even the sound of footsteps. Off to his left, a cluster of warehouses ran down to the river. Across the road the chimneys of the paper mill belched their stink into the air. Where had the bugger gone?

*   *   *

Harper had been up at Hope Brothers on Briggate, barely listening as the manager described a shoplifter. The man's mouth frowned prissily as he talked and rearranged a display of bonnets on a table. Outside, the shop boy was lowering the canvas awning against the June sun.

Harper scribbled a word or two in his notebook. It should be the beat bobby doing this, he thought. He was a detective inspector; his time was more valuable than this. But one of the Hopes lived next door to the new chief constable. A word or two and the superintendent had sent him down here with an apologetic shrug of his shoulders.

Then Harper heard the shout. He dashed out eagerly, the bell tinkling gently as he threw the door wide. Further up the street a man gestured and yelled, 'He stole my wallet!'

That was all he needed. Inspector Harper began to run.

He tipped the hat back and wiped the sweat off his forehead. The air was sultry, hot with the start of summer. Where was the sod? He could be hiding just a few yards away or already off beyond a wall and clear away in Hunslet. One thing was certain: Harper wasn't going to find him. He straightened his jacket and turned around. What a bloody waste of a morning.

He'd wanted to be a policeman as long as he could remember. When he was a nipper, no more than a toddler, he'd often follow Constable Hardwick, the beat bobby, down their street in the Leylands, just north of the city centre, imitating the man's waddling walk and nods at the women gathered on their doorsteps. To him, the decision to join the force was made there and then. He didn't need to think about it again. But that certainty shattered when he was nine. Suddenly his schooldays had ended, like every other boy and girl he knew. His father found him work at Brunswick's brewery, rolling barrels, full and empty, twelve hours a day and Saturday mornings, his pay going straight to his mam. Each evening he'd trudge home, so tired he could barely stay awake for supper. It took two years for his ambition to rekindle. He'd been sent on an errand that took him past Millgarth police station, and saw two bobbies escorting a prisoner in handcuffs. The desire all came back then, stronger than ever, the thought that he could do something more than use his muscles for the rest of his life. He joined the public library, wary at first in case they wouldn't let someone like him borrow books. From there he spent his free hours reading; novels, politics, history, he'd roared through them all. Books took him away and showed him the world beyond the end of the road. The only pity was that he didn't have time for books any longer. He'd laboured at his penmanship, practising over and over until he could manage a fair, legible hand. Then, the day he turned nineteen, he'd applied to join the force, certain they wouldn't turn him down.

They'd accepted him. The proudest day of his life had been putting on the blue uniform and adjusting the cap. His mother had lived to see it, surprised and happy that he'd managed it. His father had taken him to the public house, put a drink in his hand and shouted a toast – 'My son, the rozzer.'

He'd been proud then; he'd loved walking the beat, each part of the job. He learned every day. But he was happier still when he was finally able to move into plain clothes. That was real policing, he'd concluded. He'd done well, too, climbing from detective constable to sergeant and then to inspector before he was thirty.

And now he was chasing bloody pickpockets down Briggate. He might as well be back in uniform.

He paused on the bridge to light a Woodbine and look down at the river. Barges stood three deep against the wharves, and men moved quickly and surely along the gangplanks, their backs bent under heavy loads. It looked like a hard way to earn a day's pay, but what wasn't?

On either side of the Aire the factories were busy, thick smoke rising to cloud the sun. A deep blue slick floated on the water from the indigo works upstream, bright against the dull grey. The bloated corpse of a dead dog sailed past, carried by the current. He watched until it passed from sight.

Briggate was busy with couples, in from the suburbs and parading in their best clothes. The men were shaved so close their cheeks looked pink and shiny, and their shirt collars stood high and stiff around their necks, Their wives showed off their bright summer dresses in the latest fashions, fresh from the seamstress. Hems swept against the pavements as they walked, parasols spread, eyeing other women they passed or glancing at the goods displayed in the shop windows. The best part of four hundred thousand people lived in Leeds now, rich and poor alike; a sunny Saturday and most of those with brass were out in town to display themselves, he thought.

He wasn't in a mood to see any more smug faces this morning. Instead he cut through Queen's Court, ducking between washing that was strung out to dry between the crumbling old houses, hopeful of a glint of sunlight. A barefoot boy threw a ball against the wall, concentrating furiously on catching it. It slipped from his hand and rolled towards Harper. He picked it up and tossed it back, and the boy grinned as he pulled it out of the air.

He cut through a ginnel where someone was singing a song beyond a door, and came out by the Corn Exchange, then strode quickly across the market with a wave and a wink to the girls working behind the stall at Mr Marks's Penny Bazaar and across to Millgarth police station.

'Had a productive morning, sir?' the desk sergeant smirked. For a moment Harper was tempted to reply, then shut his mouth. Whatever he said, George Tollman would have heard it scores of times before. The man had stood behind that counter since God was a lad. He'd been there twelve years earlier when Harper had nervously reported for his first day as a young constable and he'd likely remain until they carried him out in a coffin. Instead the inspector just shook his head and pushed his way through to the office. He tossed his hat on to the desk and leaned back in his chair, closing his eyes for a moment.

'Bad day?'

'One of those when you wonder why you even bother,' he replied in disgust, glancing up at the man leaning against the wall. Billy Reed had only been a detective sergeant for six months. He was in his early forties, a good ten years older than the inspector. Reed had joined the force after fifteen years in the West Yorkshire Regiment. Harper had been the one to encourage him into plain clothes and then recommended him for sergeant. Reed had celebrated the promotion by going out to Hepworth's and buying a new suit to replace his old, fraying jacket and trousers, the only civilian clothes he seemed to own. He had his problems, a temper that occasionally flared into violence; at times the black dog would take him over, the pictures of what he'd seen out in Afghanistan with the army rattling around his head. He'd turn quiet then, sullen, filling his nights with drink, trying to forget. But he was as good a copper as Harper had known, loyal and dogged. 'First the case against Tosh Walker falls apart and now I can't even run down a pickpocket.'

They'd been trying to prosecute Walker for all six of the years Harper had been a detective. He'd started out as a minor criminal, no more than a nuisance, but he had an eye for the main chance and a ruthless streak as wide as Briggate. It had made him rich. He offered loans to businessmen who were going through hard times, then forced them out, sometimes for pennies on the pound, more often for nothing. Half a year before, the inspector believed he'd finally cornered the man. He spent months preparing the case. He had three witnesses all willing to testify. Then, just four days before the court case was due to begin, two of those who'd been ready to speak out left Leeds and the third changed his mind. Everything had fallen into tatters, leaving Harper raging and frustrated. Endless weeks of work had crumbled to nothing.

'Never mind,' Reed told him, 'it'll be busy soon enough now the gas workers are on strike.'

'They didn't have much choice, did they?' Harper observed. 'First the council sacks half the stokers at the works, then they lock out the rest and say they're going to pay them less and take one of their holidays. For God's sake, Billy, what would you do?'

'You'd better not say that when the chief's around,' the sergeant warned. 'You'll give the old man an apoplexy. By the way, one of the constables was in here earlier asking for you.'

'Who?'

'Ash.'

He wondered what the man needed. Ash covered the beat that had once been his, the poor area in the heart of Leeds, between the Headrow and Boar Lane, running west from Briggate and across to Lands Lane. Tucked out of sight behind the shops, it was full of the old, squalid yards and courts, a part of town that had barely changed in a century or more, where folk counted themselves rich if they had threepence left come payday. That was where he'd walked every day for six years. He'd known the faces there, the people, all the crime and the promises that end up as nothing. He'd carried men home to their wives on a Saturday night after they'd drunk away their money, tended wounds, and laid a sheet over the old who'd died of hunger.

Ash was still new, just a year on the force, but he seemed thoughtful and conscientious. If he had something it might be worth hearing. He stood and picked up his hat.

'I'll go and find him.'

TWO

Reed caught sight of himself in the shop window and ran a hand over his beard. Time for a trim soon, he thought. Keep it neat, not straggling on to his chest like an old man. He straightened his back and marched along Boar Lane to the Post Office. It was a grand, imposing building, always bustling with voices and people scuttling from counter to office, a symphony of footsteps on the heavy tiled floor.

He'd taken his time writing the letter, copying it over and over in his room until he was satisfied. He waited in the queue, then handed over his tuppence and watched the harried clerk toss it on to a pile.

He exhaled slowly. With luck he'd hear back in a few days. He had the rank and the experience now; it was time to enquire about positions elsewhere. Whitby. That was where he wanted to be.

He'd visited the place after he left the army. As soon as the regiment returned from Afghanistan he'd turned in his papers. There was plenty of pay in his account, enough to take a month off and walk around Yorkshire, going wherever his feet carried him. It had been an attempt to clear the pictures from his head. He needed to try to forget all the things he'd seen and done out there. But they'd still come back to visit him every night – until he reached Whitby. He'd loved the streets that rose steeply from the harbour, climbed the steps that led to the ruined abbey above the town, and sat there, looking out to sea. In the end he'd spent a week in the place, lodging with a fishing family. He'd passed his evenings in the small alehouses and for once not needed to lose himself in alcohol. His sleep had been deep and dreamless while his days had been filled with wandering. Each morning he'd felt his spirit lighten.

And then he'd had to leave. But he still ached to return, to find that peace again. It had left him once he'd come back to Leeds, seeing old pals from the service. Some of them were fine, others as troubled as he was, with thoughts behind their eyes that few others could ever understand.

The discipline of the police helped. It kept him busy, his mind occupied. Yet in the evenings he'd be in the Hyde Park, reluctant to go home to his lodgings. He didn't want to close his eyes and see it all again. For a few hours, at least, the drink could keep it all at bay.

Tom Harper had been good to him. He'd covered on the days he arrived bleary-eyed and weary from the nightmares and stopped him when his anger rose. Reed knew he was good at his job, that he solved crimes. But ever since spring he'd felt the longing for Whitby growing again, for somewhere he could sleep a whole night and wake without remembering a single bad dream. He pushed his lips together and walked back to Millgarth.

The inspector cut through the courts and alleys, up by Swan Street. He knew every paving stone around here. There were plenty of good memories and one bad. Three years before, just by the entrance to the music hall, he'd tried to subdue a thief and taken a heavy blow on his right ear. The next morning he'd barely been able to hear on that side. Every sound was muted and distant.

The day after it was no better. He was scared, but he didn't dare see the police surgeon. It would go on his record. Instead, he paid to see a doctor. He needed to keep everything private. He sweated through the examination, then sat, waiting for the verdict. The blow had burst his eardrum, the physician said. But as it healed, his hearing would probably return.

Over the next two months some of it had returned. Not all. Not even near. He'd learned to lean a little as he talked to someone, to walk on their right, even to read lips a little to understand everything. He'd said nothing about it. He never would. No one in the police could ever know; something like that could see him invalided from the force and he loved the job too much to lose it. He hid it well; he watched faces. But he was always careful when he talked to people. He had to be.

Harper found Ash outside the Theatre Royal near the top of Lands Lane, gently moving on a match girl. Once he'd watched her go reluctantly down the street, the constable turned to him. He was big, a good handspan over six feet, taller still with the cap. His uniform was crisp and pressed, buttons shining, everything regulation. His hair gleamed with pomade, and the moustache was rich and bushy above his lip.

'You were looking for me?' Harper said.

'Yes, sir.' He looked around. 'Maybe we'd better talk somewhere else. Always better out of the way,' he said gravely and led the way up the street and ducking into a court. The few people outside their doors melted away at the sight of the police.

'What is it?' Harper was curious now, wondering why Ash needed to talk out of sight of prying eyes.

The man chewed his lip for a moment before answering, his face dark and serious in the shadow.

'It might be summat or nowt, really, but I thought I'd better pass it on, sir. Do you remember Col Parkinson?'

Harper nodded. Parkinson had never done a day's work more than he was forced to. He always had some little scheme going on that usually paid out to nothing. He had a thin, ferrety face, most of the teeth gone from his mouth, those left in shades of black and brown. His wife was almost as bad as him; the only good thing he could say about Betty Parkinson was that she doted on their daughter. Martha must be about eight now, the inspector guessed. Soon enough she'd be done with school and out earning money if Col had anything to say about it.

'What's he done now? It shouldn't be anything you need me for.'

'It's not him, sir.' Ash hesitated. 'Well, not quite. It's that little lass of his. She's not been around for a week. He says she's gone to stay with his sister in Halifax.'

'Does he have a sister there?' He couldn't recall.

'The neighbours say that the first time he mentioned her was after the girl was gone.'

'What about Betty? What did she tell you?'

'She's in Armley jail, sir. Three months for receiving. Not out until the end of July.'

Harper snorted. It was hardly a surprise. If one of them wasn't in jail, usually the other was. 'You want me to talk to him?'

Ash nodded. 'He's sticking to his tale, but there's summat in there I just don't believe. And I don't want anything happening to Martha. She's a grand little girl, always happy. You wouldn't credit it with parents like hers. I just didn't want everyone knowing.'

'I'll go and have a word. Where does he drink these days?'

'At home with a jug unless he has a bob or two. That's the other thing, sir. He seems to have a little money lately.'

'What are you trying to tell me?'

'I don't know, sir.' Ash frowned. 'I honestly don't know.'

Around here he didn't even need to think of the way. He'd walked it for so long that he knew every ginnel and gap. At one time he could have said how many lived behind each door, what they did and whether he needed to watch them. Many would be new now, strangers, but there would still be plenty of people he'd recognize.

He slipped through to Fidelity Court. The place was even worse than he remembered. The cobbles were broken, half the flagstones pulled up, the windows of the cottages so grimy they barely let through any light. A dog barked as he passed one of the houses. A sign painted on the glass advertised Smiley's Barber Shop, the dirty red and white pole hanging at an angle. But the chair inside was empty and the door locked. He smiled. Johnny Smiley would probably be out at the Rose and Crown, supping whatever money he'd earned during the morning.

Harper climbed a short flight of worn stone steps and stopped outside a black door with the paint peeling away from the wood in long strips. This wasn't a place where the houses needed numbers; no one back here received letters. He brought his fist down hard, knocking long and loud then rattling the door handle.

'You can stop now. He's not there.'

The woman's voice made him turn.

'You know where he is, Mrs Dempsey?'

She had to blink twice until she placed him, then stood with arms folded across her broad chest. Virginia Dempsey was sixteen stone if she weighed an ounce and not much more than five feet tall. If anything, she was bigger than he remembered. Her fleshy arms were bare, a thin shawl covering her hair even in the June warmth.

'Well, if it in't Mr Harper. Looking flash these days, you are, Constable.'

'You'd better get it right, Ginny,' he told her with a wink. 'It's Inspector Harper now. And the suit's one of Mr Barran's specials, five bob discount to a bobby. Nowt flash about it, love. Do you know where I can find Col?'

'Got business with him, do you?' she asked suspiciously.

'What do you think? It's not like he's on my social list.'

She sniffed. 'Happen you'll find him at the Leopard Hotel. He's spent a lot of time there these last few days, what with his missus in Armley and Martha up in Halifax.'

'Halifax?' he asked as if he'd heard nothing about it. 'What's she doing up there?'

'Gone to stay with his sister.'

'I didn't even know Col had a sister.'

'Oh aye.' She lowered her voice. 'That's what he says, leastways. I've never seen her meself.'

'Martha was just a nipper when I saw her last.'

'I bet she'd still know you, Mr Harper. Dun't forget anything, that lass. Sharp as owt and twice as bright. Betty even had a picture took of her when they were flush. Up on their wall, it is.'

He nodded slowly. 'He's often at the Leopard, you said?'

'Right enough.' Her laugh came out like a cackle. 'Don't know who he's been robbing but he's not been short lately. But mebbe you'd know more about that.'

He smiled. 'Aye, maybe I would, Ginny.' Let her think that for now. If he needed more from her he could always come back.

Hotel was a grand word for it. He wouldn't have stayed at the Leopard for love nor money. He passed under the archway that led to a cobbled yard and pushed open the door to the saloon bar. The wood was ancient and dark, the white ceiling stained shades of brown and yellow by smoke.

A few of the men looked up as he entered. They had beaten-down faces, creased and tired, the look of the weary and the worn. Harper spotted Parkinson in the corner, an empty gin glass in front of him.

He sat down noisily, dragging the chair over the flagstone floor. Parkinson raised his eyes, squinting at him questioningly.

'I know you, don't I?' His gaze was blurry. Not drunk yet, Harper decided, but on his way. He'd still be able to think. And lie.

'Aye, you do, Col.' He knew Parkinson was hardly older than him but he already looked faded, cheeks sunk, the hair thinned away to nothing on his scalp. 'It's Inspector Harper. Constable Harper as was.'

'Oh aye.' Recognition dawned on his face. Harper stared around the bar, not surprised to see it had quietly emptied. It always happened. Some would have known him already, the rest would have smelled him for a rozzer.

'You been staying out of trouble?' he asked.

'Course I have.'

'I hear your Betty's in Armley again. What do they do, keep a cell specially for her up there?'

'Not her fault,' Parkinson told him. The inspector almost chuckled. It was never their fault. If he had a penny for everyone time someone had said that, he'd be a rich man.

'And how's Martha? She was no more than a bairn when I saw her last.'

'A good lass,' Col said, nodding his head for emphasis. 'A very good lass.' He patted the pockets of his tattered old jacket. 'Do you have a cigarette?'

Harper pulled out the packet of Woodbines and Parkinson's gaze followed his movements. He handed one to the man and lit it.

'Martha,' he prompted.

'She's with me sister.'

'I didn't know you had one, Col. I never heard you talk about her.'

'In Halifax.'

'Oh aye? How long's Martha up there for?'

'Till . . .' He hesitated. 'Till my Betty's out. Better that way.'

She should have been at school but he doubted Parkinson would worry about something as trivial as that.

'Better for you, you mean. If she's not here you don't have to look after her. So what's your sister's name, Col?' Harper asked idly.

For a few seconds Harper didn't answer.

'Sarah,' he said finally. 'She's married, got little 'uns of her own, too.' He took a deep draw on the cigarette.

'Where does she live in Halifax, then?'

'I don't remember.'

'You don't, Col? Your own kin? You sent Martha up there and don't even know where she's going?'

'I put her on the train. Sarah was meeting her at the station.'

'How would she know what train? Good at guessing is she, this sister of yours?'

'I sent her a letter.'

Harper laughed. 'Come on, Col. You can't write and you don't know where she lives. How are you going to send her a letter?'

'I had her address at home, on a piece of paper up on the mantel. And my Martha writes a right good hand. I had her do it.'

'How long's she been gone?'

'A week.' Parkinson shrugged. 'Day or two longer, mebbe. I don't know.' He started to rise. 'I need to go.'

Harper clamped his hand tight around the man's wrist. 'Not yet, Col,' he said quietly. 'Not when we're having a good little natter.'

Parkinson sat down again, shoulders slumping.

'What does Betty think about all this?'

'I've not told her yet. I will.'

Ash had been right, Harper thought. There was definitely something going on here.

'I think you'd best give me your sister's address. Just so I can get in touch and make sure everything's all right.'

Parkinson shook his head. 'In't got it, do I? I threw it out after we sent the letter. Don't need bits of paper cluttering up the place.' Harper kept hold of the man's arm, fingers digging hard into the flesh. Parkinson's eyes were starting to water, his eyes pleading.

'I'm off to Armley on Monday to see Betty, so you'd better

be telling me the truth.' He squeezed a little harder then let go, feeling the man flinch. 'You understand?'

'Yes.' He let go. Parkinson cradled his wrist, rubbing it lightly, his look a mix of wounded pride and anger.

'You've got money for a drink, too,' Harper noted. 'That's not like you.'

'I won it. A bet on the rugby.'

'First time for everything, eh, Col?' He waited a heartbeat. 'If you have something to tell me, you can find me at the station.' Harper stood slowly then bent down, his mouth close to the man's ear. 'I hope you haven't been lying to me, Col. If anything's happened to Martha I'll make you wish you were dead.'

Parkinson was hiding something. That was obvious. But as he strolled back to Millgarth in the sunshine he couldn't imagine what. Col might send his daughter somewhere so he didn't have to look after her, but the tale of a sister was all lies. Why, Harper wondered? What was he hiding?

As soon as he entered the station he could hear the buzz of talk and the dark undercurrent of complaints. Something had happened. In the office he looked at Reed.

'The superintendent wants you,' the sergeant said, glancing up from a report.

'What is it?'

'All leave cancelled from Monday.'

'The gas strike?'

'Yes.'

He knocked on the door and Superintendent Kendall waved him in.

'Sit down, Tom,' he said.

Kendall was in his fifties, grey hair cut short, with a long, patient face and a measured temper. He wore his jacket cut long, always black, with striped trousers, a style long out of fashion, and the top hat that used to mark out detectives hanging on a stand in the corner. When Harper became a detective constable Kendall was already an inspector; he'd taken the young man in hand and passed on what he knew. Now he was in charge of A Division, a solid policeman, utterly honest and loyal to the force. The only thing he lacked was imagination.

'When did you get back?' he asked.

'About two minutes ago.'

'Long enough to have heard, I suppose.' He picked his pipe out of the ashtray, tamped down the tobacco with a nicotine-stained fingertip and struck a match. 'There was trouble at the Wortley works last night.'

'Trouble?'

'Nothing too bad. Not yet, anyway. That's going to start on Monday. They're bringing in the replacement workers then.'

'The blacklegs, you mean, sir,' Harper said coldly.

Kendall frowned but ignored the words. 'We're not playing at politics with this, Tom. It's our job to keep *everyone* safe. We're going to make sure no one breaks the law.'

'And if they do?'

'We arrest them.' He paused for a brief moment. 'Whoever they are.'

Harper nodded.

'The train with the replacements is coming on Monday night. And I expect you to keep that quiet,' Kendall said pointedly. 'They're bringing them into the Midland goods station so we can just march the men over to the Meadow Lane works.'

It made sense, he thought. The gasworks was across the road, no more than a hundred yards away.

'What do you want me to do, sir?'

'I want you down there when they arrive.'

'In uniform?' He hoped not; he'd been grateful to leave the blue suit behind. He had no wish to wear it again.

Kendall shook his head. 'You and Reed will stay in plain clothes. There'll be a crowd waiting. Bound to be. Mingle with them. You know what to do if there's a problem.'

'Yes, sir.'

The superintendent sighed. 'It's going to be an ugly business. Probably violent.'

'Probably?' Harper could feel himself start to bristle. 'There'll be ructions, sir. Certain to be. The gas committee's getting rid of men just to save a few pennies. Of course they're angry.'

He'd seen it before. A man worked himself down to his bones to look after his family, then the bosses threw the bones aside. He thought of his own father, living with one of his sisters now.

After years on the railways he was just a husk of a man, his body no more than a memory of what it had been. When his illness started, the loss of strength, the loss of memory, the company hadn't paid for a doctor; instead, they'd sacked him for not reporting to work.

'I know where your sympathies lie,' Kendall said with an awkward smile. 'You've never made a secret of them. But I'm relying on you to do your job properly.'

'I will, sir.'

'After Monday night everyone will be on duty until all this is over. I'll have some camp beds set up.' He chuckled. 'With luck it'll all be over before your big day.'

'It'd better be. Annabelle won't forgive any of them if she has to postpone the wedding.'

'You'll be there all right, even if we have to drag you. Getting married might be the best thing to happen to you, Tom. It steadies a man. I've been married almost thirty years now and I've never regretted a day.' He grinned. 'Well, not many, anyway.'

'Thank you, sir.'

'Are you working on anything special at the moment?'

Harper thought about Martha Parkinson. 'Something odd,' he replied. 'I'm not sure what it is yet.'

'Whatever it is, you'll need to put it aside until all this is over.'

'Yes, sir.'

'You spend some time with that fiancée of yours, Tom. No need to report before Monday evening.'

'Thank you, sir.'

'Just make sure she knows she won't see you for a while after that.'

Back in the office he pulled the watch from his waistcoat pocket. Half past four. Plenty of time yet. Reed had already left, his desk neat, the small piles of paper carefully squared off, the pens lined up. That's what happens when you hire a military man, he thought. Everything in order.

He looked over at his own desk. Documents everywhere, scrawled notes, a nib that had dripped ink on some paper. But then he'd never had army discipline. He found Ash in the changing room, sitting on a bench, painstakingly updating his notebook.

'You were right about Col. Something's going on there.'

'Any idea what it is, sir?'

'Not yet,' Harper said with a quick shake of his head. 'But I want people keeping an eye on him in case he tries to do a flit.'

'And if he does?'

'Bring him in.'

The constable nodded, then said, 'Sounds like this strike's going to keep us busy for a few days.'

'Very likely. Just make sure you don't end up with your head broken.'

Ash laughed. 'Cast iron skull, that's what me ma always said. More likely they'll be the ones who are hurting.'

THREE

In the end he was five minutes late, dashing along Boar Lane, past Holy Trinity Church to meet her in front of the Grand Pygmalion. Sergeant Tollman had wanted a quick word that stretched out to ten minutes, then a detective constable needed a piece of advice. After that he'd been forced to run the whole way.

'I'm sorry,' he said, gasping for breath. She stood with her back to one of the grand glass windows, the shade of a wide hat hiding her expression.

'I don't know, Tom Harper, I'm not sure I can do with a man who's never on time.' Her voice seemed serious and he looked at her, suddenly worried. But Annabelle was smiling, her eyes playful. 'You're going to have to do better than this,' she scolded.

'I . . .' he began, and she laughed.

'Oh give over, you daft ha'porth. It took me eight months to get you to propose. I'm used to you being late, I'm not doing to drop you now.' She leaned forward and kissed his cheek. 'If you want to make yourself useful you can carry these.'

'Six packages?' Harper asked. 'What have you been doing, buying half of Leeds?'

'Just things a girl needs when she's going to be wed,' she told him. 'I could have waited for you before I started shopping, if you'd rather.'

'No,' he replied hastily. 'It's fine.' He'd been in the Pygmalion when it opened. Four floors of draperies, parasols and sailor suits. Everything was slick and well-presented, and there were more assistants than he could shake a stick at. A department store, they called it. Nothing to interest him at all. He'd been a member of the Co-op as far back as he could recall. Their big shop on Albion Street had everything he needed and the prices suited his pocket. On a policeman's pay every penny counted.

'Come on, then, we'd better get a move on,' Annabelle said. 'It's Saturday and I said I'd help out tonight. We'll be packed and I want a bite of something first.' She waited until he had all the packages and set off along the street, her arm through his. Her dress was a pale lemon colour, matching the ribbon that held the hat in place and tied in a bow under her chin. Simple clothes, but she wore them with elegance and style.

He saw men glancing at her. She had that kind of face. Not beautiful, no Jenny Lind or Lily Langtry, but she possessed a quality that drew the eyes. The first time he'd seen her he'd been unable to stop staring. At first it was just for a moment before turning away, then looking again and again until she'd stopped in front of him and boldly asked if he liked what he saw.

She'd been collecting glasses in the Victoria down in Sheepscar, an old apron covering her dress and her sleeves rolled up, talking and laughing with the customers. He thought she must be a serving girl with a brass mouth. Then, as he sat and watched her over another pint, he noticed the rest of the staff defer to the woman. He was still there when she poured herself a glass of gin and sat down next to him.

'I'm surprised those eyes of yours haven't popped out on stalks yet,' she told him. 'You've been looking that hard you must have seen through to me garters.' She leaned close enough for him to smell her perfume and whispered, 'They're blue, by the way.'

For the first time in years, Tom Harper blushed. She laughed. 'Aye, I thought that'd shut you up. I'm Annabelle. Mrs Atkinson.' She extended a hand and he shook it, feeling the calluses of hard work on her palms. But there was no ring on her finger. 'He's dead, love,' she explained as she caught his glance. 'Three year back. Left me this place.'

She'd started as a servant in the pub when she was fifteen, she

said, after a spell in the mills. The landlord had taken a shine to
her, and she'd liked him. One thing had led to another and they'd
married. She was eighteen, he was fifty, already a widower once.
After eight years together, he died.

'Woke up and he were cold,' she said, toying with the empty
glass. 'Heart gave out in the night, they said. And before you
ask, I were happy with him. Everyone thought I'd sell up once
he was gone but I couldn't see the sense. We were making money.
So I took it over. Not bad for a lass who grew up on the Bank,
is it?' She gave him a quick smile.

'I'm impressed,' he said.

'So what brings a bobby in here?' Annabelle asked bluntly.
'Something I should worry about?'

'How did you know?'

She gave him a withering look. 'If I can't spot a copper by
now I might as well give up the keys to this place. You're not
in uniform. Off duty, are you?'

'I'm a detective. Inspector.'

She pushed her lips together. 'Right posh, eh? Got a name,
Inspector?'

'Tom. Tom Harper.'

He'd returned the next night, and the next, and soon they
started walking out together. Shows at Thornton's Music Hall
and the Grand, walks up to Roundhay Park on a Sunday for the
band concerts. Slowly, as the romance began to bloom, he learned
more about her. She didn't just own the pub, she also had a pair
of bakeries, one just up Meanwood Road close to the chemical
works and the foundry, the other on Skinner Lane for the trade
from the building yards. She employed people to do the baking
but in the early days she'd been up at four each morning to take
care of everything herself.

Annabelle constantly surprised him. She loved an evening out
at the halls, laughing at the comedians and singing along with
the popular songs. But just a month before she'd dragged him
out to the annual exhibition at Leeds Art Gallery.

By the time they'd arrived, catching the omnibus and walking
along the Headrow, it was almost dusk.

'Are you sure they'll still be open?' he asked.

'Positive,' she said and squeezed his hand. 'Come on.'

It seemed a strange thing to him. How would they light the pictures? Candles? Lanterns? At the entrance she turned to him.

'Just close your eyes,' she said, a smile flickering across her lips. 'That's better.' She guided him into the room at the top of the building. 'You can open them again now.'

It was bright as day inside, although deep evening showed through the skylights.

'What?' he asked, startled and unsure what he was seeing.

'Electric light,' she explained. She gazed around, eyes wide. 'Wonderful, eh?' She'd taken her time, examining every painting, every piece of sculpture, stopping to glance up at the glowing bulbs. Like everything else there, she was transfixed by the light as much as the art. To him it seemed to beggar belief that anyone can do this. When they finally came out it was full night, the gas lamps soft along the street. 'You see that, Tom? That's the future, that is.'

'You're off with the fairies again,' she said, nudging against him.

'Just thinking.'

'You're always doing that.' But she smiled and shook her head. 'Be careful, you'll wear your brain out.'

They were strolling out along North Street, through the Leylands, the afternoon sun pleasant on his back. Omnibuses passed them with the click of hooves and the rhythmic turn of the wheels, a few empty carts heading back to the stables. The area was quiet. There'd be little noise around here before sunset, he thought. All the Jews would be at home for the Sabbath. He'd grown up less than a stone's throw away from where they were right now, over on Noble Street, all sharp cobbles and grimy brick back-to-backs, like every other road he'd known; nothing noble about it at all. Back then there'd been no more than a handful of Jewish families around, curiosities all of them, with strange names like Cohen and Zermansky that stuck on the tongue when he tried to pronounce them. The women all had dark, fearful eyes and the men wore their full beards long. Ask a question and they'd come out with torrents of words in a language he didn't understand. Twenty years on and the Leylands was full of them, working every hour God sent, sewing clothes in their sweatshops. He was willing to bet there was more Yiddish spoken round here these days than English.

'What do you want to do tomorrow, Tom?' Annabelle asked.

He shrugged; he hadn't given the next day a thought yet. 'The park?' he suggested. He liked the sense of space, of openness, up at Roundhay. The foul air that filled the city seemed like a strange memory when he was out there.

'Aye, if it stays like this,' she agreed. They'd walk to the park gates then wander arm in arm around the big lake and finish up with an ice cream. Maybe they'd carry a picnic along with them.

'I'm off on Monday, too. Until the evening.' He hesitated. 'After that I might not be around for a few days.'

'The gas?'

'Yes.'

'You just make sure you look after yourself.' She grinned but there was steel behind her expression. 'I'm not dragging a corpse to the register office next month.'

July the twelfth, he thought. No more than a few breaths away. It was odd, though; the idea didn't scare him. He trusted her completely. She was the only one he'd ever told about his deafness. 'I'll be fine, don't you worry.'

'Anyone tries to hurt you they'll have to deal with me,' she warned, and he believed her. If that didn't make him safe, nothing would.

He was back at his lodgings by ten and in bed by half past. Tomorrow he'd have Annabelle to himself. The Sunday before, his sisters had come to inspect the bride, swooping down from Bramley, Holbeck and Morley. Annabelle had entertained them and impressed them with her rooms she had above the Victoria. The women had chattered away at a mile a minute, his sisters as prattling as ever, never quiet until it was time to leave. They'd approved, that was obvious in their envious gazes. Not that it mattered; he was the one marrying her.

The banging woke him from a dream that vanished like smoke as he blinked his eyes open. He struggled into his dressing gown and opened the door. Mrs Gibson, his landlady, stood there, wide-eyed and shocked at the disturbance, a constable with a long face behind her.

'I let him in, Mr Harper. He *says* he's a policeman.'

'He is, Mrs Gibson. Don't worry.' What else would he be,

Harper thought irritably, wandering round in uniform in the middle of the night?

She scurried away. He waited until he heard her door close and said, 'What is it?'

'You wanted to know about Col Parkinson, sir.'

'Has he tried to flit?'

'No,' the constable answered slowly. 'He's dead.'

FOUR

B y the time he reached Fidelity Court the early summer dawn had arrived, pale sunlight almost making the place attractive. He took time to shave and dress properly before he left. His suit and waistcoat were brushed, a four-in-hand knot on the tie and the shirt collar carefully studded on. The body wouldn't be going anywhere and God alone knew when he'd have time to come home and change.

A uniform he didn't recognize nervously guarded the door to Parkinson's house. Neighbours had gathered across the yard, clustered around Ginny Dempsey's door.

'Is he dead, Mr Harper?' she called as he passed. She was already dressed, the shawl pulled over her hair and neck.

'How would I know, Ginny? I've only just got here.'

His words set her muttering to the others. Harper stopped to examine the door to Parkinson's cottage, the wood splintered around the lock. Inside it was still too dark to make out the face of the man standing in the corner, only the glowing dot of his cigarette end.

'Come on,' Harper said testily, 'let's have some light.'

He heard the sharp rasp as the man struck a match, then the soft, fluttering light of a candle showed Parkinson's body hanging from a ceiling beam, a chair kicked over on its side close by. Sullivan, the night patrolman for the beat, pulled off his cap in respect.

It was Col, no mistake about that, a puddle of piss on the floor underneath him and the room stinking where he'd soiled himself.

'Who jemmied the door?' Harper asked. 'You?'

'Yes, sir,' Sullivan replied, trying to keep his gaze away from the corpse. 'They said you wanted to know if he tried to run so I shone me lantern in the window when I made me rounds. I saw something . . .' His words faded away for a moment. 'It was swinging a little bit. I knocked on the door. When there was no answer I thought I'd best come in.'

'Good,' he said with an approving nod. 'Have you talked to the neighbours yet?'

'No, sir. As soon as I realized what it was I blew me whistle and waited until young Nicholson showed up. I had him stand outside, just in case, and I went to the station so they could send someone for you.'

'Right. Half the court's over outside Ginny's. See if they heard anything. Who's been coming and going here, that sort of thing.' He paused, then added, 'Send Nicholson down to Millgarth. We'll need someone to haul Col away.'

'Yes, sir.'

Alone, he walked slowly around the room. One chair by the hearth, a table pushed against the back wall. A small, dusty mirror over the mantel. No pieces of paper, no books, very little of anything except a jug of beer and a cracked glass by one of the chairs. He pushed through to the kitchen. There were a few days' worth of dishes on the table, covered with a fur of mould, a trail of ants crawling in and out. A half-empty bucket of water. Nothing useful.

He lifted Parkinson's right hand, bringing it up to the light. Fresh grazes on the knuckles. They hadn't been there when he'd seen the man the previous afternoon. More on the left hand. He dragged the other chair over, climbing on it to look at Col's face. Someone had given him a battering.

Harper was pacing the room again when Sullivan returned.

'The man next door heard noises here close to midnight, sir. Looked out and saw two men hauling Col in. Thought he was likely dead drunk. Wouldn't be the first time.'

'Did he recognize them?'

'No gas lamps back here, sir. Pitch black.'

'Anything else?'

'A couple of others heard something but they didn't bother to look.' He edged a glance at the body then quickly looked away. 'I suppose he must have woken up and done it.'

'Maybe,' Harper said doubtfully. 'Where does Col go these days, apart from the Leopard?'

'The Rose and Crown mostly,' the man answered after a little thought. 'He mostly sups at home. Doesn't stray far, our Col. Didn't,' Sullivan corrected himself after a moment.

'Right. I'll leave him with you. I'll want the police surgeon to take a close look at Mr Parkinson.'

He spent two full minutes hammering on the door of the Rose and Crown before a shape appeared on the other side of the glass.

'Who is it?' a man's voice called, still full of sleep.

'It's Inspector Harper, Arthur. I want a word.'

He waited as the bolts were strained back and a key turned. The door opened and Arthur Rhodes was looking up at him. The man was still in his nightshirt, grey hair sprouting out wildly from his head, a stout, polished branch in one thick hand.

'It'd better be important,' he grumbled. 'Do you know what time it is?'

Harper pulled out his watch. 'It's half past six on a Sunday morning and I've been up for three hours. So why don't you let me in, Arthur, and stick the kettle on?'

The man muttered but moved away, leaving Harper to follow through the bar to a back parlour.

'Essie,' he yelled up the stairs, 'get yourself out of bed. The police are here.'

Ten minutes later he was sitting with a cup in front of him, waiting as the serving girl poured the tea and left.

'Right,' Rhodes said, 'what is it? Sunday's the only day I can sleep in for a bit so I hope you haven't ruined it for nowt.'

'Col Parkinson.'

'What about him?'

'Does he drink in here?'

'Sometimes,' Rhodes conceded. 'I've not seen him in a day or two. Why, what's he done?'

'He's dead, Arthur.'

'Dead?' the man asked. 'Col?' He shook his head in disbelief. 'What happened to him?'

'Hung himself at home.' For now it was the safest thing to say.

'Poor bugger,' he said slowly. He poured some of the tea into the saucer and slurped it.

'Who does he drink with?'

Rhodes sat back, thinking. 'Let me see . . . you know Dick Smith?'

'Ginger Dick?'

'That's the one. I've seen them together a few times. And Bill Corson. Mind you, a week or so back he were with a couple of fellows I'd not seen before. Heads together like they were planning something. Nasty pair, they were.'

'Nasty?' Harper asked. 'How?'

'Seemed like they'd cause trouble as soon as blink. Well, one of them did. You know the type.'

He did, all too well.

'Do you remember what they looked like?'

'One was big, a real bruiser, head all shaved. T'other was smaller. Dark hair, maybe.' Arthur Rhodes shrugged.

'When exactly was this?'

'A week, like I said. No,' he corrected himself. 'My Jane were down with her lumbago and we were rushed off our feet. Ten days back, a week ago Friday.'

'Thank you, Arthur.'

'Who's looking after that lass of theirs with Betty in Armley?'

'She's gone to his sister's in Halifax.'

Rhodes shook his head. 'I never had Col down to do owt as daft as kill himself.'

'Neither did I,' Harper told him, keeping his voice bland.

'Was he in last night?' Harper asked the landlord of the Leopard Hotel.

John Murphy looked him up and down. 'You're the one who came in to talk to him yesterday afternoon, aren't you?'

'I did.'

'Cleared out me custom for an hour.' With his name and red hair there might have been Irish in Murphy's past, but his voice was pure Leeds. He'd taken over the place since Harper had walked the beat here.

'So was Col here last night?'

'Aye,' the man acknowledged. 'Came in around eight and stayed until I closed.'

'When was that?'

'A little before midnight. Not enough of them left to keep me from a warm bed.'

'Who was he with?'

'No one, most of the time.' He rubbed the stubble on his chin. 'Why are you looking for him, any road?'

'I'm not,' Harper said and watched the man's eyebrows rise. 'I know exactly where Col is. He's on his way to the mortuary right now.'

'Dead?' With an unconscious gesture, Murphy crossed himself, his face suddenly pale. 'Sweet God, what happened?'

'Looks as if he killed himself. So you understand why I wanted to know what he was doing last night.'

'Of course, of course,' Murphy nodded quickly. 'He must have come up not long after eight. That's when Mary called me for me supper, and he was here when I came back down.'

'And on his own the whole time?'

'Like I said.'

'How much was he drinking?'

'No more than usual. He had a word with people here and there. Then these two fellows came in and sat with him until I kicked everyone out.'

'What fellows?' Harper asked with interest.

'Hard types, you know what I mean, Inspector? One of them looked like a prizefighter. Big man, shaved his head, broken nose, scars on his face and hands.' He saw the inspector staring at him, surprised at the detail. 'I used to follow the fights,' he explained.

'Did you know them?'

Murphy shook his head. 'Not seen them before. But they were talking away and poor Col was listening and nodding his head. They all left together.'

'What was the other man like?'

'Smaller.' Murphy shrugged. 'Not someone you'd notice in a crowd. Dark hair, clean shaven.' He paused. 'But he kept touching his lip as if he'd had a moustache there lately.'

'Was Col drunk or staggering when he left?'

Murphy pursed his lips and thought. 'No,' he answered slowly. 'He was up on his own two feet.'

'Did he look as if he'd been in a fight?'

'He did not,' the landlord responded firmly. 'Was he that way when you found him?'

'Yes.'

Murphy shook his head again. 'Poor man. May the Lord look after him.'

'Had he been in often lately?'

'Most nights in the last week. A few of the days, too,' he added.

'With money to spend?'

'Enough for what he wanted. He wasn't buying rounds, if that's what you mean.'

Harper thought quickly, then asked, 'Did Col look as if he was expecting the two men?'

'I've no idea, Inspector. I was bringing up a new barrel when they arrived.'

'Is there anything else you can think of?'

'Not really, Mr Harper. I'll let you know if I do. Col.' Murphy glanced up, his eyes filled with sadness. 'He wasn't the best man but I doubt he was the worst, either.'

Outside, he felt the sun warm on his face, lit a Woodbine and smoked as he decided what to do next. He could go back to Millgarth and write up an initial report on Parkinson's death. Or he could go to Armley Jail and talk to Betty Parkinson.

She needed to know her husband was dead. She could also tell him more about Martha. It seemed to revolve around the girl. Two men appear, Martha vanishes to visit the mysterious sister and Col has a little money. Then, as soon as the police come around asking questions the two men reappear and Col stretches his neck.

Except that he didn't believe for a moment that Parkinson had killed himself. The bruising on the man's face and Murphy's story put paid to that little tale. He needed answers and Betty might be able to provide a few of them. And she deserved to hear the news from someone other than a prison guard.

Armley it was. It was little more than a mile each way and fine weather for a walk. He made his way out along Wellington

Street and climbed the slow gradient of the hill. In the distance he could make out the Wortley gasometers, both of them so low they seemed almost empty, then the huge bulk of the Mills, standing tall and dirty between the river and the canal. For once there was no smoke pouring from the chimneys to hang over Leeds and hide the sun.

From November to March soot lingered around town in clinging, harsh palls of dark fog. It made men cough and spit black phlegm, the stink of industry the price of the town's success. The snow was grey before it even touched the ground.

The Sabbath was about the only time the air began to feel clean in Leeds, he thought, the one day working men could enjoy a rest and all the factories were shut.

The jail stood right at the summit of Armley. With its tower and high walls it was meant to look like a castle, powerful and intimidating. But no one was ever going to find adventure or romance once the big gate shut. There was nothing more than misery inside.

It was almost half an hour before a guard escorted Betty Parkinson through to the interview room. Light filtered in through a high, barred window, a shaft of sun catching dust motes as they rose. There was a wooden table, its top scarred and dull, one leg shorter than the others, and a pair of plain chairs.

She looked at him with empty eyes and sat meekly on the chair, hands folded in her lap.

'Come to try and charge me with summat else, Mr Harper?'

'Not today, Betty,' he told her, and his tone made her look sharply at him.

He remembered the first time he'd seen her. It was a week or so after he'd started on the beat. She'd been fourteen or fifteen then, a real bobby dazzler all the lads wanted, full of fun and mischief and free with her favours until she met Col. He always thought they were an unlikely couple, Col so quiet and Betty loud, always ready for something. But they'd married and found a life of little crimes that suited them both, even after Martha was born.

'What is it?' she asked urgently. 'Has something happened to Martha?'

'It's Col,' he said gently. 'I'm sorry, Betty, he's dead.'

Her mouth opened wide, one of her hands flying up to cover it as the moan of pain came out. She began to cry and he passed her his handkerchief, watching as she pawed at the tears that ran down her cheeks. Her body convulsed hard with each sob.

Harper waited until she'd calmed a little, the handkerchief clutched tight between her fingers.

'How?' she began, her voice thick and stumbling, 'I mean . . .'

'It looks as if he hung himself, Betty.'

He watched as she forced herself to sit still and control her expression. Her mouth was shut tight, eyes empty with loss. Then the thought came, just as he knew it would.

'Martha? Where's Martha? Is she all right?'

He waited a moment before answering.

'Col had sent her to his sister in Halifax.'

At first she looked confused, as if she hadn't understood a word he'd said. Then the panic rose in her eyes. 'Sister? What do you mean? What sister? Col dun't have a sister. What are you talking about?'

He tried to explain, to ask more questions, but she was up and pacing quickly around the room. She fell to her knees and started screaming, 'Where is she?' over and over until the guards helped her away, her pleading echoing down the hall.

He knocked on Superintendent Kendall's door and the man waved him in. Sundays, holidays, Kendall was always at the station. Maybe that was why his marriage was so happy, Harper thought; he was never there for it.

'I heard you were called out early,' Kendall said.

'Yes, sir. Col Parkinson. I'd asked the beat to keep an eye on him.'

He explained it all, laying it out step by step. The super listened carefully, filling his pipe and lighting it, his face creased into a deep frown.

'So the girl's been missing for a week and her father's death is suspicious,' Kendall said finally.

'It's murder, sir. I'd bet my pay on it.'

'Let's not say what it is until the surgeon's examined him.' Harper understood the superintendent's reluctance. He required evidence.

'Yes, sir. But the girl . . .'

'The girl we start looking for *now*,' Kendall said. 'We need to find her as soon as we can. What about these two men Parkinson was seen with? How do they fit in with her disappearance, do you think?'

'I don't know yet.'

Kendall dipped his nib in the inkwell and started scribbling notes.

'Go back to Fidelity Yard,' he ordered quickly. 'Question everyone there, and I mean *everyone*. I saw Reed in the office, take him with you. I'll send over some constables to help you.' He ran a hand through his hair. 'You have today and tomorrow. After that I'm going to need you both for duty on this gas business.'

'Sir—' Harper started to protest. Kendall cut him off.

'That's an order from the chief, Tom. We're going to be stretched thin enough as it is, especially if it becomes violent.'

'I can guarantee you it will if they bring in a bunch of blacklegs.'

'And if they don't, Leeds won't have any gas,' Kendall pointed out. 'That's no lights, no cooking for those who have gas stoves, no power for any of the factories. This is an emergency, Tom, the council's pressing the chief constable and he's pushing hard on all of us. I don't have any choice in the matter. Not even for a missing girl.' He sighed. The inspector could see just how much the man was torn. Kendall knew that finding Martha Parkinson was the work the police should be doing. The right things; that was what he'd drummed into Harper a few years before. But his masters had other ideas and like a good man he had no choice but to obey. The superintendent ran a hand through his hair and said, 'Do as much as you can. I'll give you all the help I can find.'

'What about after Monday night?' Harper asked bluntly. 'Do we just forget about her then?' He hesitated, then added, 'If she was an alderman's daughter there'd be no question of forgetting her.'

'Tom,' he warned then shook his head. 'I'm sorry, but it's out of my hands. I'll do all I can to keep you away from it and give you some time.'

'Let me keep Billy Reed, then,' he asked. 'I'm not going to be able to do everything myself.'

'All right,' Kendall agreed. 'But he's your responsibility.'

'Yes, sir.' If that dark mood took him at the wrong time, Billy could become dangerous.

'Come back at six and tell me what you've found. If there's anything you need in the meantime, send word. Anything at all.' He looked up. 'And we'll just have to pray nothing bad has happened to her.'

'You think he was murdered?' Reed asked as they strode up the Headrow.

'I'm certain of it.' Harper had his hands bunched deep in his trouser pockets, the fingers balled into tight fists. 'Don't worry about Col for now. We need to find Martha.'

'What do you think he did with her?'

Harper waited. He hadn't said it, didn't want to say it, but he knew it needed to be out in the open.

'I think he sold her.'

FIVE

'You can't be serious,' Reed said incredulously. 'No one would do that. Not to his own daughter.'

'Of course they would. I've seen that and worse before. Why were you in on a Sunday, anyway?'

'I had to finish a report. That Kinnear burglary. I didn't have anything better to do, anyway.'

'Right,' Harper told him with a decisive nod. 'When we get there, I'll talk to the neighbours, most of them know me. I want you to look at the house again. There's supposed to be a photograph of Martha but I didn't see one when I was there.'

'You really think she's been sold?'

'Yes, I do,' Harper answered with sadness and anger as they edged through the passageway that led to Fidelity Court. A young constable still stood outside Parkinson's tumbledown house, ready to challenge the new visitors. 'Whatever you can find in there, Billy.'

The body had gone but the smell remained. The stink of death seemed to creep into every corner. Reed began his search in the main room. It was simply a matter of time and method, going through every little thing. You never knew what could be important; that was what the inspector had taught him.

He found the photograph quickly enough, down at the side of a chair. That seemed odd; it should have been out somewhere, on display. The grate was empty, all the ashes cleared with no need for a fire in the summer. He felt under the chairs, then tested the floorboards in case one was loose and made into a hiding place.

There wasn't much in the place. Parkinson owned very little. Anything worth money would have long since gone to the pawn-shop. But he still went through everything before moving into the kitchen. He held his breath, trying not to retch. There was no tap in the house, just an old bucket, half empty, for carrying water from the pump. The larder was almost bare, only part of a loaf covered with green mould and some cheese that had become food for mice and rats. On the table he separated the plates, brushing away the insects, then looked in the empty oven before feeling to the back of the cupboard. Everything he touched had a thin coating of grease and grime, as if none of it had been cleaned in years. An empty beer jug and three cracked glasses sat on the table.

Who could live like this, he wondered? At least the army had taught him the value of neatness, the need to keep things in good order. Your rifle needed to be stripped regularly. It had to treated with loving care to stop it jamming when you needed it most. And there'd been pride in a spotless uniform. He didn't have many clothes now, but he still made sure they were clean, his boots always bulled to a high shine.

The ancient stairs creaked under his weight. At the top there was just a single room, cobwebs in the corners, a chamber pot almost overflowing with piss. He opened the window, pushing hard on the sash to release it, letting in air that seemed sweet after the close stench of decay inside. The bedstead was iron, rusted in patches; it had probably stood here for half a century.

He flipped the pad that sat on top of it, tore off the sheet and felt the dirty pillows. Nothing. The girl's bed lay against the wall. It was nothing more than a pallet, straw covered with a sheet, but it was tidy, everything folded, a small old doll placed on the pillow. He picked it up, cradling it close as he continued to search.

A few ragged clothes hung from nails hammered at angles into the plaster. There was a man's shirt, the white faded to dull ivory and worn through at the elbows. A woman's dress, second- or third-hand, worn and stained, was next to it, then a dress and apron for the girl. Those had been cared for, tears and snags mended by awkward fingers, the apron washed clean.

But there was nothing in the house even to give the names of the people who lived here. So little remained of them that they might never have existed. He heard footsteps on the boards below. Harper was back. There was nothing more to find, anyway.

The inspector knocked on the Dempseys' door and heard the rush of children running to answer it. He'd known all the family by name at one time, given three or four of them a cuff round the ear when they'd misbehaved.

'I need to talk to your mam,' he told the upturned faces. At least two of them hadn't been born when he last patrolled here.

'Ma,' one of them shouted in a voice older than his years, 'there's a rozzer wants you.'

She came lumbering through from the kitchen, pushing them aside until she was filling the doorway in front of him, the old shawl gathered around her shoulders.

'How many of them now, Ginny?' he asked.

'Eight,' she replied with a chuckle. 'I told me husband, you try and give me another and I'm taking a knife to that thing.' She stared into his face. 'What is it, then, Mr Harper? They'd not have you lot asking questions about someone killing hissen.'

'It's Martha.'

'Gone to his sister in Halifax. I tell't you that yesterday – for whatever it's worth.'

'I went to see Betty this morning. Col doesn't have a sister in Halifax.'

Ginny's expression didn't change. 'How did she take it?'

'How do you think? She's lost her husband and her daughter's gone missing.' He could still hear the screams as the guards led her away. 'I need to know everything folk back here can tell me. No mucking about, none of this not helping the bobbies business.'

'They'll help,' she assured him. 'Wait a minute.' She closed the door and he heard her speaking, her voice too low to make out the words. Then her children streamed out like a flood, one after the other. 'They'll pass the word, don't you worry. Anyone gives you a problem, come and see me.'

He nodded his thanks. 'Now, what do you know about Martha?'

She thought for a second, folding her hands in front of her large body, fingers playing with the fringe of her shawl.

'You remember what Betty was like when she was young?'

'Yes.' The image of her slid into his mind.

'Martha's going to look the spit of her mam.' She tapped her head with a finger. 'But smart, not wild like Betty. She's a good lass, do owt for anyone. Always happy, a smile on her face.' Her eyes moved around the poor court. 'You find that lass, Mr Harper.'

'When was the last time you saw her?'

'A week ago Friday. She'd just come back from school and she was playing with our Eliza.'

'She's eight?'

'Nine come August.' He cocked his head, surprised she could be so exact. 'Three days younger than my Eddie,' Ginny explained.

'Did you see her go? Or see Col taking her anywhere?'

'No. The next day I just asked how she was and he told me she'd gone off to his sister's. First I'd ever heard of her,' she said with a sniff, 'but I thought it was probably better than staying with him. Col's useless, allus were. He couldn't look after himself, let alone a little one. It were Betty who did everything in that place.'

'What about strange men? Did you see any of them around the house?' She hesitated. The habit round here was to tell the police nothing. 'For God's sake, Ginny, I'm looking for Martha,' he said angrily.

'A few, mebbe,' she conceded. 'Not many ever came to see him, mind. Soapy Wilcox a couple of times. And two I didn't know.'

'One of them big, with a shaved head, the other one smaller?'
he guessed and she nodded.

'Aye. That big 'un scared me. I saw his face. His eyes.'

'What about them?'

'They were empty, like he wouldn't even care if he killed you.'

'And the other one?'

'He were smaller, not as big as you, and thinner. Like a rail.
Dark hair, a moustache, good suit like yours.' She paused, trying
to think, then shrugged.

'Did you hear any names?'

'No. They knocked and went in when he opened up.'

It was the same all over the court. Men who wouldn't usually
give him the time of day were eager to talk. A missing girl, one
of their own, outweighed any past enmity; everyone wanted to
help with this. A few had seen the two men but no one could
put a name to them. Cold, that was the way one of them described
the big one. Dangerous.

After two hours of questions there was nothing more to learn.
He made his way into Parkinson's home, the constable saluting
smartly as he passed. He could hear Reed moving around in the
bedroom upstairs. The body and the rope that held it had gone,
the tipped-over chair now neat against a wall. Only a dried stain
on the boards remained to show where Col had hung.

A photograph lay on the table. It was a portrait of a girl,
dark hair brushed until it was thick and shining. She had a shy
smile on her face, wearing a dress that was better than anything
she'd have owned around here, with a crisp white apron on
top. Martha was sitting on a chair, black stockings and shiny
button boots showing under the frock. Ginny was right, she
had the look of her mother around her eyes, but with a childish
innocence and stillness. The stamp on the back read London
Photographic Co, Queen Anne Buildings, 15 New Briggate,
Leeds.

Harper stared at the picture. Where are you, love, he thought
desperately, where the bloody hell are you?

'There's nothing here besides that,' Reed said as he clattered
down the stairs. 'It was beside the chair. I've been through the
whole house. Just filthy bedding and some old clothes upstairs.
Girl's clothes there, too. And this.' He held up an old doll, the

painted face worn off the china head, half the ringlets gone, the dress so old the pattern had worn away. Someone's cast-off and probably the only toy Martha owned. 'Can you imagine her leaving without it?'

They both knew the answer.

Harper told him what little he'd managed to learn. Reed kept hold of the doll, holding it close to his chest.

'Just what's going on here?' he asked. 'I can't make any sense of it. Why would Parkinson sell his daughter?'

'I'm damned if I understand it,' Harper admitted. He lit a cigarette, sending smoke into the still air of the room. Col would lie, he'd steal, he'd cheat, but he couldn't imagine the man doing something like that. He'd never dare, even if he had the idea. So why? What had happened? 'Soapy Wilcox,' he said finally. 'He was here in the last week, let's talk to him.'

'Sunday afternoon?' Reed mused. 'He'll likely still be dead drunk from last night.'

'Even better. We might get some truth out of him.'

They both knew Wilcox; everyone on the force did. He'd been arrested so many times, always for small offences – a pocket picked here, an item shoplifted there. When he was young Wilcox had worked at Joe Walton's soap factory on Whitehall Road. He'd come home each evening smelling sweet and fragrant for the first time in his life. The name had stuck even if the job hadn't. These days he was bloated, drunk as often as not, his fingers nowhere near as light as they'd been as his fortunes sank lower each year.

'Where was he living the last time you heard?'

'That lodging house on Swan Street.'

'Let's see what he has to tell us.'

'I know how to deal with Soapy,' Reed said.

The landlady was reluctant to let them in until Harper mentioned a missing girl. Then, without a word, she led them up three flights of rickety stairs to the attic, selected a key from the large bunch in the pocket of her dress and said, 'He's in there. If he's done owt, he'll wish he'd never been born.'

'If he's done anything he'll be in jail faster than you know it,' Harper assured her, and she nodded her acceptance.

Wilcox was still asleep, not even stirring as they walked in and pulled back the thin cotton curtains. Sunlight streamed in and Reed kicked the bed.

'Wake up, Soapy, you've got visitors.'

Wilcox grunted and turned on to his back, shading his eyes with his hands. The room stank of stale beer, sweat and smoke. A stained old frock coat and striped trousers were thrown across the chair. A table stood against the wall with a ewer and bowl of water. A straight-edge razor lay open by it, bristles still stuck to the rusty blade.

'Col Parkinson,' Harper began.

'What about him?' Wilcox coughed and sat upright, his eyes bleary, the skin slack and jowly around his mouth. He looked at the two men. 'Got a cigarette? I need a smoke first thing, like.'

Harper took one out and tossed it to him, followed by a match, and waited until the man inhaled and coughed again, groping for a dirty handkerchief under the pillow and spitting up phlegm.

'Col's dead,' Reed told him.

'Dead?' Wilcox coughed once more. 'Can't be. I only seen him two or three days back.' He looked from one face to the other. 'You're pulling my leg, in't you?'

'He died last night.' Harper sat on the bed, staring hard at Wilcox. 'He put a rope round his neck.'

'Jesus.' He shook his head sadly. 'Poor bastard. What made him do that?'

'You know his little girl?' Reed asked.

'Course I do,' he answered as if the question was stupid. 'Known them all for donkey's years.'

'Where is she?'

'Col sent her to his sister while Betty's in jail. Said it would be better for her, like.'

'How long ago?'

'No idea. She weren't there when I was at his house last.'

'Col doesn't have a sister,' Harper said.

'He must have,' Wilcox protested. 'Why else would he have said it?'

'That's what we're asking you.' Reed brought his face close. 'All we need now are some answers.'

'I don't know!' he said, panic in his eyes. 'It's only what Col told me.'

'You know some friends of his, one of them big, face all marked up like a prizefighter, the other one smaller, dark hair?'

Wilcox shook his head emphatically. 'Don't know 'em, no one like that. You think they had summat to do with all this?'

'I want to talk to them and find out,' Harper said. 'You can get yourself out of this pit and start asking around.'

'But—' Wilcox began.

Reed took hold of the man's jaw and began to squeeze. His eyes were hard. 'She's been missing a week, Soapy,' he said. 'You think about that and imagine what can happen to a little girl in a week.' His fingers tightened a little. 'Then, when you've had your think, start asking questions about those two, all right?' His fingers pressed deeper before he let go. 'You're going to do something good in your life for once.'

'And as soon as you find out, send word to me at Millgarth,' Harper instructed him.

Wilcox rubbed his face gently. 'What if I can't find owt?'

'Then you'll have to look again, won't you?' Reed told him as they left.

Outside, they walked past Thornton's music hall and through the ginnel that led out to Briggate.

'Get everyone working their informers. I want names for these two, Billy.'

'Where do you think the girl can be?'

'That's the problem. She could be anywhere by now.' He spat the words out. 'I'm going back to the station to tell the super what's happening. You see if you can find out who that pair are.'

'So you've no idea where the girl is, who these two men are or how they connect to all this?' Kendall asked.

'Not yet, sir.' The superintendent made it sound as if all his work in the last few hours had achieved nothing. He placed the photograph on the desk and waited as Kendall studied it.

'A bonny little thing,' he said.

'Bright, too, from what they say.'

'I'll send an alert to all the divisions and get them all searching.' He rubbed his cheeks with his palms. 'Where would you start looking, Tom?'

'I wish I knew, sir.' He'd asked himself the question on the way back to Millgarth.

'If she's still alive,' Kendall said emptily and put the photograph back on the desk.

They were the words he'd been avoiding all day. As long as you believed someone was alive you could hope to find them, to make them safe. Once you thought you were searching for a body . . .

'Why would they buy her just to kill her?' Harper asked. 'I can't see that.'

'You're assuming Parkinson sold her,' Kendall countered.

'I can't see what else it could be. But none of this makes sense, I agree with that. The Col I knew would never have sold his daughter or let anything happen to her.'

'Maybe these two put pressure on him.'

'It would have to be a hell of a lot of pressure, sir.'

'It's possible,' the superintendent said. 'You go home and rest. I want you back on this in the morning, then I'll need you at the station tomorrow night.'

'I'm fine, sir.'

'Look at yourself in the mirror, Tom. You need some sleep. Reed's out there and there are five constables combing the area. With a missing girl everyone's going to cooperate.'

'Someone needs to take charge.'

'Then let Reed do it for now. Go home. You're going to be putting in the hours from tomorrow.' He gestured at the papers strewn across his desk. 'I haven't been in here today just for my health, you know. Every available man's going to be on duty to stop trouble. The criminals in Leeds are going to think it's Christmas.' He shook his head. 'We won't have a single man out on the beat, they'll be able to do whatever they want.'

'We're still going to need people looking for Martha.'

Kendall shook his head. 'I asked the chief constable this morning. He wants everyone available to stop the violence when the replacements arrive and start work.'

'It won't make a blind bit of difference,' he argued. 'There'll still be fighting. You know that as well as I do, sir.'

'Tom,' Kendall said slowly, 'the council's given him his orders. This is more important to them than a missing girl.'

'A missing girl from a poor family, anyway. If the Parkinsons owned one of those big houses off Street Lane—'

'Tom!' Kendall cut him off with a warning. 'Go home. It's an order now.'

Annabelle stared at him. He couldn't read what was behind her eyes, whether it was anger or pity.

'By God,' she said finally, 'I've seen corpses look better than you.'

'I haven't,' he replied wearily. 'Not today, anyway.' He held her close, feeling the ache of tiredness rise in him. 'I was called out in the middle of the night and I've been going ever since.'

'Have you eaten?'

Harper had to think for a moment. 'No, I don't suppose I have.'

'Right.' She pulled away from him. 'You sit yoursen down and I'll heat something up. It won't be much but it'll fill you.'

They were in her rooms above the pub, the windows open to the night. The soft drift of conversation rose from the bar below. He sat for a moment but he couldn't settle, following her to the kitchen instead, watching as she busied herself with the pans, bringing bacon and two eggs from the larder.

'I'd rather have spent the day with you,' he said. 'I'm sorry.'

She smiled and shook her head. 'You apologize more than any man I've ever known, Tom Harper. Was it bad?' He nodded, letting the words flood out as she lit the gas and started to cook, hands moving deftly. When she was done she pulled the frying pan off the flame, sliding the food on to a plate, then cut and buttered two slices of bread. 'Get that in you,' she told him.

It was only when he'd finished, rubbing the last piece of bread around to catch the final stain of yolk, that he realized how hungry he'd been. All day his mind had been fixed on Col, then Betty, then Martha.

'There's cake if you want some,' Annabelle said. 'Can't have you wearing away to nothing.' He nodded, and heard her filling the kettle. He dozed for a moment then she was beside him again, a thick slice of something on the table and the tea exactly as he liked it, stewed and dark with a heavy spoonful of sugar. He took a long drink.

'That's better,' he said.

'I'm not going to have anyone say I let my man fade away to skin and bone.' Her mouth was smiling but her eyes were hard. 'They really say it's more important for those greedy buggers on the council to save a few pennies than to find a missing lass?'

'They do.'

There was fury in her long silence.

'You know who I feel sorry for?' she said finally. 'That woman in the jail. No one seems to care about her. Her husband dead, her daughter missing. The poor lass must be going mad. Can't they let her out?'

'Maybe for Col's funeral. Then it'll be straight back again.' He'd said nothing about the man selling Martha. He didn't dare, not yet, not to Annabelle.

'Bastards, the lot of them,' she said. 'And they want you to protect the blacklegs?'

'It's my job, love.'

'I know,' she said sympathetically. 'But there are folk who come and drink here who've lost their jobs because the bloody gas committee want to save a few precious shillings.'

'Bob Turnbull, Dick Green, Walter Boyd . . .' He began to list the names. He knew them all, he'd drunk and sung and laughed with them in the bar downstairs often enough.

'And they all have wives and kiddies to feed,' Annabelle pointed out, then stopped. 'Hark at us, eh? They'll be calling us anarchists next.'

He chuckled. 'I've been called worse in my time.'

She stroked his cheek and her fingers rasped against the stubble.

'Why don't you stop here tonight? Better than walking back out to your lodgings.' He raised his eyebrows. 'In the spare bedroom, before you get any ideas in that head of yours. There'll be a razor and strop around somewhere.'

At first he almost refused. But she was right; it was closer to the station and he was bone tired.

'You might as well learn it now, Tom Harper,' she told him. 'I'm always right. Remember that and it'll save a lot of grief later.'

He sat in the parlour as Annabelle made up the bed; she wasn't about to call Kitty the servant girl for something she could do herself in five minutes. There were paintings on the walls and a photograph of a younger Annabelle with her first husband, beaming for the camera, bursting with pride and joy. He just hoped he could make her that happy in time. A piano stood in the corner with music open on the stand. Solid chairs were gathered around the hearth. Everything just right. Nothing showy, but each piece was in good taste and expensive. She had money, he knew that. Her businesses were successful and she worked long hours to make them that way. But for the first time it struck him that she must be wealthy. He'd never even considered it before; she was simply Annabelle. What did she want with a bobby, he wondered. A policeman barely made enough to keep body and soul together. The only ones with money in their pockets were the ones who took bribes.

But he knew the answer. She loved him, just as he loved her.

'Right,' she said. 'It's all ready for you.'

She put her arms around him, holding him tight and kissing him hard, taking him by surprise. 'That's to keep you thinking of the wedding night,' she said, and the joy had returned to her eyes. She put her lips close to his ear. 'The garters are red today,' she whispered, and giggled as she pushed him through the door into the bedroom.

But Harper didn't sleep immediately. Instead he opened the window to the summer darkness. The long back garden stretched away, the city off in the distance. Somewhere he could hear the hoot of an owl and the call of night birds he couldn't identify. Where are you, he thought. Where the hell are you?

SIX

He felt a hand rubbing his shoulder lightly and opened his eyes. Annabelle was standing by the bed holding a cup of tea. She looked fresh, her hair already brushed, face made up, wearing a green silk dress he'd never seen before that shimmered in the half-light through the curtains.

'What time is it?' he asked with a yawn.

'Just gone five.' She put the cup on the table by the bed and he reached out his hands to her. 'No cuddles,' she warned him. 'I've already spent enough time getting ready this morning. I'll have breakfast waiting when you're done so you won't be going out on an empty belly again.'

There was a clean towel by the sink in the bathroom and hot water for shaving in a jug. The house was one of the few he'd been in with a water closet. Annabelle had insisted on it as soon as she became the landlady, she'd said. It still seemed like a novelty to him, a ridiculous luxury to someone who'd grown up sharing an outdoor privy with seven other houses.

By six, Harper was waiting at the tram stop at the corner of Roundhay Road and North Street. He'd bought a *Post* from the newsboy and thumbed through it as he waited. The front page was all about the gas problems. Editors and politicians were predicting chaos, no power for business and anarchy ruling the streets. Martha Parkinson only rated a tiny item on page three, a missing girl, the police searching for her. No mention that her father was dead and her mother in jail. But as soon as most people saw that she lived in Fidelity Court they'd move on to the next item, anyway.

He found a seat upstairs, the air fresh, the early sun almost the colour of lemon. He paid his threepence as the conductor came round, and the slow clop of the horses' hooves and the rhythm of the wheels rumbling in the iron tracks lulled him on the journey into town.

Annabelle had seen him off at the front door of the pub. Inside the smells of baking were coming from the kitchen. She held him close for a moment.

'Letting a man out first thing in the morning,' he said with a grin. 'Folk'll talk.'

'Let 'em.' She kissed him again. 'If they've nowt better to gossip about, what with all that's going on, they need their bumps felt. You make sure you look after yourself tonight,' she instructed him.

'I will. No one's going to crack my skull.'

'They'd better not,' she said fiercely, 'or I'll come looking for them.'

He folded the newspaper and stuck it in his pocket as he

alighted outside the market. The voices of the traders followed him as he strode down George Street to Millgarth. Tollman was already at the station desk.

'Anything?' Harper asked hopefully.

The older man shook his big head. 'Had a team out all night, Inspector. Nothing so far.'

It was what he'd expected. How did you find a small girl in a place as big as Leeds?

Reed was sleeping at his desk, his head cradled on his arms. But he woke as soon as Harper scraped his chair back, and sat upright, instantly alert. His eyes looked hunted and a line of spittle dripped from his mouth.

'It's only me, no need to panic.'

Reed shook his head to wake himself, then ran a hand over his hair.

'Sorry, I fell asleep,' he said sheepishly, wiping a hand across his lips.

'What did you find?'

'Nothing much. I came across someone who'd seen those two men talking to Ben East and another man who said they'd been in a pub with John Godfrey. Couldn't track either of them down last night, though.'

'I'll get to them today. You'd better go home and rest for a while. We're going to have a long night.' He pulled out the newspaper. 'Something to enjoy on the tram. Apparently the authorities believe things could become disturbing over the next few days.'

'Really?' The sergeant chuckled and rolled his eyes. 'I wonder what makes them think that?' He put on his bowler hat, adjusting it carefully. 'I'll see you this evening.'

Reed should have gone straight home, he knew that. He could feel the exhaustion rising up through him. He waited for the tram on Woodhouse Lane, determined he'd go directly to his lodgings and sleep until he needed to report for duty again.

As the tram slowly crossed the moor, rocking slightly with each turn of the wheels, he opened the newspaper Harper had given him, skimming from page to page, the ink staining his hands. There was nothing to interest him. Everything that affected his life he heard at the station. What was happening in London, around the empire and in other countries meant little. He'd been there, seen them during his years in the regiment. Paraded for the Queen in London, stationed in Gibraltar, service in Africa, Afghanistan, time in India. And he had no desire to return to any of them.

He alighted at the end of the Woodhouse Moor and crossed the street to Mould's Hyde Park Hotel. Just one drink, maybe two, before going to bed. Something to help him sleep. His lodgings were no more than five minutes' walk away.

The place smelt of beeswax, the wood glistening, the brass of the rails and pumps shining in the light that came through the window. Streaks of water shone on the black and white tiles of the floor where it had just been mopped. He often came here on the way back from work, but that was usually in the evenings. Mornings seemed different here. There was a single drinker, huddled away in the corner, and a potman whose face he didn't recognize polishing the mirror behind the bar.

'Gin,' he ordered, counting out the change from his pocket. He took the glass over to a table and let it sit for a minute. As long as he could do that, just stare at the alcohol without touching it or drinking, he was fine, he was in control.

Finally he put his fingers around the glass and tasted the liquid, feeling the fire and the taste rush into his throat. He closed his eyes, letting it burn through his body. Until he joined the army he'd rarely drunk. Not that he'd been teetotal; only his uncle was, and he was chapel. But Reed had just enjoyed beer then. He'd taken the taste for gin in the NCO mess. The sergeants had drunk it and corporals like him imitated them, seeing themselves like that in a few years.

He took another small sip, letting it linger in his mouth before swallowing it. There'd been precious little alcohol in Kabul. It was too far to bring it from India. All they had was what a few enterprising troopers could distil in the barracks. Godawful stuff, but everyone bought it. They needed it to warm them through the frigid winters and take the edge off the furnace that was summer there.

Mostly, though, they drank to forget what they saw. The troopers captured on patrol, and found later, tortured and mutilated. The lucky ones were dead. He found one on a bleak hillside west of the city, staked out among the rocks. The sun had burned his skin to blisters and blood had soaked into the ground where he'd been castrated. He was going to die, his tongue swollen, mind raving. Reed had tipped water from his canteen into the man's mouth, seeing his eyes clear for a moment.

'Kill me,' he'd said thickly. 'Please.'

He'd raised his rifle, taken aim, and the shot had echoed around the valley. That night he'd drunk himself into a dreamless sleep before the face could haunt him. It still returned, all too often, along with the other things he'd seen done, by tribesmen and English alike.

As soon as he returned to England he put in his papers to leave. He'd seen too much. He had to do it to stay sane. Too many of his friends, people he'd trusted with his life, were dead. Some men could cope with it, shrug it off. He wasn't one of them. Becoming a bobby seemed a good compromise and Leeds was close enough to his family in Bradford. He could visit yet still stay away. In this job he was keeping order, finding those who'd done wrong and putting them away. He could pick out the others on the force who'd spent time in the army. It was there in the way they looked at a street as they entered it, how they carried themselves. But he kept his distance from them. From everyone, really, except Harper.

Reed didn't have a girl. Most of the time he never missed it. He knew it wouldn't be fair to put her through the bad dreams, worse to have her there when his anger flared uncontrollably. If he needed someone, there were plenty available for a few pennies, factory girls needing a little extra money.

Tomorrow morning his letter should reach Whitby, he thought. With luck he'd have a reply on Tuesday or Wednesday. Maybe he'd find his tiny piece of paradise.

He drained the glass and went back for another, a large one. That would be all, he told himself. Then he'd go home and sleep and the gin would keep it all at bay so he could wake feeling rested.

As the hands of the clock turned to seven, Superintendent Kendall strode in wearing his best uniform. The braid and buttons gleamed, his cap badge shone and his boots were carefully polished. He waved Harper into his office.

'What do you have for me, Tom? I need to go to a meeting at the Town Hall in a minute.'

'Not much, sir.' He recounted what Reed had told him. 'I'll catch up with the pair of them today. After that I might have a better idea what to do. The night beat have been scouring all the courts and yards. The problem is that we don't even know where to look—'

'Or whether we're looking for a girl or a body,' Kendall said. 'I know. You've got until eight tonight. Then I want you over at the Midland Station.'

'Yes, sir.'

'The strikers are going to try to stop the replacements getting through. Mingle with them. If you spot anyone causing trouble, arrest them.'

Harper nodded. If he tried to arrest any of the strikers, the rest of them would tear him apart. He'd be lucky to escape with his life.

'The constables will come to help you,' Kendall went on.

They bloody wouldn't, he thought. They'd be hard pressed to look after themselves if it was as bad as everyone expected.

'Just do your job,' the superintendent told him. 'If you learn anything about the girl, send a message over to the Town Hall. I'll be there most of the day.'

'Yes, sir.'

Ben East. He hadn't heard that name in a couple of years. Another one who'd never held a real job but made his living like a magpie, stealing the shiny things he saw. All too often, though, he'd been caught. The man had been in Armley three times to Harper's knowledge, and probably more than that.

John Godfrey was a different matter altogether. He'd shared a drink with him a couple of times. Godfrey was in his forties, an honest man all his life. He worked at the dye plant on Fearn's Island, with a neat, clean home in Turk's Head Yard. What would he want with a couple of characters like that? Or what would they want with him?

Briggate was already busy with buses and carts, some piled

impossibly high with goods, the drivers urging on their horses. A hackney carriage weaved wildly in and out of the traffic, the cabbie skilfully guiding the horse between vehicles. Pedestrians filled the pavement, most walking purposefully, a few lounging and watching. As soon as they saw Harper with the grim, determined look on his face, their eyes would slide away and they'd slope off to another spot, out of sight.

In Turk's Head Yard, Whitelock's was already open, the door wide to air out the bar, a man shining the brass, the scent of wax rising as a woman polished the wood. The house he wanted was at the other end of the court, its glass clean, cheap lace curtains keeping out prying eyes.

He knocked on the door, expecting Dorothy Godfrey to answer. Instead he was face to face with her husband, a stooped, rounded man who peered at him and blinked.

'It's Inspector Harper,' he explained.

Godfrey's eyes widened. 'Hello, lad. What's the matter? Have I done summat wrong?' His voice was a wheeze and he coughed at the end of the sentence.

'Can I come in, Mr Godfrey? You don't need your neighbours knowing everything.'

'Aye, reet enough,' he agreed readily, standing aside. The parlour was clean, the boards swept, the empty grate blackleaded, but it seemed strangely bare. Two chairs, a table pushed against the wall, but none of the china that would usually fill the mantel in a house like this. He could hear noises in the kitchen; Mrs Godfrey already preparing dinner, most likely.

'I thought you'd be at work,' Harper said.

'Not these days,' the man told him with a weak smile. 'Me lungs aren't what they were, I'm allus stopping and coughing. And my eyes, can't hardly see to do owt, so they had to let me go.'

'How do you manage?'

'We've saved a little bit, but . . .'

Harper understood. Times would be hard and everything they could sell would be sitting in the pawnshop. It explained the sparseness of the room.

'I'm wondering about a couple of fellows you might know.'

'Oh aye?' Godfrey cocked his head.

'One big one, looks like a boxer, the one smaller with dark hair.'

The colour left the man's face and he began to cough again, finally bowing his head, dragging a handkerchief from his pocket and spitting dark phlegm into it.

'Who are they, John?' Harper asked softly. 'I need to know. A little girl's life might depend on it.'

'What, that little one from Fidelity Court that's missing?'

'Martha Parkinson, yes. It's important, please, tell me about them.'

Godfrey took a thin breath. The inspector watched him. He wanted to talk but he was scared of something, Finally the man made a decision and raised his head.

'They said they'd hurt my wife if I talked to the coppers,' he said quietly. 'They meant it, too. That big one, his face, he looks just like he wants to hurt someone.'

'Why would they threaten you?'

'I borrowed some money. Just a little to see us through. They came to collect it.'

'How much did you borrow?' Harper asked.

'A fiver. We'd been paying it back, two bob a week, like I'd agreed. Then these two came and said they wanted it all.'

'How much?'

'Seven quid.' His eyes looked helpless. 'We don't have that kind of brass, Mr Harper. Why would I want a lend if I had cash like that?'

'What did they say?'

'I've got two weeks to find it.' He shook his head. 'Said they were being generous, giving me all that time. And if I didn't pay they'd take it out on my wife.'

'Which one did the talking?'

'The small one. The big lad, all he needed to do was stand there. He terrified me, Inspector, he really did.'

'What were their names?'

'They didn't say. Didn't need to, really, did they?' He tried to smile but failed.

'When were they here?' Harper asked.

'Four days back. I've not slept proper since. There was a knock last night, I was scared to answer it in case they'd come back.' It explained why Reed hadn't talked to him.

'Who did you borrow the money from?' He hoped Godfrey wasn't too scared to answer.

'Henry Bell.'

He should have guessed. Bell made his fortune through his generosity, lending money to those who needed it, then charging interest that crippled them. The police had been trying to put him away for years but when folk refused to testify against him there was little they could do.

'These men, had you seen them before?'

'Never. They didn't sound as they were from here, though.'

'Oh?'

'Aye. Manchester, if you ask me. I might not see or breathe too well these days, but I can pick out an accent,' Godfrey said proudly.

'If they come back, don't let them in. Shout and yell and someone will call a constable.'

The man nodded. Harper wanted to say that he'd make sure the pair never bothered him again, that he'd be safe, but that was a promise he couldn't make. Not yet.

'Thank you, Mr Godfrey.'

'I'll not let anything happen to my missus. Over my dead body.'

'Then we'll have to make sure it doesn't come to that.'

Back in the sunlight he fitted the hat on his head. Money, fear, and those ready to take advantage of the folk who had nothing and scrabbled for a living. There were always too many who traded in those things, the Henry Bells and Tosh Walkers, who made their money out of misery.

But what John Godfrey had told him changed everything. It meant that Col hadn't sold Martha, after all. He must have owed Bell money and they'd taken her to pay off his debt. Maybe they'd even thrown him a pound or two along with a warning to keep quiet.

Then, after he'd come calling, asking about the girl, they'd returned to make sure Parkinson couldn't talk. Why? Why had they wanted the girl instead of money? He couldn't make sense of that. What had the bastards done with Martha?

Ben East was exactly where he'd expected, outside the large Co-op on Albion Street, watching for a rich pocket to pick. His

eyes darted around, alert for a uniformed constable but never
noticing a policeman in plain clothes until it was too late.

'I wouldn't try to scarper,' Harper warned him. 'I'd catch you
in ten yards.'

'I'm not doing anything, Mr Harper.' He was a scarecrow of
a man, scrawny as twigs, in need of a shave, never quite meeting
anyone's glance.

'Of course you're not, Ben. You're just taking the air and
trying not to think about those men who work for Henry Bell.'
East glanced away furtively and Harper sighed, his voice turning
hard. 'Look, you've been seen with them. Don't go telling me
you don't know who they are. I want to talk to them about
Martha Parkinson, so you'd best not bugger me around. Who
are they?'

'I don't know their names, Mr Harper,' he pleaded. 'I don't,
honest. They come round a few days back and said I had a
fortnight to pay up a fiver. Then the big one hit me a few
times.'

'Where?'

'On me belly and me chest where it dun't show.' He looked
shamefaced at the humiliation of it. 'T' little 'un said it'd be
worse if I didn't pay.'

'Have you seen them before?'

East shook his head. 'Never. New, I reckon.'

'How much did you borrow?'

'Two quid,' he answered bleakly. 'Two bloody quid. What is
it, you think they took that little girl?'

'I'm not sure, but I'm going to find out.'

'Who's the biggest, nastiest uniform we have?' Harper asked
Tollman.

'Robbie Collins,' the desk sergeant answered without hesitation. 'You must have seen him, sir. Over six foot, looks like he
could push down a wall without even trying. He used to play
rugby for Holbeck before he became a bobby.'

He knew the man. Exactly who he needed for a visit to Henry
Bell.

'What's his beat?'

'Round by Wellington Street. Why?'

'I'd like him to meet me at the corner of Briggate and Commercial Street in half an hour.'

The sergeant looked at him quizzically but nodded his head.

For a moment, Harper considered going over to the Town Hall to tell the superintendent what he planned to do. But the man was busy with his preparations. And what he didn't know about, he couldn't turn down.

Collins was everything Tollman had promised, a huge, lumbering man with large hands and the sort of face to scare small children. God only knew how he managed on the beat; everyone must have been petrified of him.

'You know who Henry Bell is?' Harper asked.

'I do.' The voice seemed to start at the man's boots, deep and booming.

'We're going to bring him in. All you have to do is exactly what I tell you. I want him to feel a little frightened.'

Collins smiled, his mouth disappearing into his thick moustache. 'That'll be a pleasure, sir. I've no time for Shylocks like him.'

Henry Bell lived in Far Headingley, in a big, new house filled with his wife and six daughters. But he did his business from a shabby little office on Commercial Street, above Kettlewell the insurance agent. Harper led the way, Collins's feet resounding heavily on each tread as they climbed the steps.

He turned the knob and entered. Bell glanced up and quickly slid a magazine away under the desk, an annoyed frown turning to a smile.

'Inspector.' He was immaculately dressed in a suit that would have cost Harper more than a week's wages; nothing off the peg for him. His shirt was a bright white, the wing collar well-starched. He wore it crisp and high under a smooth, smug face. 'What can I do for you?'

Harper nodded and Collins moved quickly around the desk, lifting Bell by his collar and slipping a pair of handcuffs on to his wrists, ratcheting them just tight enough to make the man wince.

'What's this all about?' Bell protested. 'I run a perfectly legal business here.'

'You employ two men.'

'Employ?' He looked bemused. 'There's only me here, Inspector. You can see that for yourself.'

'I want their names, Henry. And I want to know where Martha Parkinson is.' He waited a few seconds for an answer. When none came, he told Collins, 'You know what to do.'

With one big fist clamped around the man's arm, the constable marched Bell back down the stairs. Harper had no doubt that in a minute or two someone would be running over to Park Place, where Bell's lawyer, Mr Desmond, had his office. Another half hour and he'd be presenting himself at Millgarth, demanding to see his client.

But Bell wouldn't be there. Instead, Harper was taking him to Marsh Lane. With luck he'd have two good hours to work on the man before Desmond caught up and demanded his release.

SEVEN

'Y ou heard what happened this afternoon?' Reed asked. They were sitting in the waiting room of the Midland station, listening to the rain drum heavily on the roof. Crowds stood out in the downpour, restless and shouting. Hundreds of them filled the forecourt and the street beyond. It was ten o'clock; the platforms were silent, just a few railwaymen walking around. The uniforms were outside, waiting under the awning for their orders. Harper had arrived a few minutes earlier, sodden and miserable from the downpour that had begun two hours before.

'What?'

'They tried to haul a marquee over to the gasworks for the blacklegs to sleep in. The strikers stopped them and beat up the drivers. One of them's in hospital. The chief constable and the brass had to come down on their horses to make sure it got through.'

'What did the chief do after that?'

'Went back to the Town Hall, of course.' Reed snorted. 'Where have you been, anyway?'

'Trying to pry some truth out of Henry Bell.'

In the end he'd managed ten straight hours at Marsh Lane with the man, after taking him in through the back door. When Desmond finally arrived, full of bluster and righteous fury, the desk sergeant had denied Bell was there. He couldn't be; the man hadn't been booked in, the name wasn't in the log, so it was impossible. Eventually the lawyer had gone away again.

But it had proved to be ten hours of frustration. He'd asked the same questions over and over, his eyes intent on Bell's face for any hesitation or inconsistency. Every time, the man insisted he didn't employ anyone, that he didn't know anything about Martha Parkinson's disappearance, that his business were perfectly legitimate. The only time he'd looked worried was when Constable Collins asked ominously, 'Do you want me to have a word with him, sir?'

For a moment Harper had been tempted. He needed answers and Bell wasn't giving him anything. Reluctantly he shook his head. As it was he'd be in enough trouble for this. If Bell presented himself covered in bruises, accompanied by the best lawyer in Leeds, he'd be dismissed from the force.

At nine, knowing he couldn't put it off any longer, he escorted the man out of the station and left him to make his smirking way home in the rain.

Leeds was dark and dead as he walked across the bridge and down to the Midland station. The streets were like pitch with no gas for the lamps. None had been made since the stokers were locked out. And with no gas supply to power their engines, the factories had been forced to close.

'You should have called me in,' Reed said. 'I'd have made him talk and not left any marks.'

Harper lit a Woodbine and paced around the room. Anger and frustration scalded his belly.

'Next time,' he promised, and meant it. He'd be talking to Bell again, and soon. 'When's this bloody train due, anyway?'

'Not until half past two, for all the good it'll do. I saw notices chalked on the streets earlier. The strikers already know when it's going to arrive.' Reed lay back along the bench. He had the soldier's knack of being able to sleep anywhere, any time.

Harper wandered around. His footsteps echoed as he went out along the platform, looking into the night. At least the rain had finally slackened to a dull, warm drizzle.

He kicked at a pebble in frustration. Ten hours. He should have been able to break Bell in that time. He was good at his job, knew how to ask questions, how to lead someone along. But the man simply hadn't shifted. He was lying, both of them knew that. Yet no matter how many different ways he approached it, Bell clung to his story. It was more than guilt. It had to be. It was fear. He was afraid of what someone might do.

At midnight he finally settled in the waiting room, tipped the hat forward over his eyes and tried to sleep. The tramp of feet woke him. Reed was already up and stretching, glancing out through the glass.

'What is it?' Harper asked.

'They're taking the uniforms out to make a cordon to the gasworks. Poor buggers. What time is it?'

The inspector pulled the watch from his waistcoat pocket and opened it. 'Quarter past two.' He heard the crowd begin to bay as the constables emerged. Thank God he wasn't still one of them.

'What do we do?' Reed asked.

'We wait.'

From the cover of the entrance he watched as the constables formed two lines, forcing the strikers back to clear a passage. Men howled and yelled at them, knocking off caps and trying to land blows. And the train hadn't even arrived yet.

Then, from somewhere down the line came the long, sad sound of an engine's whistle and the loud rumble of wheels on the track. The crowd grew louder, more frantic. One constable went down, clutching at his face as the blood poured.

The train pulled alongside a far platform with a low squeal of brakes and a thick spout of steam. But there were no carriages behind it, only trucks. Harper waited for a minute. No passengers emerged.

'It's a goods train,' he yelled, hoping someone would hear. But the strikers' blood was up; they battered at the police, who tried desperately to hold their lines. 'It's a goods train,' he repeated, but his voice was lost in the tumult.

Slowly, as no one emerged, they all quietened. Five injured policemen were led away. Everyone waited, catching their breath before the next conflict. But nothing happened. Half past two became quarter to three, then the top of the hour. The superintendent in charge stood his men down, bringing them back inside the station. Finally, at half past three, the order came around: report to the Town Hall for new instructions. At least the rain had passed, scudding away to leave the pavements wet and puddled.

Harper and Reed made their slow way back up Meadow Lane, over the bridge. There was only the sound of the lapping water in the still night. Somewhere in the distance came a noise he couldn't make out. It sounded human, but it was more than that, different. At first he thought it was his hearing. Then they turned on to the Headrow as the moon appeared from behind the clouds.

Reed stopped.

'Christ Almighty,' he said quietly, his voice full of awe, 'look at that.'

The crowd in front of the Town Hall filled Victoria Square and Park Lane, and spilled into the streets beyond.

'How many do you think?' Reed asked. 'Five thousand?'

'At least,' Harper agreed, unable to take his eyes from the sight. Some had banners, others were standing still. They were chanting; that was the sound he'd heard.

'I haven't seen that many there since the Queen opened the place,' Reed said with a strange reverence in his voice. 'My father had me up on his shoulders, and everywhere I looked there were people.'

The crowds were thin around the rear entrance on Great George Street, just some spotters and a cordon of policemen in the tall shadows cast by the building. They went through, finding more chaos inside. Groups of councilmen talked urgently, while the chief constable huddled in a conference with the mayor and a fat man whose thick side whiskers extended to his chin.

'What's happening?' Harper asked a uniformed sergeant who was rushing past.

'They only brought the bloody replacement workers to the main station instead, didn't they? Madness.' He shook his head at the stupidity. 'We've got them all safe in the crypt. Now they're trying to work out how to get them to the gasworks in one piece.'

He moved off again just as a constable tugged at Harper's sleeve. 'Inspector, Superintendent Kendall wants you. Downstairs.'

Harper raised his eyebrows at Reed and they followed the young man. His uniform was stained and a black eye was starting to blossom. But he seemed content enough.

'Over there, sir.' He pointed to a door on the far side.

First they had to negotiate their way between hundreds of men sitting and lying on the floor. They were talking in small groups, trying to sleep or smoking their pipes in the light of dozens of candles and oil lamps.

'It's like bloody Bedlam,' Harper muttered as he tripped over a leg. Finally he pushed the door open. A man in a tattered old jacket and trousers was lying on the floor, a cloth cap still on his head. Kendall stood over him, uniform coat open, his face haggard.

'Take a look,' he said.

Harper knelt by the man, feeling for a pulse in the wrist. Nothing. He pushed the body on to its side, fingertips feeling down the man's back until he touched the blood. Still warm. He'd been stabbed. A neat job.

'Who is he?' Harper asked.

'One of the replacements,' the superintendent said.

'What happened?'

'They delivered the poor sods to the wrong station so we had to bring them here.' Kendall's voice was sober and clear. 'There were plenty of the strikers outside. We didn't have any choice but to run the gauntlet. This one made it down here then collapsed. Died about a quarter of an hour ago.' He looked from Harper to Reed. 'You two are going to find out who killed him. Chief constable's orders.'

'But—' Harper started to object.

Kendall silenced him with a look. 'Whatever you're about to say, the answer is no,' he said angrily. 'For now nothing else matters except this. This poor man comes here to work and someone murders him. That's going to look bad enough for us. It'll be a damned sight worse if we don't find out who did it.'

'What about Jones or Payne?' Harper said. 'They could look after this.'

'Sergeant Jones was hit in the head by a brick earlier this evening,' the superintendent explained. 'He's in the infirmary and he won't be back for a few days. Payne's still too new for this. Right now I have you two and a detective constable.'

'What about the other divisions?'

'This happened on our patch,' Kendall told him coldly. 'We handle it. Orders.'

'Martha Parkinson, sir,' Harper reminded him. 'This man's dead. She might still be alive.'

'This is your priority, Inspector. The chief doesn't care about Martha Parkinson until this has been solved. Do I make myself clear?'

Harper glanced at Reed. 'Yes, sir. Do we even know exactly where the stabbing happened?'

'Somewhere between the station and here. You'll have to ask his friends, they're outside. The surgeon's been called, he'll be examining the body tonight. I've arranged a transfer to the mortuary.'

Kendall turned to leave but the inspector called out, 'Just out of curiosity, sir, did the surgeon take a look at Col Parkinson?'

'He did. You were right, it was murder.' He pointed at the man on the floor. 'But this is what you solve first.' The door closed behind him.

'Dear God, where do we even begin?' Reed asked with a frustrated shout. 'What does he want us to do, go around everyone out in the square and asked if they knifed someone tonight?'

Harper was staring at the corpse. The poor bastard had come to Leeds hoping to earn a few pounds and he'd be going home in a coffin. Even if the man was a blackleg, he didn't deserve that. He raised his eyes. 'We'll do what we can.'

'We don't have a chance,' Reed said bleakly. 'You know that, Tom. All they'll end up doing is blaming the strikers.'

'Then we'd better find out who did it.' He paused. 'And I'll tell you something else, Billy, I'm buggered if I'm ignoring Martha Parkinson.'

EIGHT

Harold Gordon. That had been the man's name. His friends told Harper and Reed when they came out, desperate to know how ill he was. The two policemen exchanged a quick look.

'I'm sorry,' Harper told them. 'He's dead.'

For a moment there was a deep well of silence around them

as the men took in the news. Then the questions began, everyone speaking at once until the Inspector held up his hand.

'How?' one of them demanded, pushing through the others. His face was red with fury, lips pinched together, eyes blazing.

'He was stabbed, Mr . . .?'

'Gordon. Harry was me brother.'

Harper tipped his head and Reed stepped in smoothly, gently leading the man away to speak to him.

'Where did it happen?' the inspector asked the others.

'Just out on the steps. Just this side of the lions.' The man who answered was older than the rest, leaning against the wall. He slowly took the pipe from his mouth, tamping down the tobacco with his thumb.

'Here?' Harper asked in surprise. 'The Town Hall steps?'

'Aye,' he answered. 'Folk were pushing and swearing at us and trying to hit us, while the bobbies cleared a path. Harry were next to me, over here.' He patted his left side to illustrate. 'I heard him groan and he just fell against me. I thought summat had hit him so I put me arm around him and helped him inside and sat him down.' He looked at the others for confirmation, all of them nodding. 'Ben over there went and fetched someone and they brought him down here.'

'How did you know Mr Gordon?'

'He's me next door neighbour. Him, his wife and kiddies.' He paused. 'I'm Bob Allinson. We're all of us from the same street.' There were eight of them, he explained, laid off from the cotton mill and needing work. 'When we heard they were looking for people to work in a new gasworks, we applied.'

'New?' Harper asked, not understanding.

'That's what they said.' The men around him murmured agreement.

'There isn't any new works,' the inspector told them.

'Then why are we here?' Allinson asked, confused.

'You're blacklegs. That's why they wanted you. And that's why all those crowds are out there. The workers are on strike.' And probably why someone killed Harry Gordon, but he didn't say that. He didn't need to.

Sadness and anxiety mixed on the men's faces. They'd been duped, betrayed, and their friend had paid the price.

'Aye, well,' Allinson said finally, packing more than Harper could have imagined into those two words.

'Did you see anyone close, anyone who could have stabbed Mr Gordon?' he asked. The man shook his head slowly. 'We were just trying to keep our heads down and get in, lad. Last thing on our minds was looking at faces.'

He understood. But that didn't help him at all. They talked a few minutes more, but there was little more they could tell him.

'Do right by him, lad,' Allinson said as Harper turned to leave.

'I'll do my best,' he promised, and the other man gave him a quick nod.

Reed was waiting, looking drawn and glum. The notebook was clutched tight in his fist.

'Anything?' Harper asked.

'He told me about his brother, but nothing to help us.' They walked to the front doors of the hall, a line of police guarding them, and stared out in the early light at the crowd, still thousands of them. And spilling up the steps, the inspector noted.

'Where do you want me to start?' Reed asked wearily. 'You'd better tell me, Tom, because I don't have any idea.'

'Go back to the station and write up a report for the super.'

'What about you?'

'I'm going to see someone who might be able to help us.'

'Who?' the sergeant wondered, but Harper just gave a quick smile and left.

It was barely six but he knew there'd be people at the union office on Kirkgate; they'd have been there all night. The streets were quiet, only a few tired-looking early souls about. For most there'd be no work again today. With no gas, there was no power for the factories and businesses. Harper had heard that another train with replacement workers had pulled into Holbeck an hour before, and they'd been rushed across the street to the gasworks. But even with them there it would be many hours before more gas was produced.

No smoke plumed from the chimneys. Leeds already smelt fresher, the stink and stench dispersed by the rain and a breeze coming down from the Pennines. But soot still covered the buildings. It rubbed off on clothes, caught in the throat, floated in the air and left the stonework black as the grave.

A small crowd was gathered around the doorway across from the Ancient Orders of Foresters' hall. The small brass sign read *National Union of Gasworkers and General Labourers of Great Britain and Ireland*. Harper eased his way between the people and entered.

It was no more than a single small room with bare boards and two desks, each piled high with papers. Behind one of them sat Thomas Maguire, exactly where Harper expected. From the look of him he'd been here for a day or two, his red hair awry, suit crumpled and a fine growth of bristles across his cheeks. He glanced up with wild, intense eyes. His frown of annoyance turned to amusement as he recognized the policeman.

'Come to arrest me, Inspector?'

They'd met the previous year when Harper had been sent to observe a labour meeting at Vicar's Croft. The police were wary of trouble. They'd expected a thousand builders to attend, all of them ready to go on strike. In the end, three thousand had arrived, overwhelming the place. Maguire had been one of the speakers, a passionate, convincing man in his middle twenties, full of energy and fire. He *cared*. That much was obvious in his words. There'd been no trouble that day, and Maguire had organized the strike that won the builders an eight-hour day.

Harper had talked to the man when he was finished, only a short conversation but he remembered it clearly. And it seemed that he'd stayed in Maguire's memory, too. Like Annabelle, Maguire had grown up in the Bank; he knew what it was like to be poor. His parents were Irish, and there was still a trace of that in his voice.

'Not today, Mr Maguire. Sorry to disappoint you.'

The young man sat back in his chair and rubbed at his face with pale hands. 'Then what can I do for you? I have a strike to run, Mr Harper.'

'I know that. I've just come from the Town Hall.'

The man raised his eyebrows. 'Looking after the blacklegs? Our people are going to keep them pinned in there.'

'It's a bit more serious than that,' Harper told him. 'One of them was stabbed as he made his way in. He's dead.'

Maguire leaned forward, suddenly attentive, giving a brief glance to the man at the other desk. 'The poor, sad man,' he muttered. His eyes were shrewd and suspicious. 'You think one of our men did it?'

Harper shrugged. 'There are thousands of them in Victoria Square. They're angry, they were shoving at the blacklegs. What would you think?'

'I'd think you have a difficult case, Inspector. But I'm not sure what you want me to do.'

'I'd like you to talk to those men down there. They'll listen to you.'

'And say what?' Maguire asked sharply. 'Ask someone to give himself up so he can be hanged for murder?'

'The man who died has a wife and children. He's just like those on strike.' Maguire started to object, but Harper kept talking. 'You know what the blacklegs were told? That they were coming to work in a new plant.'

'Really?' he asked sharply. He nodded at the man behind the other desk, who picked up his hat and quickly left. 'We have a strike we can win, Inspector. And if they try and move those blacklegs from the Town Hall out to the New Wortley works there could be more people dead.'

'You know the mayor's sent for the cavalry?'

Maguire shrugged. 'Battles to be fought.'

'Think about what the papers will say,' Harper told him. 'It won't look good.'

'Come on, Inspector. When does the press ever treat the working man fairly? We're already scum to them. Listen to this—' He grabbed a copy of that morning's *Yorkshire Post* off the desk and started to read out loud: *'The town in darkness'.* That's just the headline. *On the evening of the first day we do not like the look of the contest.'* He looked up. 'They'd like to see us crushed, Mr Harper, but we're damned if we're going to be. They'll use this and I can't stop them. I'm sorry someone's died, but I need to worry about all those men out there.'

'He was a human being, too,' the inspector reminded him, his gaze steady. 'And those men are as hard done by as your own.'

'Perhaps,' Maguire allowed.

Harper turned to leave. He'd hoped for more, but this strike was war. A sudden thought struck him. 'You work as a photographer's assistant, don't you?'

'When time allows.' The man smiled and waved a hand around the office. 'Not so much at the moment.'

'Who do you work for?'

'The London Photographic Company up on Briggate. Why?'

'Do you remember a girl having her picture taken last year? She'd have been eight. Long dark hair.'

'We probably get five to ten of those a week, Mr Harper. Last year? I could pass her on the street and not know her face. I'm sorry, I can't help you.'

Harper cut through the outdoor market on his way back to the station. The first stalls were setting up, men moving half-heartedly, with muttered conversations and grumbles. No one was waiting to buy and he guessed precious few would arrive during the day. No gas meant no work and no wages; people would have no money to buy anything.

The café by the fish market was open. Like so many other places, they still cooked with an old coal stove, keeping to the familiar ways; pans boiled and sizzled on the blacklead range in the kitchen. Today, that meant constant trade. After a long wait, the harried waitress brought porridge, tea, and bread with dripping to his table. He ate gratefully, relishing the taste and wondering when he'd ever find time to eat again.

He finally pushed the plate away, lit a Woodbine and sipped at the drink. Reed had been right – how were they supposed to find a killer in that mob? For a minute he'd hoped that Maguire might be willing to help, but he was more concerned with his own men than the death of a blackleg.

Harper smoked two cigarettes as he sat and tried to think, the tea slowly growing tepid in the chipped mug. People came and went, but he scarcely noticed them as he tried to imagine what he could do, how he could even begin to solve this murder.

Finally he stood, brushing the fallen ash off his coat, stroked his moustache to clean it and walked back out to the street.

Behind Millgarth the police wagons were lined up, the horses docile in their traces. Inside, crowds of uniformed men filled the rooms, some talking, others trying to grab brief moments of rest. He saw black eyes and bruises, torn coats, a bandaged head, one constable hobbling with a stick.

The office was quieter. Reed had finished his report and was leaning back in his chair, dozing; he should do the same. But even as he tried to make himself comfortable he knew it was hopeless. His mind swirled with pictures that weren't going to grant him any peace. Harold Gordon lying on the floor with his empty eyes. Col Parkinson swinging from the beam. Little Martha out there somewhere.

Harper worked at his desk until nine, bringing his notes on the cases up to date. Not that there seemed to be a great deal to write. Much of the time he simply sat and brooded, trying to find a way ahead in his investigations.

As the clock struck the hour he finally gave up in frustration, threw down the pen and stood up.

'Work to do,' he said, tapping Reed on the shoulder. 'Come on.'

By the time he left the station the sergeant was right behind him, rushing as he crammed the bowler hat down on his head and straightened the sleeves of his suit.

'Where are we going?' Reed asked.

'We're going to pay Henry Bell another visit and see what he's remembered overnight.'

They cut through the courts between Vicar Lane and Briggate, coming out to a street that was almost deserted. Leeds seemed like an empty town. Shopkeepers stood hopefully in their doorways, vainly gazing up and down for custom. Carts, cabs and trams moved smoothly and rapidly along the road.

'You'd think everyone had left and forgotten to tell us,' Reed said.

'If they have any sense they'll all be at home. Half the businesses are probably closed anyway. And Leeds isn't any place for a woman right now, not with everything ready to explode.'

The sergeant grunted his agreement as they turned on to Commercial Street. Harper caught a glimpse of someone in the shadows at the rear of a shop, writing by candlelight. We might as well have moved back fifty years, he thought.

They clattered up the stairs to Bell's office. Harper turned the door handle and walked in. But the small room was empty.

'Maybe he's one of those who's avoiding Leeds today,' Reed suggested.

'And left his door unlocked?' The Inspector shook his head.
'I made sure it was secure when we took him yesterday. Besides,
with a strike on there'll be men needing money. These'll be busy
times for Henry.'

'What do you want to do?'

Harper grinned. 'Good chance for a nosy around, anyway.'

There was little in the battered desk. A few magazines, all of
them well-thumbed, the ink smeared, a couple of art postcards
of naked women pushed to the back of a drawer. No ledgers, no
list of debtors.

'He probably keeps everything safe at home,' the sergeant
grumbled.

'Maybe. Try that cupboard in the corner.'

He heard the door creak open, then turned quickly at Reed's
sudden intake of breath.

NINE

B ell's wrists had been tied tightly behind his back. He'd
been strangled, the fingermarks still vivid on his neck,
eyes bulging wide in terror and desperation. Harper placed
his hand against the man's face. The flesh was waxy and cool;
he'd been dead quite a few hours. He rubbed the jacket, his
fingertips feeling dampness on the wool. When he'd turned Bell
out of the station on Marsh Lane the night before it had been
pouring with rain; the man hadn't had a raincoat.

'What do you think?' Reed asked.

'This happened last night,' he said slowly. He stood, gazing
down at the corpse. 'If I had to guess, our Mr Bell came back
here last night after I'd finished with him. Someone must have
been waiting for him.'

'That still leaves who and why.'

The inspector pursed his lips. 'My money's on the prizefighter
and his friend. Look at those marks on his neck. Whoever did
that had strong hands. And he strangled Bell from the front, too.
He was staring right into his eyes as he killed him.'

'A cold man.'

'Aye,' Harper agreed slowly. 'Very.'

'That still leaves why, though.'

The inspector looked out of the window at the people passing two floors below. None of them glanced up; no one had any idea there was a body up here, the life squeezed out of it.

'They must have heard we'd taken him in,' he said, ideas taking shape in his mind.

'Maybe they wanted to see what he'd told you,' Reed suggested.

'Possibly.' He wasn't too sure. Bell had been scared. He'd tried to hide it in his bluster, to brush it off by repeating the same answers. But he hadn't succeeded, even though he stuck to his story time after time. The fear was always there in his eyes.

'Or maybe it was to make sure he couldn't tell you anything.'

He nodded. 'I think that's more likely.'

'You know, if we report this we'll be stuck writing up reports all morning.'

'We were never here, Billy,' Harper replied quietly. 'There's nothing useful, anyway. Just close that door and we'll walk away.'

Reed shrugged, pushed the cupboard door to, the corpse out of sight again, and they left.

'I've been thinking,' the sergeant said and they strode up Albion Street. 'I'll try to find some of the uniforms who were on the steps when they brought the blacklegs in last night. They might have seen something.'

'Good.' Harper nodded his approval. 'Try for names, faces, anywhere we can start. I'll talk to Gordon's friends again. They might have remembered something.'

The crowds still filled Victoria Square, thousands of them, moving back and forth like a tide of people lapping up against the Town Hall.

'God help the blacklegs if they try to take them out through that,' Harper said as they stood and watched.

'They won't,' Reed said, his voice full of military certainty. 'They'll wait until the cavalry's here and use the troops to guard them as they go.' He shrugged, suddenly embarrassed. 'It's what I'd do, anyway.'

Inside the building, a clamour of voices and footsteps echoed around the high marble corridors and stairways. The blacklegs had been moved from the crypt into the main hall. Half of them were asleep, jackets bunched under their heads for pillows. They'd been fed sandwiches and mugs of cocoa; pieces of crust were scattered around the floor.

Harper searched through the crowd for Gordon's friends, finding them huddled in a corner by the tall organ, smoking their pipes and talking in low voices. Allinson nodded a wary greeting as the inspector approached.

'Have you found him yet?' he asked.

'No,' Harper admitted, looking around the faces. Harry Gordon's brother turned away, anger and bitterness clouding his eyes. 'I was wondering if you'd remembered anything else.'

'What else would we know? It were the middle of the night, we were in a strange place and all them people looked like they wanted to kill us,' Allinson told him dismissively, his words full of reproof. 'The only thing we cared about was being safe.'

'How far up the steps were you when it happened?'

'How far?' The man took the pipe from his mouth, pushing down the tobacco as he thought. 'I'm not sure. Close to the top?' He looked at the others, waiting for something, but they remained close-mouthed and grim. 'You know what we want, mister?'

'What?' Harper answered.

'Just to be shut of this place. To take Harry home to his wife and bury him.'

'I'll see what I can arrange.'

Allinson nodded, as much gratitude as he was ever going to offer. 'We can't even go out. I wanted to write to Harry's wife but they won't let me go to t' postbox.'

'That's for your own safety.'

'Mebbe,' he muttered.

'I'll do what I can for you,' Harper promised.

He picked his way back out through the sleeping men to search for Reed. The police seemed to be gathered in a large room off the main hall, but before he could enter, someone shouted his name. Turning, he saw Kendall striding along, strain and sleeplessness showing on his face.

'What progress have you made?'

Progress, he thought? What could they have done? The superintendent knew better than that.

'Sir—'

'The chief constable needs a report to give to the aldermen.'

Harper considered what he could say. 'We've interviewed witnesses. Reed's talking to the constables who were there. We hope to know much more soon.' It meant little but it sounded hopeful. Kendall nodded weary approval.

'They expect a lot with this. The whole country's watching us.'

'We'll do everything we can, sir.'

'I know, Tom. See what you can discover today. They'll be moving these workers over to Wortley this evening.' He didn't need to say more. It was going to be madness, a procession full of howling and violence. Finding anyone in all that would be impossible. They'd be lucky if more people didn't end up as corpses along the way. 'Leeds is desperate for gas. The business leaders are already complaining to the mayor.'

'You know what chance we have of finding the killer, sir.'

'I do.' Kendall grimaced. 'But they don't. And they're the ones who give the orders.' Harper didn't need to ask who he meant. 'Do what you have to do. If you need to stretch the law, this is one time that no one's going to mind.'

'Yes, sir.'

'And although they'd like you to keep working until you find the killer,' the superintendent added carefully, 'I know you can't think worth a damn when you're dead on your feet. There's going to be little you can do tonight.'

The inspector smiled. 'I understand.'

Kendall nodded and walked away.

'Found anyone?' Harper asked. Reed was drinking a mug of tea and writing in his notebook as he sat on a bench in the tall marble hall. Knots of uniformed officers sat around on the floor, their jackets off, some of the men using them as pillows as they slept, others smoking and silent, a mirror of the workers in the other room.

'Four of them. It's strange, though. Come here, I want to show you something.' He led the way to the windows, with a view of the steps and the mass of people beyond. 'The uniforms say there was a cordon by the lions. And men up either side.'

Harper studied the scene. There were two sets of stairs leading up to the Town Hall. The carved stone lions stood on either side of the upper set. Above that it would be difficult for men to press in; they'd have needed to climb over the statues first.

'Allinson told me it happened just past the lions,' he said thoughtfully.

'The uniforms said the men were home and dry by then. No one could get to them.'

'Maybe he had it wrong. It's possible.'

'There's something else.'

'What?'

'There were men there,' Reed said.

'Who?'

'Workers from the council.'

'What, do you think one of them knifed Gordon?' Harper's voice rose as he asked the question.

Reed shrugged. 'Do that, then blame the strikers. It's possible.'

The inspector let out a long sigh and ran a hand through his hair. 'That's all we bloody need.'

If that was true, it would change everything. No one would like where it led. He knew what the council wanted: to paint the strikers as violent, desperate men who wanted to destroy society. This murder was exactly what they needed. It would play well for them in all the newspapers; it might turn public opinion. But if one of their own was responsible . . .

'See if the uniforms knew any of the faces on the steps,' Harper said.

'Already done it.' He grinned with satisfaction. 'They gave me a name.'

The inspector sighed with relief. 'It's a start.'

'So who's Dick James?' Harper asked. They'd found a woman serving cups of tea, along with slices of bread and butter, and now he was cradling a china cup and plate on his lap as they sat in one of the empty Town Hall offices.

'He's a manager at the Wortley gasworks,' Reed told him. 'That's what the uniform said, anyway.'

'That would explain why he was here. Where do we find him?'

'He's gone back out to the works to make sure everything's ready for the replacements.'

Harper snorted. 'If they ever get there. Even with the cavalry around, it's going to be a pitched battle all the way.' He swallowed the rest of the tea and stood up. 'Right, we'd better go and see him.'

They followed Wellington Road across the river and over the canal, passed blocks of dirty, cramped back-to-back houses thrown down between factories, homes to labourers and their families. Everything seemed strangely silent. There were hardly any carts or trams on the road; the streets were quiet except for the sound of their footsteps. It was as if the world was holding its breath and waiting.

Soon they could see the New Wortley gasometers against the skyline, close to empty, only the skeleton of the metal frames showing over the rooftops. A single train whistled loudly, thick smoke rising as it gained speed out of New Station and passed loudly along the bridge overhead.

'They're really going to bring them out along here?' Reed asked.

'It's the direct way.' He saw the shock on the sergeant's face.

'They can't. If the strikers have men up on that bridge . . .'

Grassy embankments rose sharply on either side; climbing up would be nearly impossible. Any force up there would be impregnable, protected by the bridge parapet and free to rain down branches, bricks and stones on everyone passing underneath.

'Maybe they'll be able to keep the strikers off it.'

'They should already have men up there to secure it,' Reed said angrily. 'Constables, soldiers, anybody.' He craned his neck, calculating the height. 'That has to be thirty feet. People are going to die.' He shook his head hopelessly.

There were small groups of pickets standing close at the works. The uniforms guarding the gates demanded to know who they were as he tried to enter.

'Detective Inspector Harper and Detective Sergeant Reed, A Division,' he said.

The young constable came quickly to attention. 'Sorry, sir.' He flushed. 'I didn't know you. All of us here have been drafted in from Bradford.'

'You'll be busy this evening.'

'So I've heard.' The man grinned, showing teeth stained brown by tobacco. 'Fine by me, I like a good scrap, I do.'

A few men were moving about the large yard. Two marquees had been erected, the heavy canvas pulled back to show rows of camp beds for the blacklegs. A young man with the first hope of a moustache above his lip was putting them together, sleeves rolled up to show arms like spindles.

'Where's Mr James?' Harper asked.

'Over there.' He pointed at a building at the far side of the works. As he spoke, his Adam's apple bobbed nervously up and down.

The wooden door was propped open with a wedge. Inside, a man sat at a desk, scribbling into a ledger. He glanced up, annoyance and questions in his eyes, as the policemen entered.

'Yes?' There was a brusque edge to his voice, the sound of someone used to his own authority. But he was dressed like a working man, with an old jacket and trousers and a waistcoat that had seen better days, a kerchief knotted around his neck. A foreman, Harper guessed.

'Police, Mr James,' he said, watching the man sit a little straighter in his chair. 'You were at the Town Hall when they brought the replacements in last night.'

'Aye,' James agreed warily. 'What about it?'

'You were standing on the steps, by the lions?'

'Well, I'd not be down in the mob, would I?' He smiled at his own wit.

'How many others were around you?'

'Others? What do you mean?'

'The officers said there were a few of you standing there, waiting,' Reed said. 'How many?'

'I don't know,' James answered, taken aback by the question, thinking. 'Ten, maybe. I didn't count. Why, what's this about?'

'One of the men who came in was stabbed,' Harper told him. 'He's dead.'

For a moment the man said nothing as the colour left his face. Then he retched twice, pulling out a handkerchief and trying to spit away the news of death.

'I . . .' he began, shaking his head. 'You mean someone in the crowd killed him?'

'It happened up by the lions,' Reed said. 'That's why we need to know who was there.'

'Of course.' He frowned, trying to recall. 'There was Simpson, he's one of the managers over at the York Street works.'

'Go on,' Harper prodded.

'Tattersall. He's a clerk to the gas committee. And Dawkins.'

'Dawkins?' the inspector asked.

'I'm not sure what he does,' James admitted, embarrassed at not knowing. 'He's often with the members of the gas committee when they visit.'

'What about the men on the committee? Were they with you?'

'They were inside.' He looked at the two detectives. 'Can you imagine what it would have been like if that crowd had seen them? I was scared for my life as it was.'

'You've given us three names,' Reed said. 'What about the others who were there?'

The man shook his head. 'Didn't know them.' He paused. 'He really died?'

'Yes, Mr James, he did,' Harper said.

'Poor sod.'

'What do you think?'

They'd slipped back out through the gate, the constable saluting promptly this time. Before Harper could answer, a cheer went up from the pickets.

'What's happened?' the inspector called out to them.

'Half the bloody blacklegs have walked out of Meadow Road,' a man answered with a broad grin. 'Said they'd been conned and they're going home. That'll teach the bastards.' He spat on the ground and turned away, rubbing his hands in glee.

'Sixpence says the rest of them are gone by tomorrow,' Harper offered as they began the walk back into town.

'I'd be on a hiding to nothing if I took that.' Reed looked up again as they approached the bridge. 'Do you know what this reminds me of?'

'What?' Harper wondered. The sergeant's face had taken on a strange, distant look.

'Afghanistan.' He pushed the bowler hat further down on to his head, as if it could protect him. 'You'd go out on patrol and you'd know the tribesmen were waiting. You might not see them, but you knew they'd be shooting soon enough.'

'So what did you do?'

He shrugged. 'Nothing. You went out and did your job and you prayed you'd be one of those who made it back.' Reed stayed silent for a while, filled with memories, then said, 'What do you want to do now?'

'You take the ones with the gas committee. They should be at the town hall. I'll go out to York Street a bit later.'

'Going to look for Martha Parkinson?'

Harper nodded. 'Someone has to. The chief doesn't care.'

'That brings us back to Henry Bell,' Reed reminded him. 'His body's still in his office.'

The inspector shrugged. 'His wife will report him missing soon enough. Let someone else find his body. Henry's no loss. It'll all end up on our desks, anyway. If you find anything, send a note over to the station.'

They parted at the bottom of East Parade. He watched as Reed strode purposefully up the street. The buildings rose high around him, smooth, sheer stone reaching up to the heavens. Banks, insurance offices, all of them filled with the calm, quiet power of money that brooked no challenge.

Tattersall and Dawkins could almost have been copies of each other, the sergeant decided. They were both in their thirties, with thinning fair hair and offices along the same high corridor in the Town Hall. And both were filled with the gospel of the gas committee's work.

He saw Dawkins then Tattersall, but he needn't have bothered; from the way they echoed each other, one would have been enough. Not that either had much to say. They'd been terrified by the crowd, more concerned with making sure the replacements arrived properly than anything else.

By the time he'd finished with them he knew little more than when he'd begun. They offered a name or two more. It was as if they'd been there but hadn't noticed a thing. Still, that was par for the course. Some witnesses gave you gold, most only had lead. He'd go back to the station, write up his notes and wait for the inspector.

For now, though, he was thirsty. He wanted a drink. Just one to wet his whistle, and a sandwich to fill his belly. The Bull and Mouth on Briggate was on his way back to Millgarth.

It was an old hotel, always full of men in Leeds on business, commercial travellers who hawked their wares the length and breadth of Britain. The bar was open but empty. There was only one man serving, checking the taps and trying to look busy. He glanced up as he heard the sharp footsteps on the tile floor, smiling to see the policeman.

'Morning, Mr Reed. What can I get you?'

'A sandwich and a glass of beer, please, Peter.' He looked around. 'Quiet in here.'

The barman shrugged. 'Early yet. Be more in by dinner. But everywhere's dead with this strike.' He poured a glass of beer and placed it in front of the sergeant. 'I'll bring the sandwich over to you.'

'Thank you.' He reached into his pocket and asked, 'How much do I owe you?' but the man waved him away. It was the same every time, a play, a show; he'd once caught a pickpocket in the pub yard and since then they'd made sure his money was no good here.

The food appeared in less than a minute, the bread cut into neat triangles, generously filled with cold roast beef sliced thick enough to keep him going for the rest of the day. He started to eat, washing each bite down with a sip of the beer.

He wiped away the final crumbs and drained the dregs from the glass. He wanted more to drink, another and then another. Instead he clenched his fists and breathed deeply. Tonight. He'd be fine until then. Instead of returning to Millgarth he'd go and ask some more questions.

Harper walked, barely giving Henry Bell's office a glance as he passed along Commercial Street, heading into the courts and yards he knew well, among the poor where he still felt most comfortable. This was where the prizefighter and his friend preyed on people and they were the ones who'd lead him to Martha.

In Fidelity Court, children who should have been at school were playing in the dirt. Three of Ginny Dempsey's brood were among them. He knocked on her door, hearing the slow shuffle of her feet inside.

'Mr Harper,' she said. 'We don't see you for years and now you're here all the time. Have you found young Martha yet?'

'No.' It hurt him to admit it. 'I'm still looking for those two men.'

'The boxer and his friend?'

He nodded. If anyone around here could help, it was Ginny. 'I can't do it myself. You know everyone back in this area.'

'I ought to. Lived here all my life,' she said proudly.

'Then pass the word that I'm looking, and Martha's life could depend on it. I want this pair, I don't care where the information comes from. They'll come around again. I want to know when they do.'

Mrs Dempsey stared at him for a few moments. 'If she's still alive,' she said. 'It's been more than a week now.'

'For God's sake, Ginny, I know that.' He could feel the frustration and sleeplessness of the last two days swirling inside. 'Don't you think I'm trying? I've got a dead blackleg at the Town Hall, and a chief constable who thinks finding his killer is more important than a little girl.'

Her face softened. 'I know you care, love. You allus did. I'll do what I can. If they come around, we'll find them. After that it's up to you.'

'Thank you.'

'I'm warning you, though,' she told him. 'If that lass is dead . . .'

'Then we'd better all hope she's not, hadn't we?'

TEN

The York Street gasworks lay behind the railways goods depot on Marsh Lane, close enough for the symphony of trains, the whistles, cries and the metallic rolling of wheels on track to be constant.

Harper made his way out beyond St Peter's Square and through the waste ground to Lemon Street. Around here the roads had never been cobbled. They were still dirt that dried into hard ruts during the summer and turned to heavy mud when the rain fell.

The houses were older, tired, clinging together to stay upright, with bricks black as bruises from years of soot. Around here was where the poor came when there was nowhere else left, where the bobbies only dared patrol in pairs at night.

A pair of uniformed constables guarded the entrance to the works but there were no pickets gathered outside. The lids on the gasometers bulged almost full as he walked through the yard. York Street was the only place in Leeds that still had gas, it seemed.

Everything on the office desk was careful and orderly. Each piece of paper was lined up exactly, all the edges aligned, pens neatly placed by the inkwell. The man who sat there carried an air of exasperation, as if the world would constantly disappoint him. He was as fat as the Prince of Wales, with the same well-tended beard and rakish gleam in his eye.

'Can I help you?' It was a voice used to giving orders.

'Inspector Harper, Leeds Police. You're Mr Simpson?'

'I am.' The man sat up straight, just as Harper knew he would, adjusting his cuffs and the watch chain over his ample belly and checking the glittering stickpin in the knot of his tie. 'How can I help you?'

'You were at the Town Hall first thing when they brought in the replacement workers.'

'I was.' Simpson frowned. 'What about it?'

'I believe you were up by the lions.'

'That's right. Your people were holding the crowd back.'

'How many of you were gathered there? And why were you all there?'

'How many?' He raised his eyebrows at the questions. 'I don't know, eight or ten of us, I suppose. People from the works and the committee. We'd been asked to inspect the new workers and greet them.'

'Did you know everyone around you?'

'No,' Simpson answered cautiously, smoothing his thin moustache with his fingertips. 'Why, what's happened?'

'One of the men who arrived was stabbed. He's dead.'

Harper watched the man's eyes, seeing shock cloud them.

'That's terrible,' he said, but there was little sympathy in his voice. 'The strikers did it?'

'It happened as he was passing where you were standing.'

'What?' His hands gripped the wooden arms of the chair. 'But . . .'

'Yes,' Harper said. 'You'd better tell me about the people around you.'

Simpson's lip twitched. 'There were Dawkins and Tattersall from the committee. And James, he's some sort of foreman out at New Wortley, I believe.'

'Who else?'

He counted them out on his fingers. 'Clay and Milner, I remember them. They're both engineers with the gas department. And two more I didn't know.' He looked up. 'That's all.'

More men to find and question in the morning.

'The ones you didn't recognize, could you describe them?'

'Of course,' Simpson told him with a self-satisfied smile. 'I pride myself on my memory.' Aye, and on most other things, probably, Harper thought. 'We all tried to keep away from them. There was something about them.'

'What do you mean?' Suddenly he was very interested.

'They only talked to each other. I don't think they said a word to the rest of us. One of them was a chap a little smaller than you, quite dapper, really. It was the other one who seemed odd.' Simpson paused a moment and pursed his lips. Someone dragged a piece of metal across the yard. Harper winced as the harsh sound filled his bad ear, drowning out speech. The others barely seemed to notice it.

'I'm sorry, I couldn't catch that,' the inspector said, waving at the door.

The man glanced at him with annoyance. 'I said one was a little smaller than you. The other one caught everyone's attention.'

'Go on.'

'He was big, the kind of fellow you'd avoid if you could. He had a decent enough suit, I suppose, but he'd shaved his head and there were scars on his face. He looked as if he'd possibly been a prize fighter. Something like that, you know the type. You wouldn't want to get on the wrong side of him, that was certain.'

'Are you sure?' the inspector asked urgently, his gaze intent on the man's face.

'Of course I am.' Simpson bridled, as if he wasn't used to his memory being questioned.

Harper could feel his heart beating faster. 'Who brought them there?'

'I've no idea,' the man answered. 'I seem to recall they were already standing there when we came out. But they must have been official,' he insisted. 'They must have come out from the Town Hall.'

Christ, Harper thought as he took a deep breath. This changed everything. But what were they doing at the Town Hall? And how did a dead blackleg connect to Martha Parkinson?

By the time he'd reached Millgarth he still didn't have any answers, only a fountain of questions in his head. The station was almost deserted apart from Tollman at the desk. Everyone else was over at the Town Hall, ready to escort the blacklegs out to New Wortley. It would be awful, it would be bloody, and he thanked God he didn't have to go there.

He scribbled his news on a note and left it on Reed's desk. He knew he should leave word for the super, but when he opened up the pocket watch he saw that any moment now they'd be starting the march out to the gasworks. Kendall and all the other police were going to have their hands full for the rest of the night. By morning he might have time to listen. A few hours would make no difference, anyway. And what he had to say was going to make the chief constable and the council very uncomfortable.

He couldn't make head nor tail of it. He felt stunned, as if someone had let off a bomb in front of him. The boxer and his friend kill a blackleg after murdering Henry Bell and Col Parkinson. They threaten people for a moneylender. And they snatch little Martha.

Had he become dim-witted? Was his mind addled? None of the pieces fitted together.

He sat at his desk, tossing his pen on to the blotter, smoking three cigarettes as he tried every which way to match things up. But however he looked at it, he couldn't find any pattern or logic. There was nothing to hold on to. He rubbed his eyes; they were gritty and bulging under his hand. Everything was a jumble in his head, like a skein of yarn that he couldn't untangle. He needed rest if he was going to try and make sense of it all; all he'd managed was an hour or two on a waiting room bench the night before. Finally he gave up in frustration, crammed the hat on his head and left.

He paid his fare, soothed by the rolling of the tram wheels on the tracks and the clop of the horses drawing the vehicle. The next thing he knew, the conductor was shaking his shoulder and grinning.

'You wanted Sheepscar, lad.'

He stood as the vehicle rattled away up Chapeltown Road, trying to rub the weariness from his face and the dust of the day off his suit.

There were only two customers in the public bar of the Victoria, old men crouched over a table in the corner playing dominoes. Daniel the barman finished filling a jug of beer for a young lad to take home to his father, and jerked his thumb towards the ceiling.

'She's upstairs, Tom. She'll be glad to see you. Just go through.'

Harper looked around in surprise. 'Where is everyone? It's usually packed in here by now.'

'No money,' Daniel said with a sad laugh. 'Besides, all those with any sense are staying at home this evening. The others are already down at the Town Hall, spoiling for a fight. Count yourself lucky you're not there.'

'I am, believe me,' he answered, meaning every word.

Annabelle was at her desk, head bent, absorbed in an account book. He paused in the doorway to watch her. He loved the shape of her neck, her hair gathered up, the movement of her wrist as she wrote. He coughed and she turned suddenly, eyes wide in surprise.

'Tom!' She smiled and came to hold him, her arms tight around his back. 'Oh, thank God. I was worried you'd have to be out there tonight.' She pulled away for a moment, scared, staring at his eyes. 'You don't have to go back, do you?'

Harper shook his head. 'Not until tomorrow.'

By eight they'd settled on the sofa, his head back against the thick cushions. He'd told her about the day, arm around her shoulders as she curled into him.

'What are you going to do?' she asked.

'Find them. That's my job.' He closed his eyes, trying to let work vanish over the horizon for a few hours. Tomorrow he could look at it all with fresh, rested eyes.

Two more weeks and he'd be living here, he thought. Every evening could be like this. He'd have the closeness of a wife, the small, intimate things that built a life together.

'This wedding . . .' he began.

'Ours, you mean?' Annabelle asked wryly. 'That wedding?' She tapped him playfully.

'Who'll be coming from your family?' Her parents were both dead, she'd told him that.

'Why, scared of who you'll meet?' she teased.

'I just wondered. You never mention them, that's all.'

'I don't really see them.' She shifted in a rustle of silk, her face serious. 'I've only one brother and a sister still alive. All the others are gone.'

'I'm sorry.'

'It happens.' She shrugged and he knew she was right. Among the poor, too many still died young. You accepted it as part of the cost of life. He'd lost a brother to diphtheria before the lad even had time to grow. 'Gerald lives in Hunslet,' she continued. 'I probably haven't talked to him in six years.'

'Why not?' He might not always like his sisters but he couldn't imagine not speaking to them.

'He's the type who thinks a woman should stay at home and look after the babies,' she answered with bitter resignation. 'He doesn't approve of a female showing any sign of thinking or independence. He made sure I knew that the last time we met.'

'What did you do?'

She grinned. 'Threw him out on his ear.'

'What about your sister?'

'Eliza? She's still on the Bank, two streets from where we grew up.' Annabelle snorted and her mouth twisted into an odd shape. 'Married to a sad, feckless bugger who couldn't find a job if it came looking for him. She'll come. So will he if there's free drink.' She paused. 'What about your sisters?'

'You've met them. They'll be here. They think I'm lucky to have you.'

'Clever women, those two,' she smiled. 'Are they going to tell me all the things you did when you were a boy?'

'God, I hope not.' He grimaced at the idea, then yawned widely.

'Do you want to sleep in the spare bed again? I can send one of the men to your lodgings for your clothes.'

Harper thought for a moment, then nodded. He was comfortable. Walking home would wake him up, make his mind work until the small hours when he really needed sleep.

She hugged him, then hurried downstairs.

She was back in a trice. 'I sent Dan. It'll give him something to do, there's hardly anyone in the bars. I told him to bring you a suit and a shirt.'

He laughed, astonished at the way she could organize anything in a moment.

'What?' she asked.

'Nothing. I love you, that's all.'

'Well, since we'll be married soon enough, I'm glad to hear it.' She arched an eyebrow. 'You're not so bad yourself.'

He yawned once more and she said, 'Come on, off to bed with you.'

'Sorry,' he told her, 'it's been a long two days. And I need to be up early.'

'I'll make sure you are, don't worry about that.' She kissed him tenderly, eyes twinkling. 'Just to give you summat to keep thinking about.'

She was there in the morning, waking him with a cup of tea, already dressed, her eyes bright and playful.

'You'd best not expect to get used to this, Tom Harper,' Annabelle warned.

'What time is it?' He could sense the pale early light beyond the curtains.

'Half past four. Charlotte's poorly today so I've been helping with the baking.'

'How long have you been up?'

'An hour or so. Those loaves don't make themselves.'

His eyes had adjusted to the gloom and he could make out her apron and old dress, sleeves pushed up, and the cap that covered her hair.

'You look like a scullery maid.' He grinned.

'And there's nowt wrong with that,' she told him archly. 'It's not that long since I was one meself. Anyway, up you get. Your clothes are hanging on the back of the door. I'll have Kitty clean what you were wearing yesterday.' She sighed and shook her head. 'How do men always manage to get everything so dirty?'

An hour later he walked into Millgarth, before the early trams were running. As he left the Victoria she'd put a heavy slab of bread and dripping into his hand and given him a quick kiss.

'You just watch out for yourself,' she told him.

The station was quiet, the night sergeant still on duty at the desk.

'How bad was it?' Harper asked.

The man shook his head. 'Terrible, sir. Ten constables in the infirmary, another twenty walking wounded, two sergeants down. We were lucky. It could have been a lot worse.'

'Sounds as if it was bad enough. The railway bridge?'

'Aye, and from there all the way to the works. It was like a bloodbath. Cavalry had to charge the strikers.'

'No one died?'

'No.' He glanced up towards heaven. 'Miracle, in't it? We got the replacements in, anyway. How long they'll stay is anyone's guess.' The sergeant gave a shrug.

The office was empty, but Reed had left a note on his desk: *What do we do now?*

What could they do now? It was a good question. He needed to find the boxer and the other man, and he needed to do it quickly. That pair had the answers, they were the ones who connected Col Parkinson and his daughter to a dead blackleg. There was just one thing missing. He strode back out to the desk.

'Has anyone been reported missing in the last day or so?' he asked.

'Not that I know of, sir. Why?'

'It doesn't matter.'

That was odd. By now he'd expected Henry Bell's wife to be desperate at his disappearance. Another mystery to add to all the others.

He knew his first duty – he had to tell Kendall what he'd learned.

Another hour and there'd be frantic conversations going on in offices as the chief and the aldermen wondered what to do. Part of him relished setting that cat among the pigeons. His copper's heart wanted to catch the boxer and his friend, to discover what had happened, and to bring Martha home.

The streets were still quiet, the pale clouds high over Leeds as he marched along the Headrow. A sunless day, another day with no gas and no work for thousands. The crowds were smaller in front of the Town Hall, no more than a thousand of them now, dropped papers and trampled placards filling the spaces between men. For a moment he thought he saw Tosh Walker's face among them and stopped, wondering why a criminal like him was here. Then he blinked and the man had vanished. Stupid, he thought, and moved on. Four constables guarded the rear entrance, saluting smartly as he entered.

After the crowds of uniforms and blacklegs that had filled the building the day before it all seemed curiously quiet, the halls and rooms empty, the floors swept clean, as if it everything in here had been some kind of dream. He stood, gazing around, finally roused by the echo of footsteps on the marble stairs. It was Chief Constable Webb.

He looked tired. He looked old. Harper felt sorry for the man. Webb had only been in the post since March, not even long enough to know Leeds and understand the way things worked here. And now he had to deal with this.

'Detective Inspector,' he said, his voice as grave and ringing as a Baptist preacher.

'Sir.' He stiffened to attention as the man approached, keeping his good ear towards the chief. Webb's uniform was creased and crumpled, stains and dirt blotching the good worsted. The lines were deep on his face, the eyes dark and full of pain.

'I trust you have some good news for us.' The voice boomed around the walls and up to the ceiling.

'Some, sir.' It was the diplomatic answer, at least for now.

Webb nodded wearily. 'Thank God for that. We need something after last night.'

'We have a good idea who murdered the replacement, sir.'

'That's progress, Inspector.' Webb favoured him with a nod. 'Now I expect you to find him.' It was a command, not a wish.

'Yes, sir.'

'Superintendent Kendall's in the clerk of court's office upstairs. Report to him.' As Harper turned away, Webb said. 'Inspector?'

'Yes, sir?'

'Is there something wrong with your hearing?'

'No, sir.' Harper stared at him, surprise and horror on his face. 'Why?'

'The way you had your head tilted, that's all.' He looked for a moment longer, then shrugged. 'Maybe it's my imagination. Off you go.'

By the time he reached the clerk of court's office his hands had almost stopped shaking. It was too close. If the chief constable had discovered his hearing problem that would be the end of his police career. He swallowed hard, knowing he needed to be more careful. Harper breathed deeply a few times then turned the doorknob. The super was staring out of the window and drinking from a mug of tea. When he sat, he looked shocked, as if he'd seen too much in the last day.

'Well, Tom?' Kendall asked.

Harper laid it all out, everything except Bell's body; that was a secret he intended to leave unspoken. When he'd finished, the superintendent stayed silent for a long time, slowly rubbing at the bristles on his jaw.

'So it wasn't one of the strikers at all?'

'It doesn't seem like it. But it was meant to look that way.'

'To pass the blame?'

'Yes.'

'Who are these men? Who are they working for?' the superintendent asked. 'And why didn't we know about them before?'

'I don't know. I really don't. They're not local, that's for certain. We'd have come across them before, otherwise. And all the other things they've done in the last few days . . .' He let the sentence tail away to nothing. He didn't know how to finish it.

'I don't understand how they ended up on the Town Hall steps,' Kendall said slowly. 'That was meant to be council employees only.'

'None of it makes sense, sir. Collecting debts is one thing. Killing someone and taking his daughter is another. But then stabbing a blackleg.' He saw Kendall wince at the word. 'A replacement worker. I don't understand it.'

'The aldermen hoped the strikers were responsible, you know.'

'I'm sure they did, sir.' He kept his voice even, looking directly at the other man.

'You need to find this pair, and sharpish.' He calculated the reserves of men. 'I can spare you three constables.'

'Thank you, sir. I heard about last night.'

'It was the worst I've ever seen in this job, Tom,' the superintendent said slowly, raising sad eyes. 'It was war, plain and simple. Us against them. Do you know when I realized how bad it was? When I had to watch the cavalry charging Englishmen. Our own people. I'm just glad no one died.' He gave a small, shamed chuckle. 'It's a terrible day when people think that seems like a victory. More of the replacements have already gone from Meadow Lane. Only a handful are left there now. The strikers climbed up on the walls and persuaded them to leave. But the council won't pay their fares home.'

Harper imagined them, in fours or fives, friends or family together, cousins, brothers, neighbours, walking down the roads away from Leeds. What would Harry Gordon have ended up doing if he'd stayed alive?

'And all for a few bloody pennies and pride,' the inspector said quietly.

'Tom,' Kendall warned quietly, then relented. 'I don't know, maybe you're right after all,' he conceded with a sigh. 'It's a bloody mess. I need you to find these men.'

'I've passed the word. If they come into any of those courts off Briggate I'll hear about it.'

'What about elsewhere?'

'I'll do my best, sir,' was all he could offer.

'I want them today. So will the chief constable.'

'So do I, sir.' Everywhere he turned, the two men were there. They were like shadows he could never quite grasp, always just beyond his reach. 'I want to know what they've done with Martha Parkinson. With respect, sir, we've been forgetting her.'

The superintendent's smile was shrewd. 'I know,' he admitted. 'But you haven't, I'm sure of that.' Harper bowed his head for a moment. 'I've known you too long, Tom. When you find this pair, just be careful. The fighter sounds dangerous.'

'The fighter's just muscle. It's the other one who worries me.' He paused. 'And whoever's paying them.'

'Never underestimate a big man,' Kendall warned him. 'You'd better make a start. Keep me informed. If you catch them I want to know immediately, understood?'

'Yes, sir.'

When Harper left the room he could still feel the fear inside him. He'd come close to being discovered by the chief constable. He'd been careless, complacent. From now on he needed to be very aware and very careful. He lit a Woodbine, eagerly drawing down the smoke before exhaling in a long stream.

Reed was waiting just inside the front doors, slouching against the wall. He looked refreshed, shaved, his eyes clear and alert.

'Find them today,' the inspector told him. 'Those are our orders.'

The sergeant gave a grim chuckle. 'Did he say where and what time we had to do it?'

'I think he might grant us a few hours' leeway there, Billy.'

'No one's reported Henry Bell missing yet,' Reed said as they walked along the Headrow.

'I know.' It was wrong. Someone, his wife, his lawyer, should have missed him long before now. A full day had passed since they'd discovered the body.

'We could pay a visit and find him.'

'No,' Harper decided. Looking for the boxer and the other man was more important. 'Let's go through the yards first. If there's nothing, then we'll go.'

But no one had seen the fighter or his friend. Ginny Dempsey had no word.

'Bell?' Reed asked and Harper nodded.

Inside the office, flies buzzed loudly and the air was heavy with the stink of decay. The sergeant held a handkerchief to his face as he pulled open the cupboard door and Bell's corpse tumbled out.

'Go out and whistle for some uniforms.' Harper glanced down at the body. 'We're going to need him out of here.'

Alone, he riffled through the papers again, checking he'd missed nothing the day before. But either the killer had taken everything valuable or Bell had kept his ledgers elsewhere.

He'd need to go out and talk to Bell's wife. Why hadn't she reported him missing? And what about Desmond, the lawyer? He should have been here first thing yesterday, seeing to his client after his time with police. It was all out of kilter, nothing added up.

'There's a wagon on the way and a uniform to keep the gawpers away,' Reed said when he returned. 'I asked in the office downstairs. They heard a few people come and go yesterday. Didn't see anyone, the windows face the wrong direction. At least they didn't see us.'

'Small mercies, Billy,' Harper said. 'We need to see the lawyer and the family. Which one do you want?'

'The lawyer,' Reed answered without hesitation. No one would break the news to a dead man's family by choice. It was the worst of all duties, one Harper had done too many times over the years; it never grew easier.

'Go through the place once more after they've carted him off, then go and see Desmond. I'm off to Far Headingley.'

He thought about taking the omnibus but a hackney carriage would be faster. The vehicle he flagged was driven by a quiet, serious man with a long, sad face, his horse sleek and shining from the brush. Inside, the plush velvet on the seats was worn, but at least it was clean. The trip seemed to take forever as they followed the road out past Woodhouse Moor and through Headingley. Well-fed wives and nannies with their charges crammed the narrow pavements. Then they were out where the real money lived.

The streets were wide and the young trees were growing tall; another few years and these would seem like shaded avenues. For now, though, everything seemed too new. It was all too raw and brash, an advertisement for new money. He had the cab drop him at the corner and waited until horse and driver had clopped out of sight.

Out here, no more than a few miles from all the chimneys and the press of people, the air was definitely clearer and cleaner. He breathed deeply a few times. This was why those who could afford it moved to the suburbs, he thought. The road was empty, no people, no chatter or laughter, no arguments. Those would all take place inside, in private and away from the neighbours.

He walked up a short, neat driveway to a house that stood on its own, the brick fresh enough to still look a blushing red, the dark paint around the windows sharp and bright. The maid who answered the door was no more than fifteen, a harried girl wearing a black dress and apron made for someone larger. The cap sat skew-whiff on her head, mousy hair tumbling down.

She left him in the parlour, and a minute or two later her mistress bustled in, eyes wide and worried to have a policeman in the house. She'd probably been a pale, pretty woman when Bell married her. Now, even covered with expensive creams, her features looked coarse and hard. She was wearing a rich dress, heavily corseted at the waist to preserve some semblance of a figure.

'Mrs Bell,' he said.

'What is it?' she asked quietly. 'Something's happened to him, hasn't it?'

'I'm sorry,' Harper said gently, hoping she'd understand, that he wouldn't need to say the rest.

'I see.' There was sadness in her eyes and her voice, but little more, as if she'd been expecting this news for a long time. No tears or screaming, just a sense of tired acceptance.

She sat down, gazing up at him. 'Where did it happen?' she asked quietly. 'How did he die?'

'We found him in his office,' Harper explained. 'It looked as if he'd been there more than a day. Hadn't you expected him to come home?'

Mrs Bell shook her head. 'Henry often stayed in town during the week. Sometimes from Monday to Friday if he was busy. I was used to it. How did he die?' she repeated.

'Someone killed him.' He didn't want to give more detail than that.

'I see,' she answered after a while. Her calmness worried him. It came too easily. She stayed silent for a long time. 'I'm sorry, Inspector, you must wonder what to make of me.' He didn't answer; he had no idea what to say. 'I know exactly what my husband did for a living. I know how dangerous it is. Was,' she corrected herself and raised her eyes to him. 'So did he. That's why he made sure we were well provided for. Do you know who did it?'

'We're looking for two men.' He described them, but there was no recognition in her eyes. 'Had he seemed scared or worried at all?'

'Not that he said. But there were plenty of things he didn't tell me, and I never asked.' There was little regret in her tone. The woman had a hard streak of realism at her core, he thought, not the loving wife of hearth and home.

'Does he have an office in the house?'

'No. Henry was very firm about keeping his work separate from home.' She'd slipped fully into the past tense, he noted.

'Might I take a look?'

'Of course,' she agreed with a gracious nod. The frightened-looking maid accompanied him.

But she hadn't lied; there was nothing. A library, but the desk there was almost empty. Finally, back in the parlour, Harper asked, 'You said he kept a room in town. Where was it?'

'He stayed with Mr Desmond, his lawyer. In Park Square. They were good friends.'

And that would be where he kept his books. They'd be safe with a lawyer. Knowing Desmond's reputation, though, he'd probably never show them to the police. Harper stood and offered her another condolence; there was nothing more to be learned here.

He caught the omnibus at the stop by the ancient oak across from the Skyrack public house, gazing out of the window as the vehicle trundled along and thinking as the houses thickened around him and leafy trees vanished into brick and soot. Close to St John's Church he alighted and strode down to the Town Hall. It was time to add to the super's worries and tell him about Henry Bell.

ELEVEN

Kendall listened carefully, exhausted eyes trying to focus. How long had the man been awake, Harper wondered? Too long, that was certain; his attention kept wandering away so that the inspector had to keep repeating himself. Kendall would only have snatched moments of rest until the strike was resolved.

He'd heard the rumours as he entered the building. The blacklegs were already heating the retorts out at New Wortley. Soon they'd be making gas. But most had already left, escaping into the crowds that waited around the walls and greeted them like heroes. Meadow Lane was nearly empty, little more than a handful of workers left. The council was losing the strike.

'No ledgers anywhere?' the superintendent asked.

'He keeps them with his lawyer, according to the wife. You know what Desmond's like.'

'Do you think he could be behind it all?' Kendall asked.

'I don't know.' He'd considered the idea on the journey into Leeds, but he couldn't believe it. There wasn't a policeman in Leeds who'd trust Desmond, but it was impossible to think of him killing his clients, and he'd been Bell's lawyer for years. 'Reed's gone to see him.'

Kendall nodded and tried in vain to stifle a wide yawn. The weariness had turned him into an old man, his hair grey and unkempt, the lines so deep on his face they could have been cut into the skin.

'These two men, the boxer and the other one,' he began slowly. 'I can see how Col Parkinson connects to Henry Bell, he'll have borrowed money. But how in God's name did they end up on the Town Hall steps?'

Harper shook his head. 'I don't know that yet, sir. I can't see how it all fits together.' He paused. 'But it all seems to hinge on this pair.'

'Find them. You know the council's still saying that the strikers are behind the murder?'

'But they're not,' Harper protested, starting to rise from his chair. 'We both know that, sir. The strikers had nothing to do with it.'

Kendall raised his hand, waiting until the inspector finished. Quietly and firmly, he said, 'Until you bring in those two and prove they did it, that's the line the council's taking.'

Harper knew full well why they were doing it. This strike was war between union and council. And in a battle like this, words could be powerful weapons. Leeds was crippled, and those in power couldn't allow that situation to last. They'd use anything they could to win, even if it was a lie. If it was repeated often enough it could become the truth.

'Tom,' Kendall said gently. 'You have no idea how bad it is out there. The cavalry's guarding the works out at New Wortley. There are crowds of strikers outside who look like they might storm the place at any time. The mayor's going to read the Riot Act later today. They're going to issue the constables with cutlasses.'

'What?' Harper asked in disbelief. He'd heard of things like that, long ago, but not now, not in this modern age.

'I never thought I'd live to see it,' the superintendent said sadly. 'They're scared it'll all go out of control.'

'Yes, but . . .' He found he simply didn't know what to say. He knew what the Riot Act meant, he'd had to learn it when he trained as a constable. After it was read, if the mob didn't disperse in an hour, the soldiers would open fire and damn the consequences. Englishmen shooting Englishmen; it didn't bear thinking about. The council wasn't just scared, it was terrified.

Kendall sighed. 'Two men from the Chamber of Commerce have agreed to arbitrate. The union's already said it's willing. The first meeting's this afternoon.'

Harper could imagine Maguire at the union offices down on Kirkgate smiling with glee as he sensed victory. The gas committee had handled everything so stupidly and arrogantly. Times had changed; working men wouldn't simply bow down and do what they were told any more. Reading the Riot Act was a last gasp of the old order, a desperate move to prove that the council was still in control by declaring war on their own people. Come the next election, folk would remember.

'You see why we need to find the boxer and the other one today?' the superintendent asked.

He nodded.

Reed was at his desk in Millgarth, a neatly-bound set of ledgers sitting in front of him. He waved at them proudly as Harper walked into the office.

'A present from Mr Desmond.'

Harper was impressed. He hadn't expected the lawyer to give them up at all.

'How did you manage to persuade him?'

'Didn't have to,' Reed replied with a smirk. 'He wanted me to take them.' His face turned serious. 'To tell you the truth, I think he's worried. I was watching his face when I told him Bell was dead. He wasn't just shocked, he was petrified. Couldn't hand over the books fast enough.'

'Did you press him at all?'

'I tried.' Reed shrugged. 'He wasn't saying much.'

'Have you gone through them?'

'I took a look, but they might as well be in French for all the sense they make to me. We need someone who knows numbers.'

'No names in there?' Harper asked, surprised.

'Just letters, jumbles of them. A code.'

That made sense, in case anyone stole them. But it would be a simple code, he felt certain of that; Bell had never struck him as an intelligent man. He opened one of the books and saw columns of figures, all small amounts, written out in a neat copperplate hand. The debt on one side and the payments next to it, as far as he could judge. Not that they added up – the payments were always far greater than the amount owed. At the top of each page, letters were strung together, seemingly at random. No words he could understand. Reed was right, it was a code. Harper leafed through. There was more of the same on every page. It was all beyond him, too.

Bell had been scared when the inspector had interviewed him. Terrified, but he hadn't talked. Desmond was scared. Everyone in Leeds seemed to be scared, he thought. The council, Bell, Col Parkinson before he was killed, all the men threatened by the boxer and his friend, there was fear in everyone's eyes. Somewhere, someone was pulling the strings behind this, someone who didn't care how many died or suffered.

'Forget the numbers for now,' he decided after a minute. 'Someone else could study those later. 'Let's go and find this prizefighter and his friend.'

'Where?' the sergeant asked.

'No idea.' Harper smiled, more in hope than anticipation. 'But if we dig deep enough and long enough we're bound to come across them.'

The superintendent had promised him three constables and he selected them carefully. Ash, who'd first suspected that Col Parkinson's daughter might be missing, knew all the yards and courts behind Briggate, and the people who lived there. It was his beat; the two others could take their lead from him.

'Talk to Ginny Dempsey,' the inspector ordered. 'She's had people looking. Follow up on everything. If anything seems strange, anything at all, start asking questions.'

'Yes, sir,' the constable replied, his eyes shining, grateful to be doing anything that took him away from the strike and back to his patch.

'And if you find them, keep hold of them. For God's sake don't let them slip away.'

'Don't you worry, sir.' Ash winked, his voice steady and certain. 'I'll make sure they don't go far. Bring them here?'

'Yes.'

Harper and Reed drifted in and out of the public houses along Vicar Lane and by Kirkgate market. There were few enough customers with money to spend, hardly any people on the streets. One shop even had a notice in the window: CLOSED FOR THE DURATION OF THE STRIKE. If it went on much longer there'd be many more of those. Another day or two of this and all the businesses would be closed, no one working; Leeds would drift to a halt.

'They're not round here,' the sergeant said. 'No sign anywhere.'

For the rest of the morning they worked their way down Kirkgate, all the way out to Marsh Lane. One or two claimed to have seen the men, but not since the start of the strike.

'What if they've gone?' Reed asked.

He didn't believe that. He couldn't afford to. If it was true, Martha Parkinson might disappear forever. He'd propped the girl's photograph on his desk at Millgarth, a reminder of what was really important in all this. More than Col, Henry Bell or Harry Gordon. They were dead; he couldn't bring them back. But he could find Martha.

He didn't allow the darker idea into his mind. He had to believe that she was still alive somewhere.

'They're still here,' Harper told him. 'I can feel it.'

They turned up the Headrow, stopping into every one of the pubs, looking down the yard to Thornton's music hall. According to the poster outside the building, Dan Leno, Vesta Tilley and the Lions Comique were appearing all week. *Strike? No Gas? The show will go on!* a note added. Maybe he'd bring Annabelle here; she loved a good laugh and a sing-song. God knew that he could use some entertainment himself.

By the time they'd worked their way along to the Town Hall hunger was pulling at them. He heard the clock strike noon.

'There's a café at the station,' Reed suggested.

Harper sat and stared out at the platforms, the bustle of people coming and going, porters moving trunks and cases. Whistles sounded loudly, then a wild puff of steam. Smoke billowed under the glass roof, the smell of coal burning hot as an engine pulled out with a shriek of wheels on track.

He hadn't been on a train in a year. The summer before, with a day off and nothing to do, he'd taken an excursion to Scarborough. The sun had shone as he walked along the beach, jacket over his shoulder, waistcoat unbuttoned against the heat. He wandered along the North Bay pier, enjoying fish and chips in the sea air, and finished with a drink or two in a fisherman's pub before coming home in the evening. Next year, perhaps, he and his wife would go there for a real holiday. He'd never had one before.

Wife. The word made him smile. All too soon he'd put the ring on her finger. He'd already bought it, a thin band of gold that had eaten deep into his meagre savings, sitting in its box on top of a chest of drawers in his lodgings.

'Penny for them,' Reed said as he chewed a sandwich and sipped from a mug of strong tea.

'Not worth the money, Billy.' He ate for a little while, barely tasting the beef or the bread. 'Go and talk to your informers when you're done. See if any of them have any word.'

'What about you?'

Harper shrugged. 'I'll keep looking until I find them,' he said. Who were these men? How could they move around so freely, with no one knowing their names or where they were living?

By two he'd found no trace, and went back into the old, shabby courts where Ash and the other uniforms had spent the day searching.

'Anything?' he asked, even as the constable shook his head.

'Not been around in days, according to this lot.'

'Since the gas strike began?'

Ash thought before answering. 'Aye, that'd be about right.'

'Give it until the end of the shift.'

'Any more word on the strike, sir?' the constable asked gravely. 'I heard the mayor was going to read the Riot Act.'

He knew Ash had been out there the other night, in the thick of it. There was no mark on him, but all that meant was that he'd been one of the lucky ones.

'That's right. But the two sides are talking. Maybe it'll all be over by tomorrow.'

'Let's hope so, eh?'

'How bad was it?'

'Bad enough,' Ash answered finally but nothing more. He gazed around. 'Eh up,' he said quietly. A boy was running towards them, one of Ginny Dempsey's brood by the look of him, in patched knickerbockers, his feet and calves bare, kicking up dust as he moved.

'What is it, lad?' the constable asked.

'Me mam said to tell you they've been seen on White Swan Street,' he gabbled.

Ash looked at the inspector.

'Let's take them in,' Harper said.

They knew this area. They could find their way around its tight corners and strange ginnels without even thinking. In less than a minute they were on Swan Street, behind the music hall.

The boxer and his friend were strolling idly along, towards Lands Lane, backs to them, as if they didn't have a care in the world.

'You cut around and go to the other end,' Harper said softly. 'Which one do you want?'

'Oh, the boxer I think, sir,' Ash said with an eager smile. 'You can have the titch.'

'Right, let's catch them before they vanish again.'

He waited, giving the constable time to weave his way around the alleys, feeling the muscles in his face and arms tense. Then Ash was at the far end, blowing his whistle, and Harper began to run.

The boxer and his friend turned, looking for an escape, then back again as they saw the inspector. There was a quick word between them and the boxer ran straight at Ash while the other man darted away, around the corner.

Harper ran hard, skidding around into Lands Lane and spotting the man twenty yards ahead. The few folk out shopping quickly moved aside, staring as he passed. He could catch this man.

The man dashed into the road, crossing the Headrow towards Woodhouse Lane. The inspector started to follow, just as a cart came hurtling along, the driver whipping his horse. He pulled hard on the reins and the animal slowed and reared, sending the load tumbling. Harper tried to duck around, but one of the falling sacks caught him full on the legs and sent him sprawling to the pavement, pinning him down. Harper tried to push it off and wriggle out, but it was too heavy.

'Ee, lad, I'm sorry,' the carter said, hefting the sack on to his shoulder as though it weighed nothing. 'We were late, that's all.' He reached out a thick hand to help the inspector stand.

His ankle hurt as he tried to put weight on it. He bit his lip as the pain shot up his leg. Never mind chasing, he'd be lucky if he could limp back to Millgarth.

The driver tossed the sack back on to the cart and climbed up to his seat, leaving with just a quick backwards glance. Harper leaned against a building, catching his breath, feeling the roughness of the stone against his palm. The boxer's friend was long gone. There'd be no catching him now.

After a minute or two he believed he could hobble. He moved gingerly down the Headrow; the first few steps were agony, as if someone was hitting his leg each time his foot touched the ground. With each one he thought he was going to fall, the effort and the pain leaving sweat pouring down his face. Slowly, as he moved, it eased up a little. He was still limping badly and he felt the ankle swelling inside his boot. But at least he could move.

It still took almost half an hour by his watch to reach the station. By the time he arrived there he was drenched in sweat. Every bone in his leg and foot throbbed. His throat felt coated with the dust from the pavement. At the desk, Tollman raised his eyebrows but said nothing as he took in the dirt on the inspector's suit.

'He's in the cells, sir. Ash brought him in. Big bugger, in't he?'

'I didn't get much chance to look at him. Do we have a walking stick in here?'

'Probably, sir. I'll take a look.'

'And a cup of tea?'

Tollman laughed. 'I'll have one of the constables brew up and bring it down to you.'

'Send someone to the town hall to tell Superintendent Kendall we have one of those men.'

The cells were miserable, ripe with the heat of the day, the smell of piss and fear embedded in their walls. He glanced through the open slot in the door. The boxer was seated on a chair, looking straight ahead. His jacket, braces, tie and shoe-laces had been taken. It was for safety, to stop men hanging themselves in prison, but it did more. It left them feeling vulnerable.

'Was there anything in his pockets?' Harper asked the jailer.

'A little money, that's all, sir. Nothing to show his name.'

The inspector gazed again. The boxer's face was impassive. His eyes were as empty and cold as everyone had said. Scar tissue discoloured his face, his nose misshapen after being broken and reset many times, one ear puffy and large from his bouts in the ring. He was a big man, just the way people had described him, with wide shoulders that stretched against his shirt and large fists, the knuckles turned into thick lumps of gristle.

'Let me in. Then don't come back until you hear me calling.'

TWELVE

Ash stood in the corner, towering over the man in the chair. He exchanged a quick glance with Harper, seeing the awkward limp, and gave a small nod.

'You can leave if you want,' Harper said. Ash shook his head.

'No, sir,' the constable answered firmly. 'He knows where Martha is. I want to make sure he tells us.' He unbuttoned his jacket, folding it and placing it carefully on the floor. A single window was set high in the wall, covered in dust and grime, giving a shadowed, grainy light. The constable rolled up his shirtsleeves to show thick, hairy forearms. 'I'm ready whenever you are, sir.'

'What's your name?' the inspector asked the boxer.

The man stared straight ahead, as if he hadn't heard a word. Harper moved in front of him, taking him by the chin and raising his head so the boxer was staring directly at him.

'I asked your name.'

There was nothing. His eyes remained blank, lips never moving. The inspector turned away then heard a sharp crack as Ash slapped the man's face.

'When the inspector asks you a question, you'd better answer.'

The boxer just rode the blow.

Harper spoke quietly, then shouted and roared again, threatening and cajoling, trying everything for a full half hour. He asked about Martha, Col, why the boxer had been on the Town Hall steps, but the man never gave an answer. He didn't even acknowledge their presence, never flinched at the blows to his face or belly.

The inspector heard the viewing slot in the door slide back; Reed had returned.

'Did he tell you anything?' the sergeant asked and Harper shook his head in frustration.

'Let me have a go at him.'

'Billy . . .' Harper warned. He knew what could happen if the sergeant's temper rose; there was already a reprimand on his record to show it. But he hadn't managed to get a single word from the boxer.

'An hour and he'll be telling us everything we want to know,' Reed promised.

The inspector glanced at Ash. The constable was sensible enough to look away; he wanted no part of this decision. Harper could see Reed's eyes glistening and eager.

'Jailer,' he called.

'An hour,' Harper told him as he entered the cell. 'And remember, he has to look presentable in court when we charge him with the blackleg's murder.'

'I won't forget.'

Reed waited until the door closed, the heavy sound so final. Then he walked around the prisoner, watching the man stare straight ahead as if he was alone and lost in a world of his own. He'd seen it before, in Afghanistan. They'd bring a tribesman in and he'd ignore them, taking himself away to another place in his mind.

There were ways to make a man scream, to make him eager to say anything and everything. He'd known men who were expert at it. They relished the challenge, inventive in their tortures and always trying to outdo each other. And if the tribesman died, that didn't matter. It was one less to kill later.

What would move the boxer, Reed wondered? Not broken bones; he'd have experienced that before. Without even thinking, he reached out and grabbed the man's ear, twisting it hard, his eyes on the man's face for any reaction. A slight flinch at the start, then he'd controlled himself to show nothing more. But he knew he had the man's attention.

He leaned over, directly in front of the boxer, taking the man by the chin and raising his head. Blood trickled from the corner of his mouth, down over his chin. The boxer tried to avert his eyes, but the sergeant jabbed one lightly with his thumb.

'You're going to talk to me,' he said softly. The man's eye was watering. 'You're going to be happy to talk to me.'

Reed loosened his tie, slid it up over the stiffness of the wing collar then knotted it around the boxer's neck. He began to tighten it, little by little until it cut into the man's throat, his neck and face reddening as the air was cut off. The sergeant kept pushing, gradually increasing the pressure until the boxer's skin was almost purple. He eased off just enough to let the man breathe.

'That was how you killed Henry Bell, wasn't it? Used your hands until he died. And you looked him in the face the whole time.'

He tightened the knot once more, leaving it a little longer, forcing the boxer to gasp for air. Then he did it again. But however close to the edge he took the prisoner, the man didn't say a word. No begging, no explanation, nothing. When he looked at the sergeant there was nothing but contempt in his gaze. He wouldn't be broken.

Reed felt the heat on his skin and the blur of anger rising inside. Almost without thinking, he flexed a fist then pulled back and hit the boxer, all his strength behind the blow, hearing the bone in the nose break and watching as blood flowed sharply over the man's mouth and across his shirt. A second blow caught the man full in the mouth. The boxer spat out teeth.

'Who do you work for?'

The man glanced at him for a moment before looking straight ahead.

Reed stood back, pushing his lips together. He was breathing heavily; he could feel every bristle of his beard against his cheeks. Very slowly he extended his arm into the man's crotch, cupping his balls and squeezing slowly.

'Tell me.'

Blood was still dribbling from the boxer's mouth. The sergeant tightened his grip. The man should be screaming. But there was nothing at all. It was as if he couldn't feel pain. Staring into the man's eyes, Reed slowly brought his fingers together and twisted. Still there was nothing. Finally, he let go.

Jesus, he thought. Any normal man would have given in by now. This one barely seemed to notice.

He needed to think but he couldn't. Everything was swirling in his mind, one picture slipping into another so they slid around, just beyond his reach. He'd never failed before. He'd always made them talk. Always. In the army, when the professionals weren't around he'd been the one they turned to. He found answers. And he would this time. This was too important. They needed to know. With a roar he hit out, short, hard jabs to the face and neck, a storm of blows, trying to pound out every frustration in his heart.

It felt like no more than a few seconds. But when he finished, when he found himself standing there, fists tight at his sides, all the scars on the boxer's face had reopened into a bloody mess and his head lolled against his chest.

Reed was breathing hard as he saw the damage. He had no memory of causing it. But the red stains on his shirt, his grazed, painful knuckles and his growing horror gave him away. Fearfully, he placed a finger against the man's neck, praying there was a pulse. At first there was nothing and panic rose in his throat. Then it was there, slow but regular.

Christ, what had he done?

He banged on the door, shouting for someone to open up.

An old walking stick was propped by his chair in the office, a cup of tea on the desk, cold now. He drank it down anyway, the liquid like balm on his tongue. He pulled out the watch from his waistcoat pocket and checked the time.

Desperation gnawed hard in his belly. In his years on the force he'd never yet come across someone who wouldn't even say a single word. Some were eager to talk, some had to be coaxed and prodded, even pushed and hit. Some said little. This was the very first time he'd wondered if they'd be able to loosen someone's tongue. The boxer seemed to have put up a wall. It was as if they couldn't reach him, that he couldn't feel any of it, couldn't even hear it. But they needed names. They needed anything Reed could pry out of the man.

He looked at the watch again. Reed was good with the stubborn ones. He'd learned things that opened mouths and minds. But he knew well enough that the sergeant could go too far. The year before they'd caught a rapist. Everyone knew he was guilty, but the man wouldn't confess. After a session with Reed he'd admitted everything and needed two broken fingers and a cracked rib set. It had all been explained away as an accident, but the superintendent had been forced to give the sergeant a warning. Leaving him with the boxer was a risk. But he had no choice, not if they wanted to find Martha; Billy was their best chance of discovering information.

He rubbed his ankle. The flesh was tender and swollen under his fingertips. He could move around awkwardly with the stick. But it'd be several days before he'd manage anything more than a graceful hobble. Harper sighed. He'd been so close to the boxer's partner. Another minute and he'd have caught him, but wishes weren't horses, and he wasn't about to ride. The man was off somewhere now. And the fighter was all they had.

Harper wrote up the report, the scratch of the pen on paper the only sound in the office. He glanced at the watch again, willing the minutes away. Finally he sat back in the chair and lit a Woodbine, blowing out the smoke and watching it rise.

The door opened with a slow creak and Reed stood there. His face was pale and sober. There was blood on his knuckles, red spots flecked across the front of his shirt.

'Tom . . .' he began.

'For God's sake, Billy, what the hell have you done?'

He grabbed the stick and hurried down the stairs, trying to ignore the pain as he landed on each step. The door to the cell was open. The boxer sat on his chair, head slumped forward. His face was ruined, teeth broken, nose squashed, blood covering his mouth and down his shirt.

Warily, Harper reached out and touched the man's wrist lightly. The pulse was there, not too strong but regular. He turned to the jailer, out in the corridor.

'Send for an ambulance, now.'

The station had one of the new telephones. He'd never used it himself, but Tollman would be able to ring the Infirmary.

Reed stood by the door, hands pushed deep into his trouser pockets, his face pale.

'He wouldn't answer,' he said shakily. 'It didn't matter what I did to him.'

'He'll live. Better be grateful for that.'

'Tom . . .'

Harper cut him off. 'We need to go and talk to the superintendent, Sergeant.'

'Yes, sir.'

There was nothing more he could do. The staff in the station would look after the boxer until the ambulance arrived. He straightened. The man still hadn't moved. His eyes were closed, his breathing shallow.

'Come on,' he ordered, making his way to the front desk. 'I want Ash to go to the hospital with the man and stay with him. Keep him handcuffed to the bed.'

'Yes, sir,' Tollman said, carefully not looking at Reed.

He set off along the Headrow, the sergeant close behind. For once, they didn't talk. Harper was tangled in his thoughts, fury and frustration roaring through his blood. He was angry at Reed for going too far, angry at himself for giving him free rein. And angry at the boxer for his blind, silent stubbornness. Every step was an effort. He was already breathing hard, his back damp with sweat, but the pain in his ankle kept his fury boiling.

At least the boxer hadn't died. Injuries could be buried in reports, as long as they lived. If he died, though, Reed could go down for murder. He'd be an accessory himself, sacked from the force if he didn't end up in jail. And it had all been for nothing.

'Billy, what the hell were you thinking?' Harper asked in exasperation.

Reed took out a cigarette and lit it. His hands were still shaking, his face sickly grey.

'I just kept trying to make him talk,' he answered slowly, his voice bleak. He blew out smoke. 'He didn't even seem to notice anything. He wouldn't say a word. I hurt him, Tom, I know I did.'

'You nearly bloody killed him,' the inspector turned and shouted. One or two people walking along the street stopped to stare. Harper lowered his voice to a hiss. 'We're both lucky he's alive. You do know that, don't you?'

The sergeant nodded and lowered his head. 'I'm sorry, Tom. He . . .' He searched for the words he needed. 'I just wanted answers. You know I can make them talk.'

Harper knew that much of the blame was his. He was the one who'd let the man loose. And he knew that Reed used the things he'd learned in the army.

'Come on,' he said, letting his breath out in a long sigh. 'Let's get this over with.'

Kendall sat in the chair, gazing at the desk as the inspector talked. Reed stood at attention. He stayed silent for a long time after the explanation had finished before looking up.

'Get out,' he told the sergeant coldly. After the door closed he gazed at Harper.

'You were stupid,' he said slowly, enunciating each word slowly, barely keeping his anger in check. 'For God's sake, Tom, you know what he's like and you gave him a man who wouldn't say a word. You didn't even stay in the room?' His voice rose as he spoke until the last words came out as a yell, spittle flying from his mouth. Tiredness showed on his face. His eyes looked sunk deep, almost hidden. He shook his head. 'He'll live?'

'It looks like it, sir.'

'You'd better hope so.'

'Yes, sir.'

'Then we'll be able to charge him for killing the replacement worker.'

'Harry Gordon.' The superintendent looked up quickly as Harper spoke. 'That was the dead man's name, sir.'

Kendall began to pace around the office. 'If this strike wasn't going on I'd suspend you both.'

'Yes, sir.' Inside, he could feel the relief grow. They were going to be let off lightly, not even a suspension.

'Instead, you'll both receive a warning.' He rubbed at the ache in his neck.

'Yes, sir.'

'And you'd better keep Reed close in future, Tom.'

'I will, sir.' He stood, leaning heavily on the stick.

'I'd rest that tonight, if I were you,' he advised.

'Yes, sir.'

The sergeant stood, looking over the marble bannister at the floor, forty feet below.

'Well?' he asked.

'We're both going to receive a warning.'

'That's all?' Reed asked, his eyes widening in disbelief.

'Do you want more?' Harper asked him. 'Be grateful.'

'I am, believe me.' The colour was gradually returning to his face. He lit another cigarette. 'What do we do now?'

'I really don't know.'

'We could try to find the boxer's friend.'

Harper gazed down at the men moving around, all of them looking purposeful in their dark suits and ties, a few still in the old-fashioned frock coats. He shook his head.

'I'd bet good money he's already packed and gone.' It was what he'd do himself, simply vanish as soon as possible. Train, omnibus, even walking; they'd never find him.

'Then what?'

'We start thinking,' he said after a moment. 'Go back to the basics. Do you know what the super taught me when I was starting out?'

'No.'

'Find out who's going to gain from a crime. Work that out and once you've done it, you've probably found who's behind everything. He's right, too.'

He started to walk down the stairs, leaning heavily on the stick. Every step was painful and he moved slowly, letting the foot take his weight slowly as he concentrated. At the bottom he took a deep, trembling breath, steadying himself before he crossed to stare out of the windows.

A mob was still scattered across Victoria Square, about a thousand, far fewer then when they'd brought the blacklegs in. But it was enough to leave the bobbies guarding the main doors of the Town Hall with furrowed, worried faces.

'So who profits from Col's death?' Reed asked.

'Whoever took Martha,' Harper answered. 'The same person responsible for Henry Bell's death.' He stared out at all the faces standing in the sunshine, every head covered with a working man's cap. 'Let's try looking at it a different way,' he said.

'How?'

'Who profits from the death of a blackleg?'

For a long moment the sergeant was quiet. 'But we don't know how that connects to Parkinson.'

'Forget that,' the inspector insisted. 'Just think about the blackleg.'

'If they can blame the murder on the strikers, it strengthens the position of the gas committee.'

Harper smiled. 'Exactly. How many on the committee? Four, isn't it?' He seemed to recall reading the figure somewhere.

'I think so,' the sergeant answered with a shrug.

'Then let's start looking into them. Maybe one thing will lead to another.' He grimaced. 'It's not like we have anything else.'

'I'll start asking.' Reed paused, turning the bowler hat in his hands. 'You should go home and rest that ankle.'

'That's what the super said,' Harper said with a small laugh. 'Anyone would think the pair of you were trying to get rid of me.'

But they were right. He could barely walk, let alone run. And he felt drained, his body exhausted. But he could feel the need rubbing inside him, wanting to know, to have this thing over and Martha safe.

'Get to work,' he said finally. 'I'll be in tomorrow.'

'I will.' He paused then added quietly, 'And thank you, Tom.'

THIRTEEN

He hailed a passing hackney at the back of the Town Hall, out on Great George Street. When the cabbie leaned down from his seat, asking, 'Where to, guv?' at first he wasn't sure how to answer. His lodgings? Or to Annabelle?

'The Victoria in Sheepscar,' he replied after a moment, leaning back and closing his eyes to let the pain ebb away for a while.

The pub was almost empty when he entered, just the usual old men whiling away the late afternoon and Dan standing behind the bar, polishing the brass to a high, bright shine. He raised his eyes as he watched Harper limp across the room.

'You look like you've been in the wars.'

'I lost an argument with a cart,' he explained with a wry smile.

'Sit yoursen down and I'll bring you a brandy.'

'Is she upstairs?'

Dan shook his head. He was a young man with tousled red

hair and an eager grin, always bustling around to find something to do. The best worker she'd ever had, Annabelle claimed.

Harper settled on a chair, stretched out his leg and felt the pain ease to a heavy throb.

Dan placed the glass on a heavily polished table and waved him away as he tried to pay.

'Give over, Tom. She'd kill me if I took your money. Call it medicine.' He grinned, showing a mouth with most of the teeth gone. 'She'll be back in an hour or so, she's gone round the bakeries.'

The inspector was still sitting there with a full glass of brandy next to the empty one when Annabelle returned an hour later.

She swept through the door in a rush, a short grey jacket buttoned tight over a white blouse that rose to her throat. The grey skirt flared, swishing as she walked. Her hair had been pulled up under a hat, just a few wild strands peeking out.

'I didn't know if I'd see you today,' she said happily, leaning over and giving him a peck on the cheek. Then she noticed the stick and pulled back, eyeing him. 'What have you done now?'

'I twisted my ankle. Nothing serious.'

Annabelle bustled around, pulling over a stool and watching as he rested his foot on it.

'Better,' she said approvingly, settled next to him and dropped her bag on the floor with a heavy jangle of coins. Without a word, Dan brought her a glass of gin and she drank gratefully.

'Good God, what's in the bag?' Harper asked.

'Takings from the bakeries,' she replied breezily.

'How much?'

She shrugged. 'I haven't counted it yet.'

'Anyone could have robbed you,' he told her, startled when she began to laugh.

'Round here?' Annabelle laughed heartily. 'They'd never dare, Tom Harper, they all know me. And if anyone tried, they wouldn't get ten yards before there'd be people all over them. Your lot would be sweeping up the pieces.'

All he could do was shake his head. He'd never known anyone quite like her, so sure, so confident. 'I don't want anything happening to you, that's all.'

'Don't you worry about me. I'm not the one with the dicky ankle.'

'I'll live.'

'You'd better,' she said, arching her brows, eyes glinting and amused. 'I'm not done with you yet.' She downed the rest of the gin in a single swallow and stood. 'Let's go upstairs and I'll put something on that ankle. No one's looked at it yet, have they?'

'No,' he admitted.

'Right, up those steps and I'll bandage it. You'll just be walking wounded by the morning.'

But morning came too soon. Early light through the curtains in the spare bedroom woke him and he limped around the floor. He tried the gas mantle, but there was no familiar soft hiss. All the supplies were gone. Instead he shaved and dressed by the light of a candle, moving quietly through the rooms to the kitchen.

Annabelle was already there, wearing an old dress and apron, hair half tucked away under an old cap, busy buttering thick slices of bread. She glanced up and smiled, leaning across to give him a quick kiss.

'I've made you some tea,' she told him. 'I heard you crashing about in there like a herd of elephants.'

He thought he'd been quiet. She pushed the food across to him and picked up her cup.

'How's your ankle?' she asked.

'A little better.' It still hurt, but he could limp around with the stick. 'I'll survive. There's work to do.' He looked at her again. 'Why are you dressed like that?'

'Kitty's gone for a few days. Her mam's been taken poorly. And there's work to do,' she echoed him with a grin, sticking out her tongue. 'The pub needs a good cleaning.' She paused, then continued, her voice still straightforward and practical as she looked him in the eyes. 'I've been thinking.'

'What about?'

'How many nights have you spent here now?'

'Three,' he answered. She knew it just as well as he did.

'And we're going to be married in a fortnight.' He nodded his answer. 'I thought you might as well just move in here,' she continued, holding up a hand before he could say anything. 'Give your notice at your lodgings. I can have Dan bring everything here, and you have the spare bedroom until we're wed.' Annabelle cocked her head. 'What do you think?'

He stood and looked at her. The way she talked, it sounded sensible. He'd be closer to the station, he wouldn't be paying for somewhere to live. Best of all, he'd be with Annabelle each evening. Slowly he smiled.

'I think it's a grand idea,' he told her, and suddenly she was hugging him, then pulling back after a moment.

'Spare bedroom,' she warned him. 'Don't get any ideas, Tom Harper. Not until that ring's on my finger.'

He put his arms around her, pulling her close, seeing her eyes spark with joy and tasting the morning on her kiss.

'Right, you,' she said finally, 'eat your breakfast then off you go to work.' She laughed. 'I sound like a right bloody wife, don't I?'

'The best one I'll ever have.'

'The only one, if you know what's good for you.' She grinned and straightened his tie. 'That's better.' She stood back and inspected him. 'That moustache needs a trim but you'll do.'

For a moment he thought of his mother; she'd never have spoken to his father that way, with the same glint of mischief in her eyes. She wouldn't have dared. He was a man who ruled his house, with the strap waiting for the slightest insolence or disobedience.

And now he was going to be living in a woman's house, above the pub she owned, her other businesses little more than a stone's throw away. His father would never have understood that. To him, it had been the man who provided for his family. His wages as a railwayman paid the rent on their back-to-back and put food on the table, just like every other man on Noble Street and all the streets around it.

Instead, Harper would have a wife who probably earned more in three months than he did in a year. She'd turned his world upside down, changed every idea that had been part of his fabric without effort.

'What are you thinking?' she asked.

'Nothing important.'

'Any more word on that girl?'

He shook his head. Martha had been the last thing he'd thought about before falling asleep, the first in his head when he woke. Each day the feeling that she was dead grew inside him. And if she wasn't . . . perhaps that would be even worse.

'You'll find her,' Annabelle told him. He wished he could believe her. They weren't even close.

Names, Reed thought. That was the place to start: find out who was on the gas committee. At least he was in the Town Hall, the right place to find the information. A few minutes later, after being sent to three different offices, he knew who they were. Harper had been right: there were four of them, with Alderman Gilston in charge, as the clerk had told him, the downturn of his mouth speaking louder than any words.

Councillors. These were people beyond his ken. They lived in a different world, one that rarely touched him. He dealt with criminals. They were poor folk for the most part, ones who'd end up in Armley Jail for a few months, maybe even a year or two for fighting or stealing – small, everyday crimes. The ones with money in the bank, the clean shirts and good suits, rarely ended up in a cell.

He stood, thinking. Who did he know who might have information on some councillors? Finally he smiled. Richard Finer. He was a man who managed to blur the lines between the different levels of society. He'd done time in the past, for fraud, but made enough money for people to be willing to forget the fact.

It took an hour to find him, holding court at the Golden Lion Hotel on Lower Briggate, down towards the bridge. He sat at the head of the table, four other men listening eagerly to every word. With no gas, candles gave a soft, diffused light to the room. Finer toyed with a glass of brandy, long fingers running around the rim. He looked prosperous and self-satisfied, his dark suit cut well enough to disguise the growing belly. The collar of his white shirt was sharp as a knife blade, a shining stickpin through the knot of his tie. Very flashy, Reed thought. Finer's bushy side whiskers extended to his moustache, starting to turn grey, but the hair of his head was still thick for a man in his fifties.

He spotted the sergeant, leaned forward and spoke a few quiet words. Without a complaint the men around him left, two of them glancing briefly at the policemen as they passed.

'Mr Reed,' Finer said with a broad smile. 'It's strange to see you here. Not one of your usual haunts, is it?' He gestured at a seat. 'Have a drink? Gin for you, isn't it?'

Tempting as it was, he refused. 'I'm on duty, sir.'

Finer leaned back in his chair, amusement dancing in his eyes. He stroked a chin so freshly shaved he must have been barbered late in the afternoon.

'It must be serious if you're turning down a drink. Well, I've done nowt, so you must want some information.' Reed knew that the attitude was an act, a mask, the blunt Yorkshireman everyone could trust. But a sharp, devious mind lay behind it.

'Very clever.'

Finer gave a small bow of his head. 'Who do you want to know about?'

'The men on the gas committee.'

'Don't ask for much, do you?' He reached into his jacket, brought out a cigar case, and made an elaborate performance of selecting one, cutting off the end then lighting it, saying nothing until he'd blown out a thick plume of smoke. 'Why?' he asked.

'I can't tell you,' Reed answered.

'Aye, I bet you can't. They're in trouble, they've already lost this strike. It'll all be signed and sealed in the morning.'

'What do you know about them, Mr Finer?' The sergeant kept his eyes on the man.

'Not much,' he admitted. 'But I'll tell you this: I'd not trust any one of them as far as I could throw him. And with two of them that'd not be no more than a couple of yards. They're like everyone else, in it for what they can get.'

'What about Alderman Gilston?'

Finer gave a dismissive snort. 'He was the one with the bright bloody idea that caused the strike. That tells you all you need to know about him. The only other one with a spine is Cromwell. I'd keep your eye on him.'

'Have you heard any gossip?'

'Nowt worthwhile.'

Reed knew that was a lie. Gossip was currency to a man like Finer. What it meant was that he wasn't ready to spend any of it yet. He wasn't going to say anything more. The sergeant stood.

'Thank you.'

'Come back when you're ready for that drink, Mr Reed.'

It was close to July dusk when he caught the tram. Half past
nine, not too late, he could stop at the Hyde Park for a quick
drink. Since Finer had offered one he'd been able to taste the
gin, to feel it on his tongue and his throat.

In the end it was after midnight when he put the key in the
door of the house on Burchett Place. It was just another street
of back-to-backs, home to working men and their families. Mr
Methley, his landlord, was a foreman at one of the tanneries
down on Meanwood Road. His wife, a fragile little woman, kept
everything sparkling, and Katie, the only daughter still living
there, was a factory girl.

They were used to his hours by now, the late nights and early
mornings. If they noticed the alcohol on his breath or heard him
on the nights he tossed and moaned in his bed, they were polite
enough to say nothing. The place suited him. He wasn't there much,
it was quiet, and there was dinner on the table every Sunday if he
was at home. He closed his curtains and took off the cheap gaber-
dine suit before he opened the letter that had been waiting for him.

It was the reply from Whitby, two short paragraphs in a neat,
flowing hand. There was no current vacancy for a detective, it
said, but if one were to come up, they would advise him.
It doesn't matter, he told himself. It was never more than a dream,
anyway. And now, with another reprimand on his record, no other
force would take him. He was here for all the years ahead.

On the tram Harper read the headlines over someone's shoulder:
the gas committee and the strikers were talking, it would be over
soon. That was what Leeds needed, a return to normal, for the
gas to flow. The men needed to return to work and bring home
their wages. They'd all learned how thin this layer of modernity
really was.

He limped down from Vicar Lane, hearing fragments of conversations, everyone hopeful that things would soon be over, that
business would improve quickly. At the station Reed was already
at his desk, neat and shaved, only the redness around his eyes a
sign that he'd been drinking the evening before.

'How's the ankle?'

Harper shrugged. 'Could be worse. Did you find anything?'

'Bits and pieces.' He rubbed his hands down his cheeks. 'I talked to Dick Finer. He said we should look at Gilston and Cromwell. The problem's going to be finding anything. These aren't criminals, Tom. They're businessmen. Rich businessmen.'

Harper understood. The activities of the police rarely touched that of the rich. They had few sources there, hardly anyone who could tell them what happened there, where to look or whose secrets were valuable.

'Desmond,' he decided finally.

'The lawyer?' Reed asked.

'He represents half the important people in Leeds.'

'He wouldn't say anything. You know what he's like.'

'He was scared enough when you told him Henry Bell had been killed – you told me that. We'll work on him.'

The sergeant considered the idea. 'I suppose it might work,' he agreed. 'We don't have anywhere else to try.'

'Maybe we do,' Harper said, gathering up his stick. 'I'll be back in an hour. Desmond won't be in his office before nine, anyway.'

Leeds smelt cleaner than he could ever recall. The air was almost sweet and clear, and the sun shone bright as he made his way slowly over to Kirkgate. There were close to a hundred men milling around outside the union office, two constables standing across the street, their expressions nervous as they shifted from foot to foot.

He pushed his way through the crowd and into the room that smelt of old, rank sweat. Papers were piled high on the desk. Maguire sat in his chair, wearing the same clothes as two days before, his hair unruly, eyes wild and exultant.

'Mr Harper,' he said, eyeing the stick and the limp. 'I hope it wasn't one of our men who did that to you.'

'An accident,' the inspector answered.

'Sorry to hear that. What can I do for you this grand day?'

'You've won?'

Maguire lit a cigarette and waved his hand, watching the smoke rise.

'All but. We're giving them a little so it doesn't look like a complete rout.' He shrugged. 'It'll be settled this morning. Tomorrow night all those men outside will be back at work.'

'Congratulations.'

'We've shown them what happens when they try to take advantage of working men. There's hope for the world yet.' He gazed at the inspector. 'But you didn't come here for famous victories, Mr Harper. More about the dead blackleg, God rest his soul?'

'We know it wasn't one of the strikers who killed him.'

Maguire raised his eyebrows and said nothing.

'The man's in custody,' Harper continued. 'I'm looking for some information.'

'Are you now?' He smiled slyly. 'And what might you need?'

'I'd like to know about the members of the gas committee.'

Maguire sat back and stared. 'Why's that now, Inspector? Or can't you tell me?'

'You've dealt with them.'

'I have,' he agreed with a nod.

'You must have found out about them, their strengths and weaknesses.'

'It's a wise man who understand his opponents,' he answered. 'Tell me, Mr Harper, are you a card player?'

'No, I'm not.'

Maguire smiled. 'Then I'd advise you stay that way. You tip your hand too easily.'

Harper laughed. 'Do I?'

'You tell me none of the strikers were involved in that murder and then you ask me about the gas committee. It doesn't take a great mind to make the leap from one to the other. You think one of them is behind it.'

'Very perceptive, Mr Maguire,' he acknowledged. 'What can you tell me about them?'

'Why? The police have hardly been our friends. Do you know how many union members have been hurt in the last few days? Your chief constable even armed his men with cutlasses against us.'

'I need to know because it could save the life of a young girl,' Harper said flatly.

'I won't ask you how,' Maguire replied slowly. 'You wouldn't tell me anyway.'

'No. But now you understand.'

'Yes,' he said, as if he'd agreed to something. He stubbed out the cigarette and lit another, the harsh sulphur flare of the match filling the air for a moment. He closed his eyes and started to speak. 'Alderman Gilston's the head of the committee. He's the one who caused the strike. A venal little man, Mr Harper, and nowhere near as clever as he believes he is. He thinks he's a man people should follow. The only trouble is that he couldn't lead his way out of a paper bag. But a criminal?' He pursed his lips and mused. 'He doesn't have the imagination. He thinks in pounds and pennies. He has gods of gold. Life's a balance sheet to him. You know the type?'

'I do.'

'Good. Wilks and Dodds will do anything Gilston wants. I doubt either of them has ever had an original thought between them.'

'They made money,' the inspector pointed out.

'They inherited money,' Maguire corrected him. 'Life's much easier when you don't have to earn a living.' He grinned. 'Or so I'm told.'

'That leaves one man.'

'It does. Alderman Cromwell. The man whose namesake decimated Ireland, if you know your history. I dare say our Mr Cromwell would like to leave his mark, too, but he never will.'

'Why not?'

'Because he's a weak fellow, Mr Harper. He'd like to be great and never will be, but that doesn't stop him trying.'

'What's he done?'

'Nothing that I know about,' Maguire admitted. 'But in your shoes I'd keep my eye on him.'

'Because you don't like him or because you don't trust him?'

'Both,' the man answered without hesitation. 'When you were a schoolboy, was there a sneak in your class?'

'A sneak?' He wasn't sure what Maguire meant.

'The one you'd make sure never heard anything. If he did he'd be straight off to the teacher to pass it on and make himself look better.'

In spite of himself, Harper smiled. There'd been a someone exactly like that at his school, his nose always runny, listening at doors and corners, shunned by all the others.

'I think Alderman Cromwell must have been one when he was a lad,' Maguire went on. 'He's just grown into his cunning, that's all.'

'What do you know about him?'

'He owns a mine in Middleton. Cost him plenty enough, too. It's a strange coincidence, though, that once it came under new ownership the mine received a contract to supply coal to the gasworks in Leeds. One hand feeds the other, Mr Harper, and if both hands belong to the same man, so much the better, eh?'

'Can you prove that?'

'The papers are on record.'

'I dare say it's legal.'

'It is, it is, even if it goes against everything most men call moral.'

'Then there's nothing I can do.'

'Oh, it becomes better, Inspector. Our good Alderman Cromwell is under investigation.' There was real, deep pleasure in his voice. 'He thought he'd increase his profits by selling the gasworks substandard coal. A greedy man.' Maguire shook his head. 'He'll pay for it, too.'

He stubbed out the cigarette and stood, stretching his back and yawning.

'If you'll excuse me, Mr Harper, I've a few men to humble and many more to please this morning.' He gave a wry smile. 'And after that I'll get roaring drunk with the lads then take to my bed and sleep for two days. He took a battered bowler hat off the rack. 'I wish you well, and I hope you find the girl.'

There was some real summer warmth to the day as he walked back to Millgarth, stopping to buy a bag of liquorice from Mr Marks's stall in the market. The sharp taste felt good in his mouth, cleansing away the bitter taste of corruption.

Reed was still at his desk, going through Bell's ledgers and making notes. Harper glanced at the photograph of Martha Parkinson, propped against the inkwell on his desk.

'What do you know about the coal business, Billy?'

'Coal?' The sergeant frowned, confused. 'Nothing.'

'I think we're both about to learn.' He pulled the watch from his waistcoat pocket, checked the time and wound it. 'I'll tell you on the way to Park Square. The speed I'm moving with this ankle maybe we'll be there by dinner time.'

FOURTEEN

The Park estate stood on the edge of the city centre, the houses simple and graceful, built around a manicured grass square. It had been there since long before he was born, but unlike all the dour yards and courts that had simply grown, higgledy-piggledy and mismatched, this had all been planned and laid out carefully, a place for people with money. It was somewhere a man could breathe and enjoy life, as long as he possessed the means.

Once families had lived here. Children and their nannies had played on the grass that stood protected behind railings, dutifully cut every week. Now it was filled with offices, with lawyers and doctors and all the professional people who could afford the rents and kept their solemn hours in the expensively decorated rooms. It felt apart from the rest of Leeds, like a place that kept the world at bay with wealth.

The door to number eleven was a deep black, and the hallway smelled of beeswax, carpeted to soften the footfalls. Desmond's name was a simple brass plaque on a polished ground floor door. Harper turned the handle and walked in.

Soames the clerk raised his head, smiling politely; two others carried on with their work, hunched over their desks. They all wore dark, sober suits, their clothes fifty years out of date, pens scribbling sharply on paper.

'Inspector,' Soames said with a small nod. 'Sergeant. Can I help you?'

'We need to talk to him.'

'I'm sorry, he's with a client,' Soames answered apologetically. It was all a game; maybe there was a client, maybe not.

'Tell him we're here, please,' Harper told him. The man glanced, then hurried away, vanishing through a door and returning a few seconds later.

'Go through, sir.'

The room was lined with bookcases that reached all the way to the high ceiling, and the tall window looked down on the square. Desmond was seated behind a large wooden desk with elaborately carved corners. The lawyer's robe and short wig were tossed idly over an armchair in the corner.

He looked prosperous, his suit the best tailoring money could buy, nails clean and buffed, cheeks so closely shaved beneath grey side whiskers that they seemed to shine. But under the sophisticated exterior his eyes were fearful and hunted.

'Mr Desmond,' the inspector said as he sat, turning his head to hear clearly.

'What is it, Mr Harper? I'm a busy man.' His tone tried for irritation, but Harper could hear the nervousness underneath. 'I gave you Bell's ledgers.' With his bulging eyes and hooked nose, there was nothing attractive about the man. But the inspector knew he had a young, pretty wife who seemed content on his arm. That was what happened with rich men, he found: it made some women blind to many faults. And Desmond had plenty of money. He earned it, too; he was one of the best lawyers in Leeds, sharp and clever, his mind precise and ruthless in the labyrinth of the law, and he charged his clients accordingly.

'Yes,' he answered, 'and we're very grateful, Mr Desmond. All in code, though, isn't it, sir?'

'Is it?' he asked. 'I never looked at it. Henry just kept it with me where it was safe.'

Harper didn't believe a word. Desmond would have been through every page of the book; he was a man who wanted to know all his clients' secrets. He delved into the nooks and crannies; it was how he knew to the guinea exactly how much to charge them. If he'd found something it could explain why he was so scared.

'I'm sure it'll tell us a great deal,' he said with a smile. 'But that's not why we're here, sir.'

'No?' The lawyer gave him a curious look, something almost like relief behind his eyes. 'Then what?'

'Some information.' Harper smiled again. 'I'm sure you'll be happy to help where you can.'

'Of course.' Desmond gave a short, condescending nod.

'Alderman Cromwell. Do you know him?'

'Of course I know him,' the lawyer answered brusquely, as if it was the most obvious thing in the world.

'Is he one of your clients?' Desmond shook his head and the inspector continued, 'What do you know about him, sir?'

'Know about him?'

'Yes, sir. We're looking into his affairs.' Harper paused. 'This is in confidence, of course.'

'I can't help you, I'm afraid, Inspector. I know Charlie Cromwell, but that's all.'

'No gossip?' Reed interrupted.

'I try to ignore gossip, Sergeant.' The lawyer pushed his thin lips into a frown.

'Never useful, sir?' Harper asked. 'I find there's often a grain of truth in rumour. I'm sure a man like yourself keeps abreast of everything happening in Leeds.'

Desmond shrugged. 'Of course.'

'Have you heard anything about the alderman, sir?'

He sat back, staring at the policemen. 'Nothing of any importance,' he said finally. 'Just idle talk.'

Harper stood, Reed following, and they started to leave without another word. The inspector let the sergeant go, then quietly closed the door behind him, walked back to the desk and put his hands on the polished wood, leaning close to the lawyer's face.

'Something's scaring you, Mr Desmond.' He kept his voice low, little more than an intimate whisper. 'I don't know what it is, but I'm going to find out. And if you've been keeping something back that could help me, I assure you, you're going to be scared of a great deal more.' The lawyer's eyes had widened but his face remained impassive. 'That's a promise. I'm trying to find a little girl who's been missing more than a week. You'd better think about that.'

He was turning the handle when the words came, so quiet he barely made them out.

'Cromwell's in debt. You should look into that.'

The heavy door closed silently.

Reed was outside, staring at the grass in the square.

'Cromwell owes money,' Harper told him.

'Who to?'

'He didn't say.' The inspector lit a Woodbine, watching the smoke rise into the warm air. 'You see what you can find out. I think it's time to have a word with the alderman himself.'

'If he'll see you.'

'He will.'

'I thought you said they were negotiating to finish the strike.'

'I dare say he'd be glad for an excuse to leave,' Harper said with a smile. 'If Maguire was telling me the truth, the gas committee's going to come out of this looking like fools.'

'Tom, talk to the super first. Tell him what's happening. After yesterday . . .'

He was right, Harper knew. He should talk to the superintendent before he did anything. They were already on a warning and Cromwell was a councillor, not an ordinary criminal. If Desmond was right, he might not have money but he did have power. He was still one of the people who controlled Leeds.

'No,' was all Kendall said.

'Sir,' Harper protested, but the superintendent cut him off.

'Not until the strike's settled. That's an order.'

They sat in an empty office on the first floor of the town hall. The crowds had poured back into Victoria Square, restive and loud, waiting for the news that they'd won and the council had been forced to agree to the strikers' demands. Soon enough there'd be a party out there. They'd all be singing and waving their flags. A victory for the workers. A rare enough thing at any time.

Kendall had changed back into plain clothes, his suit fresh, hair pomaded and moustache carefully clipped above his lip, the grey showing silver in the light. His top hat sat on the edge of the desk.

'Martha Parkinson,' the inspector said.

'Don't play that game with me, Tom.' Kendall snapped. 'I'm the one who taught you how to do it.'

'With respect, sir, we need answers and he might have them.'

'You said that about the boxer. Have you had anything from him yet?'

'No.' He didn't give the superintendent the full truth; he hadn't been to the infirmary to see the man. But he would.

'Then work on him instead. Once the strike's all done, then you can talk to Alderman Cromwell. Not before, do I make myself clear?'

'Yes, sir.' He stood, and Kendall sighed.

'Tom, I want that little girl safe as much as you do. But if we do anything to jeopardize the end of this strike, it'll be your job *and* mine. We could have a dozen like her all gone, bodies piling up along Briggate, and they'd still play second fiddle to this. Leeds is depending on it being resolved and nothing can interfere with that. Nothing. The chief constable and the mayor have made that perfectly obvious.'

'Yes, sir.'

'We're losing thousands of pounds every day. Other places in England are passing us by and laughing at us. All the business leaders are furious. We need this to be over, we need that more than anything else just now.'

Harper left, angry, coming out into Great George Street and the warm sun. The infirmary was no more than a hundred yards away, just past the confectioner's and the postbox on the corner. The grand Gothic towers and elaborate decoration outside the building always seemed to promise magic rather than medicine to him. Perhaps that was what it really was – the doctors seemed to kill almost as often as they cured. He walked in through the Winter Garden, light pouring through the great glass ceiling on to the statues that lined the walls. The chairs where the patients could sit had been moved out and tennis nets crossed from pillar to iron pillar in the hall. 'Come and join us!' a bright poster announced. 'Games every afternoon!' He moved into the tiled corridors where the only sound was of the nurses walking, the click of their heels and the swish of their uniform skirts. He hated coming here; the building was filled with the smells of illness and death and the carbolic that failed to mask it all. At least the smoke and stench of industry seemed honest. This was . . . He didn't have the words to describe it. Every time he entered the place the odour caught on his clothes and in his nostrils, and it seemed to take days to wash it away.

The boxer had a room to himself. He was handcuffed to the bedstead, and a constable sat on a plain wooden chair close by, uniform buttoned up, cap lying in his lap. He started to rise to attention, but Harper waved him down. The window was closed, the air stuffy and close.

'Has he said anything?'

'No, sir,' the constable replied.

Harper stood by the bed, looking down. Cleaned up, the fighter's face was a map of cuts, his eyes swollen, a red weal around his throat. Reed had given the man a real battering, there was no doubt about that. But he could understand it. No response, not even an acknowledgement, would be enough to make a man push harder and harder until he went over the edge.

The constable coughed. 'The doctor said he has swollen testicles, too, sir.' His raised his eyebrows. 'Very painful, he says.'

The boxer's eyes didn't flicker. He didn't turn to glance at the inspector, simply stared straight ahead. His lips looked dry and cracked.

'You're going to stand trial for the murder at the Town Hall,' Harper told him. 'As soon as you're well enough you'll be in court, then on remand in jail.' The man didn't even seem to hear him; he might as well not have been there.

The inspector turned to the bobby. 'Does he eat and drink?'

'Yes, sir. The nurse comes around and gives him a tray. All mush, though. Mr Reed knocked out most of his teeth so he can't chew.'

'How long before he's discharged?'

'Tomorrow, they said. Got my orders to take him to the cells under the Town Hall.'

'You're going down,' Harper told the boxer. 'Very likely you'll hang. Still nothing to say?' But there was nothing at all. 'Good luck with him,' he told the constable, and left.

Outside, he breathed deeply. He tried to rub away the hospital smell, running a hand over the pomade before putting the hat on his head. The visit had been a waste of time, but he'd always known it would be. If a beating couldn't make the man talk, time in a hospital bed wasn't about to loosen his tongue. He needed Alderman Cromwell.

Reed didn't know Middleton. He'd seen signposts to the place, but nothing more. He doubted that most of the people in Leeds had ever been there. It was simply a name, a place that supplied coal for them to burn in their fireplaces.

The railway station was off Town Street, along a road of neat little shops and cottages. In the distance he could see the pit works, several of them gathered close together, and farther away, rolling landscape and a big house. Newer back-to-backs stood separate, as if no one wanted them close. Now all he had to do was discover which of the pits Cromwell owned.

It was easier than he'd expected. The woman behind the counter in the grocer's seemed to know everything about the place. He selected an apple, paid for it and simply asked, 'Do you know which is Cromwell's pit?'

'Ee, love, course I do.' She was a little dumpling of a lass, with an eager smile and playful eyes. 'Come on, I'll point it out to you. Not local, are you?'

'No, I'm from Leeds.'

'Oh aye?' She led him out on to the pavement and pointed. 'You see that one over there, beyond those trees?'

'Yes.'

'That's the one you're looking for, love.' She barely came to his shoulder and stared up at his face. 'Not sure what you'd want there, though. You don't look like a miner.'

'I'm a policeman,' he told her. 'A detective.'

'First one of them I've seen,' she answered, impressed. 'What do they call you, then?'

'Billy Reed.'

'Well, you get yourself down there, Billy, and stop in on your way back. I'm Elizabeth. You'll find me working.'

As he strode away he smiled at her forwardness. He'd no doubt that the news of a detective's visit would be all over the village in an hour; it was the way these places worked. The pit was little more than half a mile outside the town. By then the houses were all far behind him and he was out in the country; there were farmers' fields, dry stone walls and plenty of dust along the dry, rutted paths.

The office was little more than a ramshackle wooden shed, the paint long since worn away. Machinery was moving, doing things he couldn't even pretend to understand, but there was no one around. He pushed the door open and entered, finding a clerk bent over his desk.

He was a stooped man wearing an old, shiny black suit, the tie knotted exactly, the shirt collar clean. A battered bowler hat hung from a nail. The man's fingers were stained a deep blue from a lifetime of ink. The writing on the page was a beautiful curling copperplate.

'Tha must be lost,' he said with a smile. There was warmth in his voice, bemusement and curiosity at the stranger.

'Not if this is Cromwell's mine.'

'Aye, you've found the right place.' He sat back, flexing his hand. 'Gets cramp these days. Never used to.' He looked to be in his fifties, most of his hair gone, the bald head shiny.

'I'm Detective Sergeant Reed from Leeds Police.'

The clerk pursed his lips in surprise. 'You here about the investigation, are you?'

Reed said nothing but gave a brief smile. Let the man make of that what he would.

'I'll tell you what I told the fellow from the council,' the man continued. 'I just do what I'm told. I put in me hours and go home at the end of the day. I didn't know the police were involved, though.'

'We're always involved in a crime.' That was true enough, although the words meant nothing here.

'Aye, well, that's a matter for Mr Cromwell. We get the orders and fill them and that's all we do here. If they say the coal's poor quality, that's none of my business. You've had a wasted trip. You need the company office.'

'Isn't this it?' Reed asked in surprise.

The clerk shook his head and smiled.

'Nay, lad, you've had a wasted trip. It's in Leeds. That's where all the business is done. It's down on Park Square.'

No more than a few yards from Desmond's office, where they'd been just two hours before. Reed sighed.

'Does the mine make money?' He didn't know what to ask now; the question was just the first thing that came into his head.

The clerk shrugged. 'It must, I reckon. We've twenty-five underground, two foremen and me, all here. So I suppose it must do fair to middling. And contracts for all the coal we can dig out.'

'From Leeds?'

'Aye, mostly. A few others, but they take the bulk. You need the office for all that.'

'And Mr Cromwell is a rich man?'

'Happen he is. I've not seen where he lives. He dresses well enough when he comes out here, like he's not short of a bob or two.' He gave a small snort. 'Not that he's here often. Five times in the last two years and you'd think it was the dirtiest place he'd ever been. But it's like they say, where there's muck there's brass. Any fool knows that.'

'What do you think of the investigation?' Reed asked.

'No idea, lad. I keep me head down, do me job and take me pay. Best thing for a man like me. For all of us as work here.'

'What do you think of Mr Cromwell?'

The man shook his head firmly.

'Not for me to say lad. I work for him, he pays me, that's it. I'll not say a word against the man who pays my wages. If I do he might not pay them any more.'

That was it, he knew, all the man would say. But he'd learned a little. Cromwell was definitely under investigation for the quality of his coal, and Leeds did buy most of it. It was all ammunition. And he'd seen the mine. There was coal dust everywhere, he could feel it as he breathed in. But what would anyone expect?

'Thank you,' he said finally and made his way back outside. The clouds had gone, leaving the sky brilliant blue, the sun hot on his face as he walked back into Middleton. He'd half a mind to duck back into the grocer's and talk to Elizabeth before catching his train but there was no need. She was out of the shop door before he had to make the decision.

'Did you find it?'

'Yes.' He gave a small bow. 'Good directions.'

'Free, too,' she answered with a wink. Bold and saucy, he thought, but in spite of himself, he was smiling. 'Are you a married man, Mr Reed?'

'Never have been,' he told her. She stood in the doorway of

the shop, arms folded, leaning against the jamb. There was meat on her, but he liked that. A pretty face, framed with ash blonde hair, lines of care and worry around her mouth. Around thirty, he judged.

'I'm a widow,' she said as if she could read his mind. 'Married ten year then he died down the pit.'

'Cromwell's?'

'Nay, one of the others. Enough of them around here. There's me and four little 'uns.' She paused and added reflectively, 'Not so little any more, mind.'

'I'm sorry.'

She shrugged. 'I'm not the only one round here. Plenty of others lost their husbands underground. What's it like being a policeman, then. You enjoy it?'

'I do,' he admitted. 'Better than a soldier. That was what I did before,' he explained.

'You've been around a bit,' she said and he smiled. He was enjoying this, a little flirtation, a pleasurable natter on a summer's day. It had been a long time since he'd felt at ease around a woman. 'Live in Leeds, do you?'

'I do.'

'You should come out here sometime.' Elizabeth nodded at the distance. 'Get past the pits and there's some grand country out there if you like Shanks's pony.'

'I've walked all over Yorkshire.'

She looked him up and down, assessing him, then nodded, as if he'd passed some test.

'They give you time off in that important job of yours?'

'Sundays if we're lucky.'

'Come out and I'll show you around properly, then. Of course, I'll have my brood with me.' She began to colour, the flush rising from her neck up her face. 'I'm sorry. That was cheeky. You've probably better things to do.'

The sergeant grinned. Why not, he thought? A new place, fresh company.

'I'd be glad to.'

'Really?' She sounded astonished, putting her hands over her mouth. 'You're not just having me on?'

'I'm serious,' he assured her.

'Well . . .' she began, then words seemed to fail her.

'I'll take the train that arrives closest to noon,' he suggested.

'Aye,' she agreed readily, her confidence starting to return. 'I'll have my lot scrubbed and on their best behaviour. Mind you, once they know you're a rozzer they won't dare do a thing wrong.' She hesitated. 'You won't change your mind, will you?'

'A promise is a promise. I'll see you on Sunday.' He was halfway along the block when she shouted, 'Better bring your stout boots,' and he smiled again.

FIFTEEN

Harper mingled with the crowd outside the Town Hall. Their numbers had been growing throughout the morning until they were packed tight under the hot July sun. Men in their working clothes, some looking serious, waiting for news, a few already celebrating the victory that was certain. Rumours rippled through the crowd. It was over. It wasn't over. There'd be an announcement in half an hour. There wouldn't be any announcement until the afternoon. The words spread like fire, voices rising briefly before returning to a constant murmur.

They could have sat at home and read their newspapers, the *Mercury* or the *Post*, but the inspector knew why many of them were here. With factories and business closed all over Leeds, this was something to do. And they'd know right away when it was all over, that they'd soon be able to go back to work and start earning again. He glanced at the faces, all of them lean, so many eyes hungry and distant, simply waiting. Some wanted to see the council defeated. Most just wanted money in their pockets once more.

The air felt dusty but the sky was clear. The pall of smoke that usually covered the town had all gone. It would return soon enough, once the gas was back and the chimneys were belching out their smoke once more.

Someone asked if he had a light and he struck a match, the sulphur sharp in his nostrils.

'Did you hear what happened to Gilston?' the man asked, blowing out smoke.

'What?'

'Almost attacked on the street yesterday.' The man laughed, showing stained teeth. 'The bobbies had to come and break it up. The bugger had to run into the Liberal Club or they'd have torn him apart. Shame they didn't, if you ask me.' He glanced at the entrance to the Town Hall. 'Any time now,' the man said eagerly. 'You wait.'

'Probably not until this afternoon,' Harper told him, but the man wasn't really listening. A small group passed a jug of beer around, one of them making enough space to dance a jig.

The inspector slowly made his way across Victoria Square and round to Great George Street, leaning heavily on his stick. It might be a mob out there, but they were in good humour. There'd be no violence, just an hour or two of joy before they all dispersed and Leeds could start to breathe again.

The constables on guard saluted as he entered. The building was cooler than the street and he was aware that he'd been sweating, the cotton of his shirt sticking to his skin.

'What's the news?' he asked a passing clerk. He'd know; everyone in the building would.

'All done except for the council,' the man told him. 'They're meeting at four. I wouldn't want to be a member of the gas committee for that.'

'The strikers got everything?'

'They might as well have. Two days' less holiday and they'll shovel more coal each shift.' He shrugged.

'What about the blacklegs?'

'They're still deciding on that one. That's why they haven't said anything yet.'

Loud cheers came from outside and the man hurried away, joining other clerks and constables at the windows to watch the union delegation making its way through the crowd to the Headrow. Cockayne, the local secretary, was in front and Harper picked out Maguire at his shoulder, talking nineteen to the dozen. Others followed, a line of them heading off to the union offices on Kirkgate.

'They've gone to explain the terms to their members,' someone explained. 'They'll be sweeping up the drunks down there later.'

He found Kendall at the top of the marble stairs, standing with his hands folded across his chest, smoking a briar pipe and staring out of the tall windows.

'It's done, then?'

The superintendent turned. 'Except for the council meeting to decide how much to pay the replacements.' He nodded down at the square. 'They'll be back making gas tomorrow. By Monday everyone will be working again.' He shook his head. 'And they'll forget this ever happened.'

'Not all of them,' Harper said.

'Give them time and they will.' He sighed, the pipe wobbling up and down in his mouth. 'They always do. And this is the worst I've seen in all my days here.'

'Cromwell,' the inspector said.

'I told you. After the council's met.' His voice was firm. 'He's all yours then. And once the replacements have gone you can have every spare man to find the girl.'

But there'd be few men to spare, Harper knew that. Most of them had been working since the beginning of the strike; the ones who hadn't been wounded would all be due leave for a day or two.

'The chief's glad to have the killing on the steps solved so quickly,' Kendall continued diplomatically. 'It saves a great deal of embarrassment to Leeds. Has the boxer said anything yet?'

The inspector shook his head. 'I doubt he will, either. He'll probably stay silent all through the trial.'

'You were lucky. The pair of you.' The words came out as a warning.

'I know, sir.'

Kendall took the pipe from his mouth and slipped it into the pocket of his jacket. His shirt was beginning to look grubby, all the crispness and starch gone, and his face seemed worn.

'Tonight I might even be able to sleep in my own bed.' He seemed almost to sigh in anticipation. 'And tomorrow we can return to normal.'

No, Harper thought. Not normal, not with an eight-year-old girl taken and still out there somewhere. Even if she came from

Fidelity Court and not somewhere genteel like Moortown or Headingley.

'How long do you think the council meeting will last, sir?'

'An hour, maybe two. They'll be done by six. Just enough time to tear a few more strips off the gas committee. Be careful with Cromwell, though. He's still a councillor, you'd better not forget that.'

Harper took the watch from his waistcoat pocket. Half past two. There was plenty of time before he'd have his chance with the alderman. 'I'll go back to the station,' he said.

'I'll be in tomorrow morning. You can tell me then what you get from him.'

Reed was at his desk, the bowler hanging from the hook behind him.

'Anything out in Middleton?'

'The company offices are in Park Square, all the business is done from there. I stopped by on my way back. Closed for dinner.'

The inspector studied his face. 'For a man who's had a pointless trip you look very happy.' Reed tried to shrug, but the blush gave him away. 'Come on, Billy, spit it out. I could use some good news.'

'I was talking to someone there and I'm seeing her on Sunday.' He shrugged again, trying to make it into something unimportant.

'Well, well, well.' Harper grinned. 'Good for you. Nice, is she?' he asked and the colour deepened on Reed's face. 'You could use a woman in your life.' He paused; the sergeant didn't want to say more, that was obvious. He picked up the stick. 'You can tell me about the pit as we go over to the office. They should be done eating by now.'

Park Square seemed hushed in the afternoon sun. A gardener tended the bushes, the only sound the quiet clip of his shears. The rumble of wheels and the clop of hooves seemed muted and distant. In a city that was always noisy, this was like a haven.

When they knocked on the door a man answered quickly. He was short, dapper, his collar so tight that the wings seemed to slice into his neck, hair so heavily pomaded that it glistened in the light, the parting perfectly straight and exact.

'Yes?' he asked, looking at them both.

'I'm Inspector Harper, Leeds Police. We'd like to ask you a few questions, sir.'

For a few moments the man simply stood there, flustered, before moving back to let them enter. It was a plain, simple office that belied the expensive frontage and address. The man moved behind the safety of a desk piled with papers.

'Mr?'

'Smith.'

'You manage the office for Mr Cromwell?'

Smith nodded. He looked to be in his forties, his expression wary, mouth tight under a bushy moustache that seemed out of place on such a precise head. 'I do.'

'I understand the company's under investigation by the council.'

'It is,' the man allowed after a small hesitation.

'For supplying coal that wasn't the specified quality?'

'Yes.' It was a quiet, chastened answer. The inspector smiled inside. This was someone who'd talk. He took a small step backwards on the polished wooden floor, knowing Reed would understand the sign and take over; they'd worked like this often enough before.

'Who negotiated the contract with the council, Mr Smith?' The sergeant deepened his voice, giving it richness and resonance in the room.

'Mr Cromwell and his lawyer.'

'And your role, sir? What do you do?'

'I take care of all the bills and invoices and make sure the wages go out to the pit.' The man seemed to shrink into himself as they watched.

'I see.' Reed let the sentence hang in the air.

'How long has the councillor owned the mine?' Harper asked.

'About two years,' Smith replied in a quiet voice.

'And when was the contract negotiated?'

He hesitated. 'One year and nine months ago.'

The inspector raised his eyebrows. 'Was Mr Cromwell aware of the quality of the coal at that time?'

'I don't know.' Smith was almost squirming on his chair.

'But there were complaints after?'

The man nodded.

'How long after?'

'Three months.'

'Did you make him aware of them, Mr Smith?' Reed took over again.

'Yes,' the man said.

'And what did he do?'

'Nothing,' Smith admitted after a long silence.

'What did you urge him to do, sir?' Reed wondered.

'It's not my decision. All I can do is advise.' It was a feeble answer and they all knew it. But it let Smith avoid the responsibility and place it squarely on Cromwell's shoulders. A sheen of sweat had appeared on the man's forehead. He pulled a handkerchief from his pocket and wiped it away with two quick swipes.

'How long has the council been investigating?' Harper asked.

'They started back in April.'

Three months. If the police worked that slowly the city would be overrun with crime, he thought.

'Does the mine make money?'

'It does. There was a good profit last year.' The man seemed eager to cooperate and answer now.

'All to the alderman?'

'He's the owner. There are three other directors, but they only have tiny shares.'

'And who are they?' Harper smiled. He could already guess the answer.

'Other councillors.'

'Gentlemen on the gas committee?'

'Not all,' the man answered guardedly.

Harper let the silence build, standing by the window to look out at the trees in full leaf.

'Do you know anything about Mr Cromwell's financial affairs, Mr Smith?' he asked finally.

The man shook his head. For all that he supposedly managed this office, he was nothing more than a clerk receiving his wage at the end of each week.

'Then you're not much use to me. Good day.'

Outside, the square seemed to trap the sun. The warmth was stifling, with no breeze to move the branches on the trees. Harper lit a Woodbine.

'What did you think?'

'He's telling the truth,' Reed answered. 'He knows Cromwell's going to sink and he doesn't want to drown with him.'

The inspector nodded. The councillor's time in office was almost done. He'd end up quietly resigning his position, then in court. If his friends on the bench were feeling merciful he'd stay out of jail. But the waves were building around him. All Harper needed was to make sure he had his information before the man went down for the final time. He pulled out his pocket watch. Half past three. Still plenty of time.

'Let's find somewhere for a cup of tea,' he suggested. 'I'm parched.'

His ankle still hurt, but it was a throb now, not the sharp pain he'd had yesterday. Still, he could feel it straining against his boot after a day of walking and he leaned heavily on the stick as they walked.

There was no café on Park Square; the place was far too genteel for anything as common as that. They finally found somewhere on East Parade, still doing eager business with men darting across from the square outside the Town Hall. Harper settled on to a chair with a loud sigh of relief.

'We're still no closer to finding Martha,' Reed said, spooning sugar into his drink. 'And every day—'

'I know, Billy.' He cut him off sharply. It had begun with Martha and she was still out there. But each day that passed made it less likely they'd find her alive. He was all too aware of that. He knew he'd failed her.

Harper didn't know how Cromwell was tied to Martha, but the connections were there. They had to be, one to another to another, like steps along a hidden path.

'What are you going to ask the alderman?' asked Reed.

He wasn't completely sure himself yet. 'About his financial troubles. Who he owes money to.'

'You think he'll tell you?' the sergeant wondered.

'I think so,' he replied after a few seconds. 'He's going to be rattled enough by losing the strike. We know he's in debt and that he's under investigation. He'll crack. If he doesn't today, he will tomorrow.'

'What did the super say?'

'Reminded me that the man's still a councillor. I should treat him with due deference.' Harper smiled.

'Do you want me there?'

He considered the idea. Two policemen could seem very intimidating. He needed the man to open up quickly, to tell him everything he needed.

'Not this time,' he said eventually. 'If we question him again, then yes. You might as well go home early for once.'

'I'll wait until you see him. I can catch the tram on Woodhouse Lane.'

He knew what that meant; Reed wasn't relishing an empty evening and was in no hurry to leave. It would mean less time at the Hyde Park Hotel, fewer drinks, a steadier head in the morning.

'So you're meeting someone on Sunday?' The words came out lightly but the sergeant still blushed again.

'I told you, it's nothing. Just a walk with her and her children.'

'Ah, a widow woman.' He grinned. 'We all know what they're like. She'll have her claws into you before the afternoon's done.'

'Like Annabelle did with you?' Reed countered with a sly smile.

'That's right. Cast her spell over me, she did.' He was joking, but there was some truth behind it all. There was something magical about her, a force that drew him.

'Won't be long before you're a married man yourself.'

'I'm looking forward to it,' he admitted proudly.

'She already has you wrapped around her finger.'

He acknowledged the fact with a nod. Why try to deny it? He knew it was true enough and it made him happy. He'd taken Billy out to the Victoria to meet Annabelle one evening. The sergeant had tempered his drinking and been good company, light-hearted and joking for once. But when he left, she'd turned to Harper and said, 'That friend of yours, he has troubles, doesn't he, Tom? I can see it in his eyes.'

He'd never understood how she'd known; he'd told her little about the man. But that was Annabelle. She sensed these things. More than that, she always seemed to be right.

They lingered over the tea, making it last until it turned cold. Finally he said, 'Time to go.'

The crowd outside the Town Hall had melted away leaving no more than a few hundred stragglers; all the others had gone off to celebrate victory. The ones who remained were lingering to hear details about the settlement with the blacklegs, all of them hoping the men would be sent away with nothing.

That couldn't happen, of course. To Harper it was obvious. They'd taken the jobs in good faith then been badly treated and cheated by the council. They needed to leave with something in their pockets. The only questions were how much they'd get and how soon. As long as they remained in Leeds there'd be no stokers going back to the gasworks.

He hobbled around the edge of the mob and through the front door, past a pair of saluting constables, standing at attention and sweating in their woollen uniforms, caps at an exact angle, eyes forward on the people, ready for anything. Not that there'd be much they could do if the crowd decided to surge.

Reed was close behind him. 'You go home Billy,' he said. 'I'll be fine from here.'

The doors to the council chamber were closed. The voices on the other side sounded weary and defeated. Not long, he thought. They'd be winding things up, ready to go home to their wives and children and put the nightmare of the strike behind them.

He rested his weight on the stick and waited, smoking a Woodbine and letting his mind wander. Any minute now. The first sound of scraping chairs came from inside the room.

'Sir?' He turned, seeing a young, embarrassed-looking bobby. 'Do you know where—?' He glanced down at his open notebook. 'Where Sergeant Reed is?'

'He just left for the day. Why?'

The man reddened. 'I've been ordered to bring him in for questioning, sir.'

'Questioning?' He echoed the word disbelievingly. 'What for?'

'It's the prisoner in the hospital. He's died.'

SIXTEEN

'What? He can't have,' Harper protested, his shout loud enough to make heads turn for a moment. It was impossible. The man couldn't be dead. 'I only saw him a few hours ago. They were going to discharge him into custody.'

'I don't know, sir,' the constable apologized. 'They only told me he'd died and to fetch the sergeant.'

'Sergeant Reed's on his way home.'

'Yes, sir.' There seemed to be gratitude in the man's eyes; if the sergeant wasn't here, it would be someone else's job to bring him in.

The door to the council chamber opened and the first people began to file out, men in well-cut suits, looking prosperous but sobered by the last few days. There was little conversation between them.

Harper was aware of the constable standing at his side, wanting orders. Cromwell emerged, tall and thin, cadaverous with his lean face and black suit, the jacket cut long in the older fashion, a frock coat that showed a short, tight waistcoat and high-waisted trousers. His shoulders were stooped, as if the world was pressing down heavily on him.

'Who's in charge of the investigation?' Harper asked the constable quickly.

'Inspector Beaumont, sir.'

Harper knew Frank Beaumont well. He was from B Division; competent, a thorough policeman, but not always quick on the uptake. He pursed his lips, trying to think rapidly as he watched Cromwell walk away. He desperately needed to know what had happened to the boxer. But right now he needed to talk to the alderman.

'Can you tell him I'll personally make sure Sergeant Reed reports to him first thing in the morning. Is that good enough?' he asked.

'Yes, sir.' The constable looked happy not to have to pursue anything further. 'I'm sure he'll take your word.'

'Good.' He began to hobble away after Cromwell, moving as quickly as he could. 'Councillor,' he called. 'Sir.'

The man turned, looking as if he'd been pulled from dark thoughts.

'Yes?'

'I'm Inspector Harper, Leeds Police. Might I have a word, sir?'

'What do you need, Inspector? I'm about to go home.' His voice was as tired as his face.

'I'll be as quick as I can, sir.' He gave a smile. 'If we can just find an office . . .'

Cromwell nodded his condescending acceptance. After trying two doors, Harper found one open. It was small, but with a table, two chairs, and a window for light it was all he needed.

The councillor settled on one of the chairs. Harper took his time, leaning the stick carefully, moving around a little. All little things to leave Cromwell uneasy. Finally the inspector sat, turning so his good ear would catch every word.

'Has everything been resolved about the blacklegs?' he began.

'The replacement workers,' the alderman corrected him impatiently. 'There'll be mediation in the morning. We'll make sure they don't go away empty-handed.'

He had the air of a man surrounded by defeat, hands clasped around a briefcase on his lap.

'I believe you own a mine in Middleton, sir.'

'I do.'

'And you're under investigation for selling poor quality coal to the council.'

Cromwell cocked his head to the side. 'Where did you hear that, Inspector?'

'Here and there, sir.' He gave another smile. 'It's a pity about the replacement worker who was murdered.' The change of subject was deliberate, a way to keep the man off balance.

'It was terrible. But I understood you'd found his killer.'

'We did,' Harper agreed with a ready nod. 'But it raised some questions.'

'Then you should ask the man you arrested,' Cromwell said irritably.

'Unfortunately, sir, he's died.'

Shock paled the councillor's face, then a flicker of relief that quickly vanished. 'That's unfortunate.'

'I agree, sir, it is.' He took a breath. 'I hear you're having financial troubles, sir.'

'You seem to hear a great deal, Inspector.' Cromwell's voice was cold.

'It's my job, sir. Hearing things and making connections.'

'And what do you want with me?'

'It seems to me that it would have looked good for the gas committee if the blackleg had been knifed by a striker. It might have turned public opinion.'

'What are you trying to insinuate, Inspector?'

'Nothing, sir. It's just an observation. But I'm sure you'll admit that a man with a great deal to lose might have wanted that solution more than anything.' He stopped and sat back in the chair.

'Are you accusing me?'

'No, sir. Of course not.'

'That's just as well. If you implied I had anything to do with a man's death I'd make sure you were straight off the force.' His eyes were furious, but there was a sheen of perspiration on his face.

'Is it true, sir? That you're having financial troubles.'

'It's none of your business.' He stood, looking down on the policeman. 'I take it we've finished, Inspector. I'll be having a word with the chief constable. I'm sure he'll be talking to you.' He tried to make his words threatening, but he couldn't put much weight behind them. The door closed loudly as he left.

Tomorrow, Harper thought. Cromwell knew something. In the morning he'd press the man and discover what it was. But now he needed to turn his attention to the dead boxer. He'd seen the man. He'd been awake and aware, recovering; he clearly remembered the bobby at the bedside say he had orders to take the man to the cells later.

Something was very wrong. He had to find out the truth before morning. If the death really related to the beating, he wouldn't be able to save Billy. The sergeant would be in the dock for murder, and he'd hang. Harper himself would be bounced off the force and probably end up in jail. But he couldn't believe that. He daren't believe it.

The doctor at the Infirmary had already left for the evening and the body had been taken over to Hunslet for the police surgeon to examine. Finally, Harper found a nurse who'd been on duty. She was harried, coming to the close of a twelve-hour shift. She looked to be in her forties, strands of grey hair peeking from her cap and splatters of blood across the white apron.

'I thought he was improving,' he said.

She looked around cautiously before answering.

'He were, love. We were going to discharge him in t' morning. The doctor said so himself.'

'What happened?' he asked.

'That bobby needed the privy. He asked us to keep an eye on the man while he was gone.' She paused and he guessed what she was going to say next. 'We were busy. Mr Johnson down on the wards had one of his fits and it teks three of us to hold him down.' She looked up at him apologetically. 'By the time your constable come back the man was dead.'

'Any idea what killed him?'

'It's not my place to say, love. I'm not a doctor.'

But she probably knew. He waited.

'It looked reet enough like poison to me,' she said quietly after a short while. 'But I didn't say that.'

The surgeon would discover it soon enough. Christ, he'd better. 'What about the doctor?'

'He just signed the death certificate.' She sighed loudly. 'There's someone else in the bed now. There's never enough room for patients in this place.'

'And never enough nurses?'

'Nay, love.' She gave him an exhausted smile. 'That, too.'

He took a hackney from the Infirmary over to Hunslet, willing the vehicle onward through the heavy flow of traffic along Briggate and over Leeds Bridge. Carts piled high with goods trundled along, horses' heads low in their traces. A carriage slipped in and out between them.

The springs were poor in the cab and the rattlejack and bouncing along the road vibrated dully through his ankle. By the time they arrived at Hunslet Lane climbing down was painful; it took a few yards to shake off the worst of it.

The B Division building was less than ten years old; some red brick still showed through the soot. Inside, though, it smelt like every other police station in Leeds, the mingling aroma of unwashed bodies, fear, vomit and urine that seemed to have seeped into the walls.

He made his way down the steps to the cellar, every bad thing he could imagine roaring through his head as he passed through an unmarked door away from the holding cells. It was quiet here, cool after the heat of the day. With no gas, candles provided the light, offering deep shadows and mystery.

This was the Kingdom. That was what everyone called it, although few on the force ever visited it, and Dr King ruled it absolutely. He was the police surgeon and had been for the last thirty years.

He turned at the footsteps, waving a saw menacingly. Harper took a step back.

'Come to see the new one, Inspector?' He waved the saw at the table, his loud voice booming in the room. King was a man who relished his work, uncovering details and surprises, happier among the dead than the living. He was seventy if he was a day, but still stood erect. His hair had gone, leaving only a few wild, wispy grey strands over the ears, but the eyes still twinkled intelligently, and he had the longest, most graceful fingers Harper had ever seen, hardly a sign of age on them.

'The one from the Infirmary?'

'That's him.' A thin sheet covered the body.

'Do you know what killed him yet?' he asked urgently.

'Of course.' King dismissed the question. 'Obvious as soon as I took a look at him.'

'Poison?' Harper asked hopefully.

'Cyanide. He'd have died very quickly.'

He let out the breath he didn't even know he'd been holding. Thank God. They were safe. Neither of them would face charges. Billy hadn't been responsible. But who had killed the boxer? Had his friend stayed in Leeds, staying out of sight and biding

his time? Or had there been someone else? And why? What
scared them so much that they needed the man dead? Did they
believe he might break his silence? He shook his head. Wherever
he turned in this tale there were no answers.

'What else can you tell me about the body?' he asked after a
moment.

'He'd taken a heavy beating, but I'm sure you know that. I
can open him up in the morning and take a closer look if you
like,' the surgeon offered.

'Will it tell us much?'

'Probably not,' King said with a shrug. 'There's one other
thing. Your corpse didn't put up a struggle when he was given
the poison. There's no sign of it.'

'So . . .'

'Either he was happy to die or he trusted the man giving him
the liquid. Take your pick.'

More to think about.

King took off his bloody apron and threw it on to a desk.
'You've brought me too many bodies lately, Mr Harper. That's
the third. I do hope it'll stop soon.'

'So do I, Doctor. So do I.'

'I'll have a report for you tomorrow. As long as you don't
send me any more corpses,' he added pointedly.

Inspector Beaumont was still in the detectives' office, sifting
through a pile of papers and scribbling in his notebook.

'Evening, Tom,' he said when he'd finished, blotting the page
lightly. 'I thought you'd be bringing me your sergeant.'

'You can have him in the morning if you want, Frank. Have
you seen the boxer's body yet?'

'Not had time, we're catching up after this bloody strike.'

'He's downstairs. King says he was poisoned. Cyanide. And
I was over at the Infirmary. Whoever was watching him went off
for a piss. When he came back the man was dead. Nothing to
do with Billy Reed at all.'

Beaumont sighed and ran a hand through his long side whiskers
and across his chin. 'You're sure?' he sighed.

'Positive.'

'All right, have him come over tomorrow, just so we can make everything official. I'll find out who was on duty at the hospital and give him a roasting. Are you any further on your case?'

Harper shook his head. 'There's still the missing girl.'

'Just hope you find her alive.' Their eyes met. They both knew the chances of that. 'I hear your big day's soon.'

'Less than a fortnight now.' He hadn't thought about the wedding since they'd left Park Square. Everything seemed to be racing, moving so fast that he could barely keep pace.

'And she has a pub, is that right?'

'Yes.'

'By God, you're a lucky man,' Beaumont said with a heartfelt grin. 'There's plenty who'd want someone like that.'

Harper smiled and stood. 'I should probably go and see her now. It's been a long day.'

'Another day or two and we'll have gas again. Small mercies, eh?'

'Good night, Frank. Don't work too late.'

The bed felt pleasantly cool, the cotton sheets crisp against his body. The window was open and he heard night birds calling and the hoot of an owl on the hunt. His ankle throbbed slowly.

He'd taken another hackney back to the Victoria. It seemed like a luxury, but he didn't have the stamina to walk back across the river then wait for the tram. He was weary; the fire and fever that had pushed him through the day drained away. Billy was safe. He was safe. For an hour he'd wondered how much longer he'd be on the force, imagining himself as a prisoner in Armley and his sergeant on the gallows. At least that bloody nightmare had vanished.

Annabelle had taken the bandage off his ankle, easing it away from his skin. The iceman had been during the day and she'd kept some to rub on his skin. It felt like balm and he sighed, his leg resting on a footstool. When it was dry she wrapped it again.

'You rest that properly,' she told him. 'Not that you will.'

'I can't. I need to find her.' He had to believe Martha was still alive.

She sat next to him and he drew her close.

'You will.'

He stroked her hair, feeling her settle and the warmth of her breath against his neck. She was his; he still couldn't quite believe it. Soon she'd have his name. Annabelle Harper. The thought made him smile.

He trusted her completely. With his life. He'd never felt like that about someone before. He'd courted, he'd even thought he'd wanted to marry, but there'd been no staying power to his feelings. This was different.

All he knew about her was what she'd told him. That hadn't been much. She seemed to want to keep her childhood out of sight and out of mind, hidden behind a curtain. He knew he could ask the bobbies who patrolled the Bank. They'd have known her family, could have given him chapter and verse. But he was content to let the words and the history come from her, if she ever wanted to tell him.

'What are you thinking?' Annabelle asked quietly.

'Nothing,' he told her. The truth wouldn't serve any purpose. He was here, he was happy and looking forward to life with her. All the days and years ahead seemed to stretch out like a warm, inviting road he wanted to walk. For the rest of his life. He was certain of that, just as certain as he'd been when he took the oath to be a policeman.

He'd always been one to take his time over the big decisions. He weighed everything first, to test it and be sure it was what he wanted. He'd be a good, faithful husband, just as he'd tried to be a good bobby and detective.

He looked down at Annabelle, her hair wild around her shoulders, eyes closed as she snuggled against him, a smile on her lips, and knew he'd made the right decision. He remembered Lucy Thorp. They'd walked out for the best part of a year and she'd been eager enough to become Mrs Harper. He'd enjoyed the time he spent with her. But every time she mentioned marriage he felt as if the sky had clouded over. He still saw her sometimes when he was working, behind the counter of the hosiery shop she ran on the Headrow. If she spotted him she pointedly looked away. He'd been fair with her, he'd been honest.

And there had been the other girls over the years, none of them quite right for him. Lovely, every one of them pretty, a few free with their favours, others reticent. But he'd never been able to see himself with any of them in ten, twenty, thirty years. Annabelle was different. She joked that it had taken him six months to propose, but he knew that it had taken him that long to pluck up the courage, scared she'd turn him down.

He felt her stir.

'I don't know about you, but I'm ready to sleep.' She glanced at the clock on the mantel and stifled a yawn. 'It's only ten. I must be getting old.'

'You work hard.' He knew she'd be up a little after four, ready to work, to do whatever was needed, and she'd keep going until evening. She wasn't one to leave a job to someone else if she could do it herself. If she finished a day not feeling exhausted, she wondered what was wrong.

'Someone has to look after this place. And the bakeries.'

'Better get your rest, then.'

'Tom, I've been thinking . . .' she said, and he knew it would be a while before he was able to rest.

'Go on.'

'You told me about that moneylender.'

Henry Bell. Another of the boxer's victims. 'What about him?'

She rose and started to pace around the room, the way she always did when she was thinking, her crimson skirt swishing around her ankles, the white blouse as crisp and clean as if she'd just put it on.

'They charge plenty of interest, don't they?'

'They gouge the poor,' he said firmly.

'What if someone was to lend money at little or no interest?' Annabelle asked.

'Then every Tom, Dick and Harry would be at their door.' He was about to say more then realized what she meant. 'You?'

She nodded. 'I could help them.'

'And you could lose a lot of money.'

'I'd be careful,' she said. That he was willing to believe. She spent when she wanted, but she knew where every penny went. 'I'd only lend to people I knew, people I could trust.'

'What if they didn't repay?'

'Do you have any idea how many people round here live on tick?' He knew; most of them only survived because of it. At the butcher, the baker, the grocer. 'If they didn't have that, they wouldn't be able to put owt on the table,' she continued. 'The wives won't stand for that. If they don't pay I'll make sure no one gives them credit and everyone knows why.'

'Just local?'

She nodded. 'I won't deal with anyone I don't know well.'

'It's a dangerous business,' he warned her. He thought of Tosh Walker, a moneylender by a different name. A predator.

'And I'll have a copper for a husband.' Her eyes twinkled. 'What do you think, Tom?'

'It has possibilities,' he admitted reluctantly. And many pitfalls, he thought. 'Just don't rush into it.'

'I'm not going to. I wanted your opinion.' She smiled. 'After all, we're going to be married soon.' She reached out, pulled him to his feet and kissed him. 'And I'll be glad when that's all done. I've been for three fittings for the dress. Three.' She shook her head. 'I'll only wear the thing once.'

'I thought it was going to be a small wedding.'

'It is,' she insisted. 'But if you think I'm not going to look my best you've got another think coming, Tom Harper. Not on a day like that. Do you have your suit yet?'

He shook his head. There was plenty of time. He'd call in and see Moses Cohen. They'd grown up together in the Leylands and the man had taken over his father's tailoring business. He'd sew something good together in a couple of days, something smart, better than Barran's or Hepworth's, a suit that would do his wife justice. With a fresh shave and a new shirt and tie from the Co-op he'd look respectable.

'Just make sure you take care of it.' She yawned again. 'I'm off to my bed.' She kissed him again and said, 'You'll solve it, Tom. You always have.'

Not always, he thought as he lay in his own bed. There was a brief, tiny shriek. The owl must have found its prey. There were many times he'd never found the culprit. Those were the ones he never forgot. Back when he was starting out as a detective constable, Kendall had told him it would be that way. At the time he hadn't believed it; he knew better now. Most of the successes didn't take much work. It was usually a husband, a wife, a fight that moved out of control. The failures were all firm in his mind, a series of pictures that galled whenever he thought about them.

But Martha Parkinson wasn't going to join them, he was going to make certain of that. No matter what waves it caused.

SEVENTEEN

H e came to, woken by a hand shaking him. It was still dark, the room so black that he couldn't see a thing.

'Tom,' Annabelle said urgently, 'There's a bobby downstairs wants you.'

He sat up quickly, running a hand through his hair. He heard the rasp of a match, then a candle guttered slightly before the flame took hold. She was standing by the bed, her hair down, a robe wrapped tight around her nightdress.

'I'll talk to him,' he said.

He hobbled down, relying on the stick, his ankle throbbing with each step. The bar smelt of old beer and stale smoke. All the glasses had been washed, the ashtrays wiped clean, the spittoons sluiced out. Dan the barman stood in the corner. He lived in a room at the back of the building.

The constable was so young that he barely looked old enough for his ill-fitting uniform. He looked embarrassed to be here, to see a senior office in his nightshirt.

'What is it?' Harper asked. The last time someone had disturbed his sleep, Col Parkinson was dead. This had to be as important.

'I'm sorry, sir.' The man was tripping over his words. 'I went to your lodgings and they said you'd be here.' He blushed and Harper laughed inside. The lad thought he'd been having a dirty night. 'The desk sergeant said you'd want to know. It's about Councillor Cromwell.'

He felt his stomach lurch, knowing what he was about to hear.

'Dead?'

'Yes, sir.'

'How?'

'Shotgun. He killed himself at home.'

'Right. I'll be at the station as soon as I can.'

Within five minutes he'd thrown on his clothes, given Annabelle a quick kiss and was walking along the deserted street. No respectable person would be out and about at this hour. All the cabs would have gone home, the horses in their stables, and the next tram wouldn't be along until dawn. He gritted his teeth, moving as fast as he could.

Millgarth was quiet, all the night patrols out, the drunks sleeping it off in the cells. Candles burned on the counter, a reminder that, although the strikers had celebrated, Leeds wasn't back to normal yet. The sergeant stood behind the desk, big and firm as a rock. He picked up a piece of paper and held out his hand.

'The address, sir. C division are already out there.'

He looked. It was out beyond Harehills, off Roundhay Road, and sighed; it would have been quicker to go there directly.

'Is there anyone to take me?' He tapped the stick lightly against his leg.

'I'll see what I can find. It'll take a few minutes, sir.'

Harper asked the question that had been bothering him since he left the Victoria. 'What made you call me out?'

'There was a note, sir. I believe Mr Cromwell had written your name on it.'

He nodded. Interesting. 'Who's covering it?'

'Detective Sergeant Gutteridge,' the man answered. The name came out politely enough but still managed to convey a word of distaste. The inspector understood why. Gutteridge was a clumsy ox of a man, who could break something just by walking past it. He was always dishevelled, his suit covered in small stains, his hair and moustache too long. Even worse, he was lazy, forever sloping off somewhere, returning with the smell of beer on his breath that no mint imperial could quite cover. Harper had never understood how he'd become a detective, let alone a sergeant. He shook his head sadly. 'I believe you might be able to find a cup of tea down in the changing rooms while you wait, sir,' the desk man told him with a wink. 'Some of the men have rigged up a small stove.'

Twenty minutes later he was sitting on the board of a cart as the horse pulled them past Sheepscar. The pub was dark, curtains closed, everyone asleep. The cart was the one they used to take bodies to the mortuary, and he half-believed he could smell death in the wood. But it was a damned sight better than walking.

The only sound was the slow clop of hooves and he looked around. There was enough of a moon to make out shapes and silhouettes. Once they passed Harehills the houses thinned, and the buildings became larger and more imposing. Off to the right, Gipton Woods loomed, menacing in the darkness. The last time he'd been out this way he'd walked up to Roundhay Park with Annabelle on a bright Sunday afternoon at the beginning of April. The daffodils had been in bloom, brilliant patches of yellow scattered across the land.

A little before Oakwood he spotted lights burning in the windows of a house and pointed. At the end of the drive he alighted, sending a disappointed driver back to Millgarth and work.

A flustered maid answered the door, the tracks of tears still plain on her face. She showed him through the house. He noticed the heavy, expensive furniture that cluttered the rooms. Lanterns burned brightly. A sob caught in her throat and she turned away.

The uniform guarding the door to the garden saluted quickly once he recognized the inspector, and led the way through the garden to a wooden summer house. Inside, Gutteridge was crouched over a body that lay on the floor, a shotgun at its side. The air still smelt sharply of cordite.

'Suicide?' he asked.

Gutteridge looked around, then pushed his bulk up with a wheeze. 'You can look for yourself, sir, but I'm sure it is.'

There was nothing left of the face beyond scraps and an eye that dangled awkwardly. Blood and pieces of bone clung to the ceiling and walls. The corpse lay on its back, legs splayed, the first finger of the right hand still curled around the trigger of an expensive shotgun.

He was right; there was little doubt that Cromwell had come out here and taken his own life.

'When was it reported?' Harper asked.

'Servant found a bobby just after eleven o'clock,' Gutteridge recited. 'She'd heard the shot and came out to look. Sent the younger maid to find one of ours, then collapsed.' He glanced down at the body. 'Can't say I blame her. He's not a pretty sight, is he?' He pulled a cheap cigar from his pocket, struck a match and lit it, the fumes covering the other smells in the small room.

'What about the wife?'

'The doctor's already been and given her a sedative. Just as well, too, she was almost hysterical by the time I arrived.'

'Who else is in the house?'

'Just the two servants,' Gutteridge said. 'The children are grown and gone, two daughters and two sons.'

'I heard that Cromwell had written my name somewhere.'

'That's right. It's why I had them call you out.' He pulled a folded piece of paper from the inside pocket of his worn jacket. Harper took it, feeling the grease marks that made it transparent and glanced at the sergeant.

'My fault. I'd been eating before I came here.' He gave an apologetic shrug.

Chief Inspector Harper had been written at the head of the page in a shaky hand. Nothing else.

'Where did you find it?'

'On the desk in the library. According to the maid he'd been working there before he came out here.'

'No other note?'

'Nothing I've seen.' He hesitated. 'Do you want the case, sir? Only we have plenty on, what with the strike and all. Suicide, there won't be much here, anyway.'

'I'll take it,' Harper agreed. 'You can leave.'

The man was wrong. There would be plenty here. The trick would be finding what it meant.

Gutteridge looked grateful as he lumbered away. Alone, the inspector knelt and started to go through Cromwell's pockets. It was a gruesome task, wiping away messy pieces of brain and flesh and fragments of bone, but after ten minutes he had everything.

Seven pounds in notes, another couple in coppers and silver. A handkerchief, still folded. The councillor's pocket watch was gold, inscribed on *To George, with all love, Hannah* inside the cover. There was a fountain pen and a few scrawled notes, all to do with council business and information on the strike. Nothing useful, nothing to show why he'd taken his own life.

'See if you can find a sheet and cover him,' he told the constable. 'I'll be in the house.'

The servant who'd let him in was sitting at the kitchen table, a cup of tea in front of her. She appeared calmer now, the tear tracks scrubbed away from her cheeks. But her eyes were still rimmed with red from the crying and she sniffled as she spoke.

'Is there another in the pot?' he asked, taking the chair across from her. She poured for him and he took a drink. Strong enough for the spoon to stand up in it; just what he needed.

'A terrible business,' Harper said.

'We all heard the shot.' The girl spoke as though her mouth was dry and she had to force every word out.

'How have things been here? Any arguments, any worries?' The servants knew much more than their masters ever realized. They could often tell him what was happening in a house better than a man's wife. The girl hesitated before shaking her head. There was something, he decided. 'What's your name?'

'Marie, sir.' She looked about sixteen, tall and gawky in her uniform, with most of her hair tumbling out from the white cap.

'Well, Marie, I'm Inspector Harper. I'm going to be here for the rest of the night, going through papers. Your mistress is asleep, I believe?'

'Yes, sir. The doctor give her summat to knock her out. She were screaming and crying to wake the dead.' She realized what she'd said and put a hand over her mouth in shock.

'What about the other servant?'

'He give her the same, sir.'

'It's bad when something like this happens, Marie. But you'll be helping everyone if you tell me what you know.' Her eyes blazed for a moment, but he continued gently, 'I know it seems like you're betraying your employers if you tell me all their confidences and secrets. But not in this case. We need to understand. Does that make sense?'

She nodded and he waited. The girl would talk, he was certain of that.

'I know he had problems,' she began hesitantly. 'Wi' t'mine. And the strike, course.'

'But?' He sensed there was more.

'Money. I heard him talking to people a few times.'

'To his wife?'

'No, sir,' Marie answered.

'Was it bad?'

'I think so.'

'Did anyone visit the councillor this evening?'

'Yes, sir. Two men.'

For a moment he felt his heart beginning to beat faster. But it couldn't have been the boxer and his friend; one of them was in the mortuary already.

'Who were they? Did they give their names?' he asked quickly.

'No, sir. They said Mr Cromwell was expecting them. I hadn't seen them before. I showed them through to the library.'

'What time was this?'

'About eight o'clock.'

'How long did they stay?'

'I heard the master show them out about half past.'

'Did you hear any of the conversation?'

The girl shook her head.

'What did Mr Cromwell do after that?'

'He went back into the library and stayed there until . . .' She didn't want to complete the sentence.

'Did he see his wife at all?'

'No, sir. She was in the parlour until ten and then she went to bed.'

'She didn't go in and say goodnight?' he asked.

'No, sir.' She paused. 'It's not their way.'

He took a deep breath. 'The men who came tonight. Can you describe them?'

She thought for a long time.

'They were both normal, I suppose,' she said, eyes half-closed as she tried to picture the man. 'One a bit smaller than you, maybe. He had dark hair.' She touched her nose. 'That was sharp. Handsome enough, but . . .' She shrugged. 'He kept looking at me. I didn't like that. But he din't say owt.'

The boxer's friend. That was his first thought. A poisoning in the afternoon, a visit to the councillor in the evening, after which Cromwell kills himself. The man seemed to carry death around with him.

'What about the other man?'

'He were well-dressed. A gold ring here.' She held up her left hand and waved the little finger. 'Big side whiskers, bigger n' yours. Going grey above the ears.'

'Anything else?' She could have described one of thousands of men in Leeds.

'He had a little scar on his forehead down to his eye. An old one.'

'Which eye?'

'His right.'

Harper knew someone who had a scar exactly like that. Tosh Walker. The man he'd been trying to prosecute for years, the one who made witnesses vanish or recant their words.

'You've done very well,' he told her. 'Can you show me to the library?'

The room was wrongly named, he decided as he settled down with a candle. It had polished oak bookcases that ran from floor to ceiling along one wall, but hardly any books on the shelves. Cromwell obviously hadn't been much of a reader; the few volumes he had all dealt with business. There was a padded leather club chair and a small table next to it with a decanter of whisky and a single glass.

The desk was full of papers. He started with the ones on top, scanning through them quickly, discarding most and keeping a few to examine later. Every drawer was full. He was surprised the councillor hadn't bothered to lock them. Some documents were council business, the minutes of meetings and committees. The summons to appear before an investigation looked interesting, as did the letters from the man's bank. From all Harper could make out, Cromwell was close to bankruptcy; only the contract for coal from the mine had been keeping his head above water, and that just barely.

He was a perfect victim for Tosh Walker. And with that name, things began to fall into place. Harper could readily imagine Walker forcing himself into Henry Bell's moneylending business, bringing in the boxer and his friend to collect the debts. It would explain why Bell had been too scared to say anything when he'd been questioned. And why he'd had to die – before he could tell what he knew.

And Cromwell? That seemed simple enough. If the strikers

could be discredited, the gas committee would win the strike. The investigation into the substandard coal would vanish and he'd remain afloat. So, an arrangement with Walker for one of his men to commit murder. But it had all gone wrong; it had come to an end after the devil had come to exact his price. Whatever he'd paid, it had left the councillor desperate enough to blow out his brains.

The only piece that didn't fit was Martha Parkinson. Tosh Walker was many things, but there'd never been a whisper of anything to do with children. He wanted money and power. Children didn't fit into that.

He put it to the back of his mind as he worked through everything in the desk. Two hours later he had a small stack of papers to take with him, the rest spread haphazardly across the desk. He made his way back to the kitchen. The maid had gone. Out in the garden it was light. The constable guarding the shed tried to hide a cigarette in his cupped hands, waving away the smoke as the inspector approached.

'Don't worry,' Harper told him. 'It's been a long night.'

The bobby had found a sheet to hide Cromwell's body and give him some dignity in death. The inspector drew it back, checking to make sure he'd missed nothing earlier. Suicide. He had no doubt. He covered what was left of the head again and glanced at his pocket watch. Almost six.

'I'll send the wagon for him,' he told the constable and made his way along the drive to Roundhay Road. At least his ankle hurt less this morning.

Harper sat in Kendall's office. As soon as Reed had arrived he'd sent him across the river to answer the questions about the boxer's death. It was no more than a formality, but Billy had still looked nervous as he left.

'I want to bring Tosh Walker in.'

'The question is how soon he'll walk out of here again,' the superintendent said.

'The maid will pick him out as a visitor to Cromwell's last night.'

Kendall rubbed the back of his neck. He looked refreshed in a clean grey suit, the black tie carefully knotted at the throat, moustache precisely clipped, his hair parted in the middle and pomaded down.

'There's no law against visiting a man who commits suicide later, Tom.'

He knew what the man was doing. They'd played this game often enough, one of them acting as the devil's advocate, testing the weaknesses in an argument or a case.

'I believe the man who was with him was the boxer's friend. I'm as certain as I can be that he went into the Infirmary and killed the boxer.'

The superintendent shook his head. 'It's all speculation. Even if you're right, Walker will have this man hidden away. From what you've told me, there's nothing you can prove. Is that right?'

'Yes.'

'Then you don't have anything, Tom. And what about the girl? How does she come into this?'

'I don't know, sir,' he admitted.

'Find something. Show me any connection between her and Tosh Walker, anything at all, and you have my blessing to put him in the cells. I've wanted that bastard for a long time,' Kendall said with feeling. 'If he's been doing something to little girls, I'll see him hang.'

Harper stood. It was almost eight, and he already felt exhausted. His eyes were gritty from lack of sleep. 'I'll find it. It's got to be there.'

'Anything you need, just ask. I'll need men to escort the replacements to the station this afternoon, but apart from that, the strike is over.'

'The blacklegs are going to be paid?'

'They are,' Kendall answered firmly. 'They did what was asked of them, it's only fair. None of them knew what they were letting themselves in for.' He paused. 'And this time we'll secure the bridge over Whitehall Road. Not that I expect any problems when they're going. The stokers will be back at work tonight. Not before time, either.' He shook his head. 'A stupid bloody mess.'

'A pointless one.'

The superintendent sighed. 'I'll agree with you there, although I'd never admit it to the chief. You're sure everything's taken care of with Reed?'

'Positive, sir. Frank Beaumont will give him a good talking-to and then he'll be back here.'

'Maybe this will drum some sense into him. Tell him, Tom, the next time there's a problem, he'll be gone from the force.'

EIGHTEEN

R eed walked back across Leeds Bridge in the sunshine. Nine o'clock and it was already warm, the sky a clear, pale blue. This was the way July was meant to be, the way he remembered it when he was a child. In the Army, when he'd been stationed somewhere hot, the heat never seemed to vanish. For months on end the days would bake his bones under his flesh. His woollen uniform would itch and his pack become too heavy to bear.

For now he felt grateful simply to be walking free. The interview had been brief enough, no more than the formality he'd been promised. At the end, though, Inspector Beaumont hadn't dismissed him. Instead he'd made Reed stand as he ranted and roared. It was the kind of dressing down he'd seen in the regiment. All he could do was stand at attention and take it, feeling the man's spittle across his face as he yelled. It took a full five minutes before the inspector grew hoarse. By then, everyone in B Division knew about Reed's faults, his drinking, his violence, the weakness that left him in the black moods. Like a good soldier he'd stayed still, letting the words wash over him and away, staring straight ahead until he was told to go, marching through the station without looking at anyone else.

By tonight, he knew, it would be all through the force. Humiliation. But that was what Beaumont had wanted. Out on Hunslet Road he took the packet of cigarettes from his pocket and lit one, hands shaking badly. He wanted a drink. He needed a drink. But he wasn't going to have one until he was off duty. He breathed out slowly, forcing himself to calm as he walked, his face like thunder. What really galled was that so much of what Beaumont had said was true. He knew he drank too much. He knew things haunted him, the pictures and faces that wouldn't go away, no matter how much he tried. He knew his failings well enough, the anger that could grip him and come out through his fists.

The sergeant gave himself time before returning to the Millgarth. When he settled at his desk he let out a long breath.

'Bad?' Harper asked. Reed just nodded. 'But no charges?'

'No.'

Harper leaned close to the sergeant and hissed. 'Think about what would have happened if you'd been the one who'd killed him.'

'I have.' The sergeant raised his eyes. 'Believe me, I have, all the way back here. I'm sorry, Tom.'

'It's done now. But for God's sake, Billy, you're going to need to keep a lid on that temper.'

'I know,' he said quietly. 'Believe me, I know.'

Harper gave a brief nod; the business was over.

'I talked to the super about Tosh Walker,' the inspector said. 'He won't let me bring him in yet. We need proof. I'm going to talk to Cromwell's widow and see if she can tell me anything.'

'What do you want me to do?'

'What doesn't fit into all this?'

'The girl. Martha,' Reed replied without hesitation. 'Walker's never had anything to do with young girls.'

'Nothing that we've discovered,' the inspector corrected him.

'What do you mean? Come on, we both know she's probably dead somewhere.'

'What if she isn't, though?' Harper asked. 'What if there are other girls with her?'

'That's impossible.' He dismissed the idea. 'We'd have heard if other girls had gone missing.'

'Would we?'

'Of course we would. Don't be ridiculous.'

'But what if they'd vanished from orphanages or the workhouse?'

'Even then,' Reed insisted.

'And if they were the fractious children? The ones who never did what they were told and caused trouble. Think about it. The guardians breathe a sigh of relief, say nothing, and still collect money from the council for the children.'

'I don't see it,' the sergeant said after a while. 'That would
be a—'

'Conspiracy? Crime?'

'Yes.'

'Then prove me wrong. Go to the orphanages. Go to the
workhouse. Ask some questions and make sure the numbers add
up.'

Reed nodded in reluctant acquiescence, then said, 'I still think
you're wrong.'

'Maybe I am,' Harper told him. 'But at least we'll know. And
if I'm not . . .'

It was stuffy on the lower deck of the omnibus. The windows
wouldn't open, and the leather seats made Harper's back sweat,
shirt clinging to the skin. They passed the Victoria, its doors wide
to air the place out, and the horses drawing the vehicle clopped
slowly up Roundhay Road.

The inspector was tired, ready to nod off. He pulled the watch
from his waistcoat. Almost ten. He'd been up since one and he
still hadn't eaten. He felt the low growl of hunger in his belly.
Dinner time, he told himself. He'd have something then.

The house was quiet. The drive was empty, all the curtains
drawn as a sign of mourning. The body would have been removed,
the copper off on his duties.

He knocked on the door. Marie, the sad maid from the night
before, answered. There were dark circles under her eyes and
her face looked strained. All of this was beyond her understanding.
Wherever she'd grown up, people managed, they dealt with things.
They didn't take a shotgun, point it at their face and pull the
trigger as an answer.

'Hello, Marie. Do you remember me?'

She nodded, then recalled her place. 'Yes, sir.'

'Is Mrs Cromwell awake?'

'Yes, sir. But . . .'

He knew. She didn't want to see anyone. But he needed to
see her, to ask questions while her memory was sharp, even if
it was painful.

'Can you tell her I'm here, please? It's important.'

The girl showed him through to a parlour, everything shaded

and shadowed by the curtains, a room in half-light. But it had the feel of somewhere that was well used, with pictures on the walls, comfortable furniture gathered around an empty hearth and a piano in the corner with sheet music scattered around. Knitting sat on a small table, next to a novel, *The Master of Ballantrae*, a length of yarn as a bookmark. Epic adventure and romance for the wife, he thought.

Photographs stood in silver frames. The prominent ones on the mantel showed Cromwell in his alderman's robes, with the mayor and other figures. The children, two boys and two girls, were consigned to the top of the piano, studio portraits showing serious faces. But there was no picture of Mrs Cromwell to be seen.

He'd been waiting almost half an hour when the door handle turned and she entered, dressed all in black, her widow's weeds. She was surprisingly small, not even reaching to his shoulder, her hair grey and gathered in a bun. She stood in shadow, away from him, the details of her face hidden.

'My condolences, Mrs Cromwell,' he began. 'I'm sorry to call on you, but I'm hoping you can help me.'

'Help you?' Her voice was fragile, a husk of a thing with no weight behind it. 'I don't understand, Inspector.'

'The gentlemen who visited your husband last night. Did you see them at all?'

She shook her head, a tiny gesture. She was gripping a handkerchief between her fingers, and turning her wedding ring.

He tried again. 'Did your husband talk about his business with you?'

Mrs Cromwell looked at him with confused eyes that seemed unable to focus fully.

'Business? She rolled the word around as if she'd never heard it before. Grief, and the sedative the doctor had given her, had left her distant, removed, he decided. 'No. He never did. And I didn't ask. That was Charles's world.'

Of course, he thought. Her domain would have been the four walls of the house, the servants and the social calls on friends and family. A different orbit altogether. For a moment he was tempted to tell her that her husband had been in trouble, that there might be nothing left for her, but what good would that do?

She was already grieving. She didn't need that fear on top of it all.

'I'm sorry to have disturbed you,' he said, picking his hat off the chair. As he passed her she placed a hand on his arm, the touch so light he barely noticed it.

'Inspector. Tell me.' She cleared her throat with a cough. 'Do you know why he . . .?'

There were many things he could have told her, truth and lies. Instead, he replied, 'I'm sorry, I don't. Not yet.'

The other servant, a sturdy lass named Beth who doubled as the cook, kept breaking into tears at every question. She'd been away in her room, had seen nothing and heard nothing until the shot tore her from sleep. She knew nothing of her employer's affairs and preferred it that way: a woman who knew her role and was content with it.

As he waited for the omnibus back into Leeds, he decided this had been a wasted trip. But if he hadn't come, he'd never have known.

Orphanages, Reed thought. Only two came to mind. One was out in Headingley, where the children could enjoy the clear air, and the other on Beckett Street. The Moral and Industrial Training School, they called it, but it was an orphanage by any other name. It was a part of the workhouse: a school to turn out dozens of factory hands and servant girls each year. Still children, but able to earn a wage.

It was quicker to walk out there than wait for an omnibus. The streets were quiet, no gas to power machines yet, no work for so many. And after a week without labour and no pay packet to collect, plenty of folk would be seeking credit at the shops.

He took the York Road, then up through Burmantofts. A woman donkey-stoning the doorstep of her back-to-back house looked up and winked at him as he passed. The municipal cemetery lay across the street from the workhouse. Headstones and marble monuments were dotted around acres of ground, men cutting the grass around them to keep it all neat. Respect for the dead, he thought, and that took him back to the comrades he'd lost in the army.

Back then it had been simple. You killed the enemy. If he had information, you discovered what it was first. And when you fixed a bayonet and charged, a murderous rage could keep you alive. It was all different back in England. Things were nowhere near as easy and obvious.

Inside, he was still shaking from everything Beaumont had said over at B Division. He was angry because the man had spoken no more than the truth. He had to learn to control his temper. He needed to cut down on his drinking. All last night he'd been looking forward to Sunday, to seeing the lass in Middleton again. Now it seemed like a bad idea. Elizabeth would be better off without someone like him, someone who couldn't keep himself in check. If he didn't arrive she'd be sad for a few minutes. Then life would pick her up and carry her along. She'd forget about him by tea time.

The training school was an imposing building, but it was meant to be. Towers and turrets and columns stood behind a fence of metal railings. He climbed the steps to the front door and entered, his footsteps echoing and booming on the floor.

A girl dashed out to him, almost tripping in the maid's dress and starched apron that were too big for her. She couldn't have been more than eight or nine, the same age as Martha Parkinson, he thought. She looked up at him with nervous eyes.

'Please sir, can I help you sir?'

'I'd like to see the master,' he told her gently.

'Yes, sir.' Not sure what to do, she bobbed a small curtsey and led him along a corridor with green and white tiles along the walls. Finally she knocked on a plain wooden door and backed away, not wanting to be seen.

'Enter.'

He turned the handle and walked into a spacious office, immaculately clean, all the wood polished. The man sat behind a large desk, peering through thick spectacles. His head seemed little more than skull, his features thin and pale, only a few strands of greasy hair clinging to the sides of his scalp. Long, bony fingers were laced together on his lap, resting on the black waistcoat.

'Yes?' he drawled, looking down his nose.

'I'm Detective Sergeant Reed, sir.' The man sat a little more upright, suddenly attentive. 'You're the master here?'

'I am,' the man agreed with a short nod. 'Nathaniel Frith.' He didn't extend a hand. 'How might I help you, Sergeant?'

'Just a few questions, if you'd be so good, sir.' He smiled genially.

'Of course. It's a duty to help the police. That's what I tell the boys and girls here.'

Reed noted the cane sitting prominently on the desk. He had no doubt the man told his pupils forcibly. He had the weak look of a bully.

'How many children do you have here, sir?'

'It varies,' Frith answered slowly. 'Between fifty and sixty.'

'How many girls, sir?'

'Usually about twenty-five,' he said after some consideration. 'Why?'

'Do any abscond?' Reed ignored the man's question.

'One or two.' He raised spindly brows. 'There are always recalcitrant children, Sergeant. A good beating and withholding meals can help them see their errors, I find.' His eyes seemed to twinkle as he spoke.

'How many girls haven't come back, sir? Say in the last few months.' He let the question hang in the air.

'I'll say again, Sergeant: why do you want to know?'

'Inquiries, sir.' He tried to make the words sound affable, but with a steel threat behind them.

The man sighed, pulled off the spectacles and cleaned them with a handkerchief from his pocket. He held them up to the light then replaced them on his face and tucked the linen away before answering.

'Two of them. My men couldn't find them.'

'How long ago was this?'

'Nine weeks on Sunday.'

'Did you inform the police, sir?'

'No,' the man admitted quietly. Of course not, Reed thought. He'd already checked the records; no child had been reported missing from the place. It could have led to awkward questions into Frith's methods and how many more had vanished during his time.

'Their names, sir?'

'Amelia Elizabeth Thornton and Cassie Osbourne,' Frith said after a small hesitation.

'And how old are they?'

'Nine and eight.' What colour had been in Frith's face had vanished. Reed wanted to be the bad dream Firth experienced at night. The sergeant had expected more backbone from the man, more resistance, but he'd crumpled at the first question. Not that the truth would have been too difficult to discover. 'Amelia was always a wayward child. Even beatings couldn't teach her.'

'And the other girl, Cassie?'

'A disciple of the other one.' He shook his head. 'Hopeless, the pair of them. And better off gone from here before they could influence the other girls.'

'Why didn't you report them missing, sir? There's no knowing what might have happened to them.' He paused for a moment. 'It was your duty.'

'Duty?' Frith said. 'My duty is to prepare these children for the world, Sergeant, to make them useful and productive and obedient. Some are beyond that.'

'I'll be informing the proper authorities, sir,' Reed told him, and relished the words, watching them sting. 'Now, you're going to tell me more about the girls.'

The matron at the Cliff Road orphanage was made of harder stuff. It took half an hour of questions, flattery and threats to persuade her to disclose that a girl had gone missing eight weeks before. A seven-year-old named Jane Grayson.

By the time he'd uncovered the information the matron was in tears, begging him not to report it, pleading that she'd lose her position for a lack of diligence and never find another. He pressed her, and got a description and more. Jane had always insisted that her mother was still alive. She'd run off to find her before, but on every previous occasion she'd been found and returned.

Christ, he thought as he came out blinking into the hot sun, how many others had gone from here and vanished without word, with people either not missing them or too afraid to report a disappearance? He walked back down to Woodhouse Moor and caught the tram back into Leeds, a horizon of chimneys touching the sky ahead of him. But no smoke filling the air. Not yet. On Monday it would all be business as usual. The fires and factories would be open. Men would be grateful to be earning a wage again. They'd have money to spend and profits would roll back into the bank accounts of the wealthy. He might never agree with Tom Harper's politics, but he had to concede that the man had a point. It was the workers who laboured and then had to fight for every right.

'Well?' the inspector asked as soon as Reed entered the room.

'Three girls gone in the last three months. Two from Beckett Street, one from the orphanage.'

'Not reported?'

'No.'

Harper frowned. 'We'll deal with that part later. How old were they?'

The sergeant laid out what he'd learned. Harper listened closely, scribbling notes on a sheet of paper.

'All long before Martha,' he said finally. 'But these other girls have disappeared, too.'

'It doesn't mean—' Reed began, but the inspector waved him down.

'I know. They could have left Leeds or be begging or anything. I know that. And we haven't found any bodies. But come on, Billy, you know how easy it is to hide a corpse. Especially a small one.'

'There's still one thing, though.' Harper looked at him, waiting. 'Why would Tosh Walker take young girls? We looked into him very thoroughly. We both questioned him when we had him in before. And we never saw any sign of that, did we?'

'No,' Harper agreed slowly. 'But we weren't looking in that direction.' They'd been concerned with putting him in the dock for forcing a man out of his own business. One case. They'd looked into Walker's affairs, the accounts he had with the Yorkshire Penny Bank and Beckett's. They'd talked to everyone they knew, bent and straight, and never heard a hint or a whisper about children. But their interest had been elsewhere. 'Perhaps it's time we did,' he said.

'We don't even have a real connection, Tom. Maybe the boxer and his friend took Martha for themselves. Have you thought about that?'

He had. It was possible. But deep in his gut he didn't believe it. Call it instinct, call it anything, but he was certain there was something more behind it all. He didn't know if Martha was still alive, but he was going to find out what had happened to her. He owed Betty Parkinson that much. Stuck in Armley Jail, helpless, hopeless, her husband dead and her daughter gone, the least he could give her was an explanation. And if he could, he'd bring Martha home.

'Time to start asking questions again,' Harper said.

NINETEEN

B ridge End felt like a desperate place. Even in the sunshine, with fresh cobbles on the street and the afternoon traffic passing, it seemed dark and empty, as if all the people inside were dead. Large posters pasted on the sides of the houses advertised an auction of materials used to refinish the roads. The doors on the buildings were all closed, windows grimy. Close by, the stench from the river rose in the heat as the water moved by sluggishly. Barges and boats lay moored, masts rising, the chatter of the men there a constant noise in the background.

The shop he wanted stood right on the corner. The glass in one dirty window was cracked, just as it had been for the last five years. Light filtered in through the cobwebs that covered the windows. The bell over the door rang as he entered, and a man emerged silently from the back room. He wore an old shirt with a soft collar, a thin black tie and waistcoat. A grubby apron was tied around his waist.

John Call needed a haircut and a shave. The stubble had grown dark across his cheeks, blending into the heavy moustache over his top lip. His fingernails were always bitten to the quick, his skin rimed with dirt. He stood behind the counter, arms folded.

'Something I can help you with, Mr Harper?'

The same goods seemed to have been on the shelves and under the glass on the counters forever. Jars of hair tonic, restorative pills, liquorice root in a jar, bottles of liquids in greens and reds and blues with thick layers of sediment at the bottom, all of it covered with a layer of dust. But no one bought what was on display. People came here to sell the property they'd stolen.

Call had spent time in jail for fencing. He'd never made much money; he only dealt with petty thieves. Now he'd become a good source of information for Harper. It was easier than taking him in and charging him again and again, and he'd led them to quite a few arrests.

'Tosh Walker,' the inspector said.

Call shook his head. 'I'm saying nowt.'

'You'll say plenty.'

'Not Tosh.' Call kept his voice firm. 'You asked me last time and then he walked.'

'And you said nothing last time, either.'

'I like to stay alive. Nowt wrong with that.'

'This is different, John.'

'Oh aye?' the man said doubtfully. He hawked tobacco into a spittoon behind the counter. 'How's that?'

'Young girls.'

'Tosh?' He laughed in disbelief. 'Get on with you. I've never seen him with a woman, let alone a young girl. Or a fella either, if that's what you're going to ask.'

'What about him employing a boxer and another man?'

Call shook his head. He knew the way to stay safe and living – you didn't say anything about Tosh Walker.

'Who'd be willing to talk?' Harper asked.

'No one with an ounce of sense.'

'Who?' he pressed.

'Mebbe try Jem Arkroyd. But don't say I sent you.'

'I won't.' You kept your narks safe and protected. That was the way it worked. It had taken time to bring Call around, to make him into something useful. There were years of secrets left in him yet. Harper wasn't about to waste that.

'He's not afraid of Tosh. Daft bugger.' He spat again.

Harper knew Jem, a big man with ropes of muscle in his arms and his neck. He'd been a stevedore once, carrying hundredweight sacks of this and that on and off the barges on the river. Back then he'd thieved from the cargos, and was big and violent enough that no one was going to stop him.

It had grown from there into a small empire along the waterfront. If someone wanted to be employed loading barges, they went through Jem. He kept things in order, made his agreements with the boat owners and the warehouses. On the surface it was legal enough, and Harper had never tested the depths. Soon enough the union would come. That would be a real battle for Arkroyd to fight.

Not his first, though. Tosh Walker had tried to take over his racket and been sent packing. When he'd sent tough lads in, Jem had beaten them with his own hands. No charges had ever been pressed but hatred had stood between them ever since.

The man's office was a ramshackle shed on the riverbank, the door open wide. Workers were busy, a bustle of activity, men stripped to the waist and sweating in the heat as they laboured, picking up the heavy sacks as if they weighed nothing. The lack of gas made no difference to the work out here.

Arkroyd was sitting in his hut, sipping from a cup of tea and sucking on a pipe, boots up on a chair. His shirtsleeves were rolled up to show powerful forearms covered in faded tattoos, and a kerchief was knotted around his throat. He'd be out there himself, bending his back and leading by example if there weren't enough workers or the men were moving too slowly. He weighed half as much again as Harper and all of it was muscle.

Jem was clean-shaven, his head cropped short, his broken nose set at an angle. He was the only man the inspector knew who never wore a hat. He looked dangerous and he was.

'How do,' he said.

'Mr Arkroyd.'

'And you're that copper. Harris, is it?'

'Harper. Detective Inspector.' Arkroyd knew his name; this was just his way of showing he was in charge. The river was his manor and Harper was a guest; that was how Arkroyd would see it. The inspector knew better; any problem and he'd bring down the law quickly enough. Nowhere in Leeds was going to be off-limits to the police.

'Well, everything's above board here. Your lot come down often enough to make sure of it. You have any questions you can talk to my lawyer.'

'And who's that?' he asked, although he could guess.

'Mr Desmond in Park Square.'

Harper smiled. 'I'm not here about any irregularities.'

'Then what do you want?'

'Tosh Walker.'

Arkroyd snorted. 'That lickspittle arsehole?' He fixed his gaze on Harper. 'Why come to me about him?'

'Because you hate him and you're one of the few who isn't scared of him,' the inspector said simply.

The man acknowledged the facts with a small nod. 'And what do you think I can do for you?'

'Information.'

Arkroyd considered the idea. 'If I have any, what's in it for me?'

'Revenge.'

Jem thought for a long time, blowing out smoke and slurping the thick, dark brew.

'Ask away,' he said finally.

'What do you know about Tosh Walker and children?'

'I know he dun't have any. Not him and the missus of his. There's been talk of a bastard or two here and there . . .' He shrugged.

'You know what I mean.'

'Do I?' He raised a pair of bushy eyebrows. 'Happen you'd better tell me.'

'Children for sex.'

Arkroyd shook his head. 'Not heard owt. And I'll tell you this much, if I'd heard anything like that I'd kill him with my own fucking hands. Why, you think he is?'

'I don't know. I'm trying to find out.'

'And you want me to ask around?'

'Yes.'

'If I find he is, you'll not see him again and you'll never find the body.'

'No. If he is, you'll let me know.' They stared at each other, neither one saying a word. 'I mean it, Jem. You don't and I'll have more men down here than you can handle. We'll shut you down.'

'Then you'll shut down the docks.'

'I dare say the union will be glad to move in.' It was more than a threat, it was the future, and Arkroyd was smart enough to know it. He'd still lose in the end but cooperation would buy him a little more time.

'All right, then,' he agreed grudgingly. 'But I'll not promise the state he'll be in.'

'You just tell me if you learn anything and I'll take care of the rest.'

It wasn't a request. It was an order.

Just the name Tosh Walker seemed to turn them silent, Reed thought. Their eyes became empty and they forgot whatever they might have known. He doubted that anyone in Leeds inspired more fear.

He'd gone from person to person, wearing out shoe leather hither and yon in Leeds, from a respectable parlour on Blenheim Terrace down to Mabgate. In St Peter's Square he stopped to watch a group of ragamuffin boys kicking a ball around over the cobbles. Their shirts were off, ribs showing through thin chests, socks fallen around their ankles. Then he walked under the imitation arch with the glass sign over the front step. It was a failed attempt to give some culture to another back-to-back in a long row of them. Inside was a Turkish bath house, one of the first in the kingdom, a notice said. The air was hot and steamy, and caught in his throat. A young man sitting on a chair, a pile of grubby towels behind him, looked at him without interest and held his hand out.

'Sixpence for the bath,' he said.

'And nothing to see Mr Ross.'

The young man glanced up again sharply, this time seeing him for who he was. 'Upstairs,' he said.

Ross had made the front bedroom into an office. He was staring out at the street and turned at the footsteps. The smile on his face was so false it could have dropped away in a second.

'The police?' he asked.

'Detective Sergeant Reed.'

There were rumours about Ross, nothing more than that. No one had managed to prove anything. His skin seemed impossibly pale, the freckles standing out like spots, his red hair a shock that oil couldn't tame.

'What can I do for you, Sergeant?' He gestured at a chair but Reed stood.

'Tosh Walker.'

Ross looked at him quizzically. 'Who?'

'Someone who might like young girls.'

'And what does that have to do with me, Sergeant?' Ross drew himself up, straightening his back.

'From what I hear, maybe the two of you have plenty in common.'

'I run a respectable business, Mr Reed.'

The sergeant smiled. 'I dare say you do. But it's not what goes on here that concerns me. Sir.'

'I don't know the man,' Ross answered. For a moment, Reed almost believed him, until his eyes flickered and he looked down briefly.

'I think you do.' He felt the heat rising inside and his fists starting to clench. Very carefully he took three long, deep breaths. 'I think you do,' he repeated.

'I don't know why you'd imagine that,' Ross said.

'Because you're lying to me.'

The man cocked his head. 'I don't understand.'

'It's a simple question,' Reed told him. 'I asked if you knew Tosh Walker. You said no.'

'That's correct.'

'And I say you're lying.'

'How can you presume . . .?' Ross's face had reddened with anger and guilt.

The sergeant gave himself time, letting the calm flow through him. 'Because that's my job.' He moved forward a pace, close enough to feel menacing. 'Now, sir, why don't you just tell me the truth? It'll be much easier for us both.'

'I told you, I don't know the man.'

'Tosh Walker,' Reed said.

'That's right.' He stared at the policeman. 'I'll say it again. I don't know him. I'm sorry, but I can't help you.'

They both knew it wasn't the truth. But Ross wasn't going to shift, at least not on this visit. Not without more force than he dare use.

'Then I'll wish you good day. But I hope you'll have a think about it before I come back and ask again. And I will be back, sir, you can be sure of that.'

It wasn't far to Millgarth. He could almost see it from St Peter's Square, the top of the roof peeking above the houses. On the way back to the station he stopped at the cobbler's shop on the corner, paid his one and sixpence and carried out his good boots in a brown paper parcel. Resoled and reheeled, ready for Harper's wedding. And for Sunday in Middleton, he thought. If he went.

By late afternoon the station was busy, every available uniformed officer called in to escort the remaining blacklegs from the Wortley gasworks back to the station. Reed pushed his way through them and into the office.

'They're ready for trouble,' he said.

'Too late,' Harper answered. 'There won't be any this time. People will be glad to see them go. Found anything?'

'Yes and no.'

They'd baited the hooks. Now all they could do was wait and hope the fish would bite.

The light seemed brilliant and clear as Harper emerged from the door of the station. At least his ankle was improving. The swelling was down; it still throbbed but he could put some weight on it and walk more normally.

He cut through the squalor of Pollard's Yard, out to Lady Lane, then along North Street to the shop that sat at the edge of the Leylands, between the old grandeur of Sheepshanks House and the Hope Inn. It was no more than two hundred yards from where he'd grown up on Noble Street. Even with the machinery silent for days, he could still smell the malthouses that supplied the Brunswick Brewery. It took him back to the years of rolling barrels day after day, memories he'd as soon put behind him.

It seemed so long ago now. And he was happier as a policeman than he'd even been back then. He was a man with a future and love in his life. But you could never escape your past; he knew that by now. This visit was like stepping back in time. He glanced at the sign over the door, M. Cohen and Sons, Tailors, and entered.

The man who bustled out of the back room, pins sticking out of his waistcoat, was as familiar as family. He was the same age as Harper. They'd gone to the same school, played together on the cobbles, their houses separated by nothing more than a few walls.

'Tommy!' Moses grinned. No one had called him that in years. It was like being in knickerbockers and long socks again, sitting through lessons and waiting for the bell to ring.

'Hello, Mo.' He looked around the shop. Bolts of fabric lined every shelf in blues, blacks, greys and browns, everything from the best worsteds to cheap gaberdines. 'Looks like you're doing well for yourself.'

Cohen gave a small, eloquent shrug. He was wiry, three or four inches shorter than Harper, with dark hair slowly receding from his forehead and dark eyes covered with spectacles. His parents had arrived from Russia with their two children, Moses and his brother Isaac, everything they owned in three small, battered suitcases. At first the family only spoke Yiddish, trying to make themselves understood with signs and pointing. But the boys had quickly picked up a kind of fractured English and translated for their parents.

By the time they were nine and leaving school, Moses spoke the language better than Harper. He'd gone to join his father in one of the sewing sweatshops while Harper started at Brunswick's, but they still saw each other from time to time. At sixteen Moses had married, a girl whose parents had fled the persecution in Lvov. Harper had gone to the wedding, one of only three *goys* invited. He'd been fascinated by everything, the words he couldn't understand, the smashing of the glass and the wild dancing.

But too many years had gone by since he'd seen Cohen. He'd joined the force and taken lodgings away from Noble Street. His mother had died; his father, ruined in body and mind, had gone to live with one of his sisters. There was nothing to bring him back here. The old bonds had broken. But never completely.

'I need a suit,' he said.

Moses eyed him professionally. 'A good one or just *schmatte*?'

'A good one,' he said with a smile.

'Promotion?' Cohen guessed.

'I'm getting married.'

'Oy.' He shook his head comically. 'You didn't learn from my mistakes.'

The last he'd known, Moses was devoted to his wife. He had two boys of his own, probably sewing away in the back room.

'I'm a lucky man, Mo. She keeps telling me that.'

'Only because she doesn't know you, Tommy.'

He laughed. 'She does. And she still loves me.'

'Then you'd better do her proud. See if you can fool her longer.' He strode to a shelf and brought out some grey cloth, expensive, close-woven worsted. 'Wear a suit of that and she'll think she's marrying a lord.'

'It's wonderful,' Harper agreed, feeling the smoothness under his fingertips. 'But I can't afford that. Policemen don't earn much.'

Cohen waved away his complaint. 'How long have I known you, Tommy? Years and years. Call it my wedding present.'

'Are you sure?' He could hardly believe it; the gesture was so generous. But any pound saved was important on his wages.

'Of course I'm sure,' Cohen answered in a voice that brooked no argument. He pulled a tape measure from the counter and pulled off the inspector's jacket. 'Now this is *schmatte*. Barran can make them cheap but he can't make them good.' He shook his head again. 'You should come to me for your suits. A few shillings more but they last you forever.'

He began to take his measurements, scribbling figures on a grubby piece of paper.

'How are your parents? Still on Noble Street?'

Cohen nodded, the pencil between his teeth as he knelt, checking the length of Harper's legs. 'They'll never move. They ran from Russia. They stopped running when they arrived here.' He shrugged again. 'They kvetch but they're happy. Me, I live over the shop. Keeps it simple. So tell me about this woman who's foolish enough to marry you.'

Harper told him as he worked, watching him nod and scribble, taking measurement after measurement until he stood, coiled the tape and put it away.

'You better be good to her, Tommy.'

'I will,' he promised.

'She sounds like the type to throw you out if you're not.'

Harper laughed. He could easily imagine that.

'When do you need the suit?'

'The wedding's a week on Saturday.'

'How about Tuesday?' Cohen asked. The inspector knew there'd be no work done after the sun set today until Sunday. Moses might be one of the new English Jews but he'd never ignore the Shabbat.

'Fine. And thank you again, Mo.'

He was drained. He'd been up since one, seen dead bodies, talked to the living and travelled all over Leeds. He'd done his duty and been measured for the wedding suit. All he wanted now was a meal, a drink and an early night. He waited for the omnibus outside the Public Dispensary on North Street, watching the sick come and go. By the time he alighted in Sheepscar he could almost feel his eyes closing.

The bar at the Victoria was almost full, men laughing and joking. Celebrating the end of the strike, he realized. Soon they'd all be back at work, with a little money in their pockets. He pushed through a door and climbed the stairs.

The windows were open wide and Annabelle was busy in the kitchen. She came through as he entered, smiling, happy to see him.

'I saw you get off the bus. Kettle's boiling.' She stood and stared at him. 'You look like summat the cat's dragged in.'

'Just tired,' he told her.

'Well,' she said, 'have a cup of tea and a wash. We're going out tonight.'

'We are?' It was a stupid question. Annabelle had made up her mind and she was going to sweep him along with her.

'You're taking me to dinner at the White Horse and then we're off to see the new acts at the Scarborough. I fancy letting me hair down for the evening.' She saw his face. 'Come on, Tom. When was the last time we went out?'

He tried to remember. Almost a fortnight. It had been a sunny Sunday, they'd taken the omnibus to the end of the line then walked across Adel Moor to Verity's tea rooms. She was right, it was too long. She looked at him, her eyes wide and hopeful and he knew he couldn't refuse her.

Annabelle had dressed quickly, in a pale grey skirt and white blouse, pulling up her hair under a summer straw hat, her arm through his as they walked, a floral parasol over her shoulder. They took the tram back into town, strolled to Boar Lane then up the stairs to the restaurant above Fairburn's druggist.

The White Horse meant chops. The meal was excellent, plates filled with mashed potato and carrots, the meat tender and perfectly cooked. At first Harper wondered if he was too weary to feel hungry, but with the first mouthful he realized he'd barely eaten all day.

It was dusk as they turned the corner on to Bishopgate. The Scarborough was no more than a few yards down the road. They arrived just in time for the second house. He ordered a glass of beer for himself, gin for Annabelle. She'd been right; she was in a mood for fun. From the moment the master of ceremonies appeared, she was loud, calling out like all the others, her face flushed with laughter from the comedians, joining in with every song, her voice brassy and tuneful.

And he enjoyed himself. It was worth it all to see her happy. By the time they climbed into a hackney carriage at the stand in the middle of Briggate she seemed content, sitting back and leaning her head against his shoulder with a sigh.

'I needed that. You can't beat a good night out.'

'It was fun.'

She kissed his cheek. 'You held up well. Thank you.'

He smiled. 'I'm always proud to be seen with you,' he said honestly.

'That's a lovely thing to say.'

He looked out of the window as the cab moved slowly along. Still no gaslight, but plenty of figures flitting in and out of the shadows, singing and laughing with none of the usual violence of drunken men. The public houses were doing good business, people still out celebrating victory in the strike. And well they might.

'Penny for them,' Annabelle said.

'I was just thinking about the strike.' But every thought about that took him one pace further and then another and another, and they all led back to Martha Parkinson. He knew the super was right, that she was probably dead. But he couldn't let himself admit it until he saw her body. Somewhere inside he felt guilty that he wasn't out there now, looking for her. But he'd done all he could. And he'd be back out there again tomorrow.

'No you weren't,' she said, and he had to chuckle at the way she could read him like the pages of a book open in front of her. 'The girl?' Annabelle asked. He nodded. 'That's why I made you come out tonight.'

'I thought you wanted a good time.'

'I did,' she admitted. 'But I also wanted you to stop thinking. You do too much of it, Tom.' She was right and he knew it. But thinking, making connections, that was part of his job. It was what made him a good detective. 'It'll all still be there in the morning.'

It would. But he wanted it over, he wanted answers. And he wanted Tosh Walker for this. They had no evidence but he could feel it inside. The man was guilty. He knew he should go back out to Armley and see Betty Parkinson again. Not going was the coward's way. But he had no news, no hope to give her. She must be going a little more mad each day, and there was nothing he could do. Not yet.

He paid off the cab outside the Victoria. Candles and lanterns lit the back but the customers had gone. Dan was cleaning up, wishing them goodnight as they climbed the stairs.

Annabelle bustled around, taking off the hat and tossing it on the table, propping the parasol in a stand and loosening her boots with a sigh of relief.

'You've no idea what we go through to look good for a man,' she complained. 'Shoes too tight, corsets that pinch you in, glop all over your face.'

'You look lovely.'

'Aye, but do you mean that?' she challenged him.

'Every word.'

Her lips curled into a sly smile. 'Happen you'd better prove it, then.'

'Prove it?' He didn't understand.

'We're getting married tomorrow week.'

'I know.'

'I want everything to be right.'

'So do I,' he agreed, still mystified.

'Everything.' She arched her brows and he began to understand. Very slowly she walked over to him, then gradually raised the hem of her skirt to display her stockings, higher and higher until he could see the garters above her knees. 'Do you remember what I said when we first met? I told you they were blue.'

TWENTY

He felt her leave the bed. The darkness beyond the curtains was starting to fade. He knew he ought to rise too, dress and go down to the station. But he was warm and comfortable, not ready to move just yet.

Annabelle had been passionate and willing, and he'd sloughed off his tiredness for a little while. When it was over, he'd rolled on to his back, her head on his chest, hair tickling him as their sweat began to cool. Before he'd fallen into a deep, dreamless sleep, in a very small voice she'd said, 'Tom, I know your job takes a lot. But make sure you leave some time for us, please.'

He eased his way out of bed, fumbling around in the blackness for his clothes. By the time Annabelle returned with a candle he'd found everything but his boots.

'What time is it?' he asked, groping for his watch.

'Just gone four.'

He pulled her close and kissed her. Her hair was down, uncombed and wiry against his hand. She pulled away and smiled.

'There'll be time enough for that tonight,' she told him teasingly. 'Cassie lit the fire earlier so the kettle's on.' She marched across the room, letting the nightgown fall behind her. He watched as she dressed, enjoying the view of her body as she put on bloomers, corset, skirt and blouse, finishing with the soft sensuality of rolling stockings up her legs. 'Liked that, did you?' she asked with a wink.

'Very much,' he replied, his voice husky.

'Come back tonight. Play your cards right and there'll be a repeat performance.'

It was six by the time he reached Millgarth; the day men were starting their shift, a parade of constables leaving for their beats.

He settled at his desk, checking through reports. There was nothing to interest him.

Reed arrived a few minutes later, the bowler perched at a jaunty angle on his head and a smile on his face.

'You look happy,' Harper observed. 'Better than yesterday, any road.'

'I'm just in a good mood. Something's going to happen today.'

'Let's hope. Made up your mind about tomorrow?'

'Tomorrow?' Reed asked, confused.

'Middleton,' the inspector reminded him. 'To see that lass.'

'See how I feel in the morning.' It was a lie. He'd already decided to go. He'd agreed and she'd be waiting; he owed her an appearance and a few hours of his time. The chances were they'd never meet again after that. 'I'm off to see the man at the Turkish bath again this morning. He knows something, he just won't say.'

'Do you want me there?' It was more than an offer; it was a warning.

'I'll be fine.' He was about to say more when Tollman, the desk sergeant, came through with an envelope.

'For you, sir,' he said to Harper. 'A lad brought it.'

The inspector raised his eyebrows and ripped it open, eyes skimming across the words. Then he stood, reaching for his hat and his stick, pushing the note into his jacket.

'Come along, Billy,' he said. 'We have someone to see.'

'Who?' the sergeant asked as they made their way through the throng of early Saturday shoppers. Commercial Street was already busy, carts parked at the roadside as they delivered packages.

They turned the corner to Lands Lane under the towering sign for the Salvation Army Temperance Society, then along Albion Place, passing the printer's and finally stopping outside Moore's Belfast Linen Warehouse on Albion Street. Harper inclined his head.

'Up there,' he said.

The sign in the windows showed Radcliffe and Wills, Chartered Accountants on the second floor of the building.

'Tosh Walker's accountant?' Reed guessed.

'Robert Radcliffe.' He produced the note he'd received and

passed it over. 'It's from John Call, that fence down at Bridge End.'

The writing was spidery, an awkward, uneducated scrawl across the paper.

Look at the places Walker owns. His accountant knows. See Robert Radcliffe.

'Do you think there's anything in it?'

'We won't know until we ask.' He pushed open a small door and climbed the stairs. There was just a small brass plaque on the wall to announce the business.

Three clerks were hunched over their desks, going through figures in ledgers. One raised his head.

'Can I help you, sir?'

'Is Mr Radcliffe in?'

The man bit his lip for a moment before replying. 'No, sir.'

'When do you expect him?'

The other clerks had put up their pens. The first man glanced at them.

'I'm not sure, sir.'

'I'm Detective Inspector Harper, Leeds Police.'

For a moment the man seemed to give a sigh of relief. 'Mr Radcliffe received a note yesterday afternoon and left without a word. We haven't seen him since, sir.'

Harper could feel the hair rise on his arms. 'Who brought it?'

'A young man. I'd never seen him before.'

'And Mr Wills? Is he here?'

'Mr Wills been dead for five years, sir.'

'Where does Mr Radcliffe live?'

'Chapel Allerton, sir.'

'Can you find me his address, please?'

As the man turned away, Reed asked, 'Is he married?'

'No, sir. His wife died two years ago.'

'You're the accountants for Tosh Walker, I believe,' Harper said.

The man dipped his head in acknowledgement. 'We are, sir.'

'And Mr Radcliffe took care of that himself?'

'Always, sir,' the clerk answered carefully. 'His personal business.'

'Are all Mr Walker's files still in the office?'

'Yes, sir.' He hesitated. 'Mr Radcliffe took nothing with him.'

'Show them to the sergeant, please.' He turned to Reed. 'You know what to look for, Billy: all the properties Walker owns. I'm going to search for Radcliffe.'

The omnibuses to Chapel Allerton only ran every hour on a Saturday. He didn't have that time to waste today. Instead he hailed a hackney, and the driver urged the horse on as he negotiated the traffic along North Street then the more open spaces of Harrogate Road. The case was costing him a fortune in fares.

The accountant had done well for himself, he thought as he paid the cabman. A detached house of stone set back from the main road, close to the bowling green of the Mexborough Arms.

He rang the bell, hearing it jingle, and waited. Finally the maid arrived, looking at him curiously.

'Is Mr Radcliffe at home? I'm Detective Inspector Harper, Leeds Police.'

'No, sir,' she answered in surprise. 'He hasn't been here since yesterday morning.'

'Were you expecting him last night?'

The girl nodded and Harper thought quickly. 'Does he sometimes go off without warning or not come back?'

'Not since the missus died, sir. He might come back late from work or a night out but he always comes home.'

'Does he have any family?'

'Two sons and four daughters, sir. But they're all grown and married, scattered across the county. He wouldn't have gone off to see any of them just like that.'

'When he returns, can you ask him to get in touch with me? I'm at Millgarth Station.'

'Yes, sir.' She hesitated. 'Do you think anything's happened to him?'

'Probably not,' he lied. If he was right, Radcliffe had run. Very far and very fast. A note and he'd been on his way. But leaving Tosh's accounts was a big mistake.

There were no hackneys in Chapel Allerton. Precious little of anything, really, only a few shops along the main road and a couple of pubs. He waited impatiently for the omnibus to take him back to town. A few carriages passed, heading into Leeds.

It was quiet out here; there was a gentle pace to life. He hated it. Give him people and noise any day of the week.

It was more than an hour before he was back at the station, desperate to move on. Reed had two large ledgers open on his desk, each filled with beautiful copperplate writing.

'Did you find him?' the sergeant asked.

'Never went home,' Harper said. 'He's done a flit. I think we can guess who sent the letter.'

'I'd like to know what was in it,' Reed said. 'I sent someone to check that Walker hasn't vanished, too.'

'Not Tosh,' the inspector replied with certainty. 'He won't go anywhere.'

'Why would he tell Radcliffe to run, then stay himself? That doesn't make sense.'

'Because he's an arrogant bastard. He's beaten us before and he thinks he can do it again. He'll brazen it out. Tosh just wants to be sure there's no one else around to tell on him, that's all. What have you found?'

'Walker's been a busy lad. He owns small factories, shops, you name it.'

'Houses?'

'I've counted two so far. I'm still looking.' He was halfway through the second book.

'Do you have the dates he acquired them?'

'I'm making notes. I'll be finished in an hour or so.'

'I'll come back and we can look.'

The market was busy. Sellers yelled their goods to the crowds, everything from plates and cups to vegetables and meat. Old women dressed in constant mourning haggled over the price of a potato; every farthing saved was precious in their purses. He picked his way through the people, sliding by a girl hawking bunches of fragrant lavender. There was an air of happiness. The strike was over. The stokers had reported back to work the night before and by Sunday evening the gas should be flowing again.

The workers had won, and that would bring a smile to everyone with an employer. It gave hope to them all. He made his way through to Kirkgate by Old Crown Yard, the smell from the tripe shop next door almost overpowering, and across the street to the union office. There were few enough men around this morning, and the ones remaining looked bleary-eyed but triumphant, unshaved and battered by a long night.

Maguire was holding court on the front step, a bottle of whisky in one hand, the other leaning lazily against the door jamb. His loud check suit was wrinkled, the worse for wear, and his expression was wild and gleeful, a man enjoying his victory.

'Mr Harper!' he cried, speech slurred. 'Come to help us celebrate?' He raised the bottle in a toast.

The inspector smiled. 'It looks as if you've managed very well without me.'

'Lads, lads.' Maguire addressed those around him, wavering as he stood. 'Inspector Harper here isn't just a policeman, he's a grand fellow, too.' They looked at him sceptically. 'He believes. He's a friend.' They still looked uncertain, but parted to let him among them.

'I need a word with you,' he whispered in Maguire's ear and the man nodded.

'Go home now, lads,' he said. 'Go and sleep the sleep of the just and the brave.'

The office was stuffy, the shutters still closed, clouds of dust motes floating in the air. Maguire slumped into his chair and leaned back, yawning. He loosened the collar of his shirt, revealing his neck lined with grime.

'What can I do for you, Mr Harper?' He took another swig, washing it around his mouth before he swallowed it. 'You want some?' The inspector shook his head and Maguire roared with laughter. 'It's only ginger beer in a whisky bottle. I'd never have lasted if I'd been drinking spirits. But people expect me to be a certain way and I can't let them down.' He cocked an eyebrow. 'So?'

'You heard what happened to Councillor Cromwell.'

'I did.' He shook his head. 'I loathed the man but I'd never have wished that on him. Was it shame, do you think?'

'I think it had more to do with Tosh Walker.'

Maguire nodded slowly. 'Ah, a very bad man, from all I hear.'

'Do you know him?'

'I've managed to avoid the pleasure.'

'Does anyone in the union know him?'

Maguire shrugged. 'Maybe. Why do you want to know?'

'Police business.'

'That old chestnut.' He smiled.

'But true,' Harper said. 'Can you ask and see if anyone knows anything?'

'I will. It might take a few days.' He gestured at the empty room. 'They're all sleeping it off, at least the ones who aren't already back at work.'

'You know where to find me.'

'I'll send word,' Maguire said and winked. He'd never willingly set foot in a police station, Harper knew.

Before he returned to Millgarth he stopped at the café by the market. He'd left the Victoria before breakfast, with just a cup of tea to fill him. He could feel his belly beginning to rumble.

Reed was finishing up the second ledger. His suit jacket was over the back of the chair, his sleeves rolled up.

'Almost done,' he said. 'It's quite a list.'

A few minutes later it was complete.

'What are we looking for?' he asked.

'A house, not a factory or a business.'

'Why?'

'We want somewhere he might take girls, somewhere no one will see or hear things.'

'If we take out the back-to-backs, we're left with five. I don't know what they're like but they're all out in the suburbs.' He took his pen and underlined the addresses.

'That one's where Walker lives,' the inspector told him. 'Forget that.'

'Four, then. Which ones do you want?'

'I'll go east, you go west.'

'Meet back here?' Reed asked as he put the bowler hat on his head.

'Yes.'

Harper was about to leave when Tollman, the desk sergeant, called his name.

'There's a telephone call for you, sir.'

The inspector had been here when the instrument was installed. Like everyone else he'd looked at it in a mix of wonder and fear. But he'd never used it, never needed to. He eyed the machine warily.

'It's the governor at Armley jail,' Tollman continued.

Harper picked up the receiver, not sure which end was which until the sergeant nodded at him. He held it against his good ear and said, 'Hello?'

At first the sound in his ear crackled and sputtered. He knew it was science, that being able to talk to someone sitting miles away was progress, the future. But it seemed strangely like magic. There were so few telephones around that hardly anyone at the station had ever used one. The voice cleared and he could finally hear the governor.

'. . . we've had to put her into Menston.'

'Who?' he asked. 'I couldn't make out what you said.'

'Betty Parkinson.' The man sounded exasperated. 'She's become more and more hysterical since you told her about her husband and daughter. The doctor saw her again today and committed her to Menston. I wanted you to know.'

'Thank you,' he said and added, 'Goodbye' before returning the handset to the cradle, very gently in case it broke.

'Bad news, sir?' Tollman asked.

'Yes,' he answered slowly, 'it was.'

Menston, he thought. That was what everyone called the place. It had only opened a couple of years before, the West Riding Pauper Lunatic Asylum as it was properly known. He'd never been there, but he knew enough about it to understand that Betty would probably be a patient for a long time.

Behind the market, he found a hackney at the stand and gave the cab driver an address in Oakwood. As they went up Roundhay Road he began to feel he'd been this way too often lately. And he wondered if it would have helped Betty if he'd gone back during the week to see her. But what could he have said? Even now they weren't any nearer to finding Martha, alive or dead.

The cab passed Cromwell's house. The curtains were drawn and the place seemed empty. No more than three minutes later, the cab turned into a street of solid, respectable houses, each set well apart from the other. Number five was new enough for the stone to retain its pale golden colour. It seemed substantial, planted in the ground. Harper walked along the path and knocked at the door.

The maid eyed him warily, even when he gave his rank.

'Who lives here?' he asked.

She looked at him as if he was stupid. 'Dr Binns and his family,' she said witheringly. 'Don't you know who you've come to see?'

'Thank you,' he told her, tipping his hat and walking back to the cab.

The second address was on Street Lane, the other side of Roundhay Park. Another large house, the front lawn elaborate and neat. As soon as the maid opened the door he could hear the sounds of a family inside, made his excuses and left.

All the way back to Millgarth he hoped Reed had found something, anything. He'd bet so much on this. He'd been so certain that he was right, that Walker was behind it all. If they came up with nothing they'd have to look at the other properties. And if nothing came up from that search, what then?

'Well?' he asked as the sergeant entered the office.

'Both rented to families. You?'

'The same with mine.' Harper had been looking at the list, putting marks next to several more addresses. 'I'll have the constables check these. We should know by the end of the day. Go through those ledgers again and see if you missed anything. Are you sure that's everything of Walker's?'

'It's everything the clerk gave me.'

Harper could feel the tension throughout his body. Every fibre seemed to prickle inside his skin. He was right, he *knew* he was right. He had to be right. It was Tosh Walker, he was certain of it.

But right now he could almost hear the man laughing at them.

TWENTY-ONE

'Nothing,' Reed said in exasperation, throwing the pen across the desk.

'You're sure?'

'I'm bloody positive.' His voice rose. 'For God's sake, I've been through it all four times. There's nothing else in Walker's name.'

Through the afternoon the uniforms had reported in on the other addresses. Every one was used legitimately.

'I—' Harper began but the sergeant cut him off.

'Tom, maybe it's not Walker. Have you thought about that? We could be wasting all this time.'

'It's him. I'm certain of it.'

'Tell me where, then. Because I'm buggered if I know.' Reed glanced at the closed door to the superintendent's office. 'Kendall's left for the day. Why don't you go home and come at it again on Monday?'

'Tomorrow. I'll be in tomorrow.'

The sergeant shrugged, arranging all the papers on his desk into careful, exact piles.

'You do what you want. I'll see you on Monday morning.'

Harper leaned back in his chair. Outside he could hear the day shift ending and handing over to the night men. He didn't want to believe he was wrong. He didn't want to believe that Martha was dead. Just a week had passed since Ash had told him the girl had gone to her non-existent aunt. A week; it felt like a month. Maybe Billy was right, he should just leave it for today, put work out of his mind for a while. But he knew he wouldn't. It would nag and worry at him. Tomorrow he'd be back here, and every day until he had an answer.

Until he walked out of the door of his lodgings, Billy Reed still wasn't absolutely certain he was going to Middleton. Saturday's sun had given way to Sunday cloud, but the air was still warm, humid enough to have him sweating in his suit before he'd walked all the way down Woodhouse Lane.

He'd stopped at the Hyde Park Hotel the night before, his head swirling from the day. His search had taken him to Horsforth and Meanwood, and the dressing down he'd received on Friday still rang in his ears and stung in his heart.

It was one reason he'd stopped after a single drink. He'd been about to ask for another, the coins jingling in his fist. Then he looked at the sparkling glass and decided he'd had enough. He'd strolled home, eaten supper with his landlady and gone to bed early.

The train reached Middleton exactly on time. He pulled back the door to the compartment and stepped on to the platform, one of just five passengers alighting as the engine stopped in a thick hiss of steam.

Elizabeth was waiting beyond the barrier, just as she'd promised, with the children lined up in front of her. Four of them, he thought. He'd been trying to imagine all this on the journey. He'd spent so little time around children. He hadn't really known a family since he left to join the army. He wasn't even sure the idea held much for him. He'd been so used to being solitary; it seemed safer that way.

'I wasn't sure you'd come,' she said, her eyes nervous, all the confidence of the other day vanished from her face. 'This is John, Emily, Edward and Victoria.' She tapped each child lightly on the head as she named them. They were all looking up at him expectantly, the older girl about ten or twelve, the younger boy little more than four.

One by one he formally shook their hands.

'Hello,' he told them. 'I'm Mr Reed.'

By the time they'd walked through the village the children had found their spirit again, running and laughing, hiding and jumping. He walked next to Elizabeth. She'd said little since they'd left the station beyond the English small talk of work and weather.

'When the train pulled in I thought I'd made a fool of myself,' she said suddenly.

'Why? I'm here.'

'I know, but . . .' She began to blush. 'I'd been so forward with you. I wonder if maybe you'd decided . . .' She shrugged. 'You know.'

'But I came.'

'Yes.' Elizabeth beamed. 'You did. And I'm glad.'

Three hours later they returned to the same spot. He'd have bought ices for the children, but this wasn't Roundhay Park and there was no one selling them. There was little enough of anything in Middleton, and it was all closed for the Sabbath.

Elizabeth's shyness had slowly vanished as they'd walked and talked. The pithead wheels were still, the village quiet. She told him about the husband who died in a pit accident. No compensation; the owners had insisted it was his fault and she had no means to fight it. She'd moved away from the house where she'd been a wife and gone back to her mother, two women raising four children. But she wasn't sorry for herself. It was fact, it had happened, she accepted it all.

He said little about army life, just a few humorous tales, and even less about his time in the police. Mostly he listened; that was much easier than talking. The children ran and played. Some games he remembered from childhood, others they'd conjured up themselves.

By the time they reached the station, the boys and girls in a ragged line behind them, she was the girl he'd met a few days before, eyes full of mischief, her mouth in a smile.

'Do you fancy doing this again, then?' she asked. It was bright and bold, but he could hear the hopeful note underneath. She didn't look at him as she spoke.

'I do,' he answered, and meant it. He'd enjoyed every minute. This seemed to be the way things ought to be, so normal, so ordinary. So unlike everything he'd known. He wanted it. 'Next Sunday?' She nodded and he continued, 'Why don't you all come into Leeds? We can go to the park.' He saw four sets of eyes widen even as Elizabeth's seemed to sadden. It was expensive to take a whole family on a train. Gently, he drew her aside. 'If I'm asking you all out, I should pay,' he told her, slipping coins for the train fare in her hand. She said nothing at first, weighing them in her palm. For a moment he wondered if she'd throw them back at him in anger. The she smiled and nodded.

'Thank you.'

He said his farewells, addressing each of the children by name, then looked at her.

'Next Sunday,' he said. 'Noon at the station in Leeds. Thank you for today.'

'I've loved it,' she said, and he believed her.

He wasn't ready to go back to the room in Woodhouse, and he didn't want to spend the rest of the day drinking at the Hyde Park. He could still smell the fresh air on his clothes, so different from the soot and stench of Leeds. Instead he walked along Boar Lane and Duncan Street, down Kirkgate and behind the market until he came out at Millgarth.

He'd study the ledgers again, just to see if there was anything he'd missed. Victoria, Elizabeth's younger daughter, was the same age as Martha Parkinson. Reed couldn't share Tom's belief that the girl was still alive. After a fortnight with no trace she had to be dead somewhere.

He didn't know if Tosh Walker was responsible. He could see him for so many things – ordering Col's killing, Bell's strangling, the knifing of the blackleg. But not children. It just didn't fit with everything they'd learned about the man.

He opened the door to the office and found Harper sitting at his desk, the books already spread out in front of him.

'I told you I'd be in,' the inspector said with a rueful grin. 'What's your excuse?'

'I thought I'd go over everything one more time.'

'You're welcome, but there's nothing I can see. I've been here all afternoon.' He rubbed his eyes. 'Did you go out to Middleton?'

'Yes.'

'Well?' Harper laughed. 'Is that all you're going to say? Come on, Billy. Are you seeing her again?'

'Next Sunday,' he admitted reluctantly. 'She's bringing the children and I'm going to take them up to Roundhay Park.'

'So you're stepping out with her?' He grinned. 'You'll be the one getting married next.'

'Give over, you daft bugger.' He knew he was blushing. 'What do we have?'

'Nothing. Absolutely sod all.' He shook his head in exasperation. 'There are no more properties that I can see. Whatever he's done, he's hidden it well.'

'Or maybe it's not him,' Reed said quietly.

Harper didn't reply. He just looked grim and returned to the book.

They'd been working for almost half an hour and twice Harper had come close to throwing the ledgers across the room in frustration, when Tollman came through and coughed.

'There's a gentleman out here wants to talk to you, sir,' he told Harper.

'Who is it?'

'He wouldn't give his name. Says a Mr Maguire sent him. Is that the rabble rouser?'

The inspector shot a quick glance at Reed. 'The union man, yes.' He watched Tollman's bushy eyebrows rise. 'Show him through, will you?'

The man looked ferrety, a closed, bony face under a flat cap, and an expression that made it clear he was unhappy to be anywhere close to a police station. The inspector stood to shake his hand and gestured towards a chair.

'Sit down, Mr . . .'

'Morgan,' the man said. He sat, and glanced around at the pale green walls, smudged by years of wear. 'Frederick Morgan. Mr Maguire said to come and see you. I were down at t' union office this morning after I finished me shift.'

'Gas stoker?' Harper guessed.

'Aye,' the man said proudly. 'There'll be gas back by this evening. We needed to get retorts hot enough first.'

'You have information about Tosh Walker?' He sat forward, tilting his head to make sure he caught every word.

Morgan shifted uncomfortably on the chair, pulled on the cap and began to knead it in his lap.

'Aye.' He glanced up, pursed his lips and began to speak. 'It's not me, really, it's me brother. He's a labourer but just casual, you know, not a union man.' He waited as Harper nodded. 'Last year he were hired on for this job on a house. No one living there, getting it ready, big place, off by itself.' He paused, licking his lips to wet them.

'Go on.'

'They were all supposed to get a bit extra if the job were finished early. They'd been told the job were for Tosh Walker's brother, so he reckoned there could be a nice little bit in it for him, Tosh having money an' all. Not that they ever saw the man there, like.' Harper glanced over at Reed, seeing the man watching intently. 'They finished a month before it were due, and turned up the next day thinking they'd go home with a few extra quid in their pockets. But there were these two big lads who just turned them away. The others left but me brother, he kept saying he wanted to see Mr Walker, he wanted what he was due.' He paused and took a breath. Harper didn't interrupt, just letting him continue in his own time.

'They beat him. Beat him so bad we had to tek him to the

dispensary. He ha'n't been able to work since.' Morgan held up
his right hand. 'Crushed. He can't grip owt. And whatever they
did to him, his head en't been the same since.'

'Why didn't you tell the police?' Reed asked.

Morgan snorted. 'Aye, and what would you lot do?'

'We'd have arrested the men who did it.'

'And ten minutes later they'd have been free again. They told
him not to do owt, that Tosh had friends in t' police. If he did,
they'd come back and do it ten time worse.'

'So why are you telling us now, Mr Morgan?' Harper asked
quietly.

'Mr Maguire reckons you're straight. He says you're after
Tosh. Says you want to see him sent down.'

'I do.'

'There you are, then,' Morgan said, as if that closed the
argument.

'Where did this happen? What was the address?' the inspector
said.

The man recited it. Harper looked at Reed, who shook his
head; it hadn't been in the ledgers they'd taken from the
accountants.

'Thank you, Mr Morgan,' Harper told him. 'You might have
made a big difference.'

'I hope you lock up the bastard and throw away the key. Our
Ray's never going to be reet again.'

'If I can, I will.' It was the most he could honestly promise.
Morgan nodded his acceptance and left.

'What do you think?' Reed asked when they were alone.

'It's the place,' the inspector answered with certainty. 'I can
feel it.'

'Maybe it really was for his brother.'

'I know Tosh inside and out from when we went after him
before. He doesn't have a brother. Do we still have a man on
Walker?'

'I never pulled him.'

'Good.' He stood, cramming his hat on his head. 'Come on,
Billy, we're taking a hackney ride.'

It seemed as if almost every mile he'd travelled in the last few
days had been along Roundhay Road. Harper said nothing as

they passed the Victoria, then past the grime and bitterness of the cheap back-to-back houses that seemed to climb on each other, thrown down around businesses. Beyond Harehills everything seemed cleaner, fresher. Greener, he thought. There were gardens and trees. There was money.

At Oakwood the cab turned along the Wetherby Road, at the back of Roundhay Park. There were few buildings out here, houses, a farm. Someone here would have privacy to do whatever they wanted. Harper had the cabbie slow a little as they passed the address. A long driveway, trees all around the house, leaving it in shade. The place seemed quiet, empty. There was no sense of life about it.

A quarter of a mile later he ordered the carriage to turn and go back. As they went by the property once more, he could see that the shutters were closed. The place stood private and alone.

'Looks vacant,' Reed said.

'It's not.'

'You don't know that, Tom,' the sergeant protested.

'I do.' He could sense it. There were people in there, people who didn't want to be seen. Things happened there that should never occur. 'We're coming back tomorrow with some uniforms. I'll talk to Kendall in the morning.' He leaned back against the worn leather as the cab jounced and jolted along. 'I'll get out at the Victoria. Just be ready tomorrow.'

Annabelle stared at him, then narrowed her eyes

'You look, I don't know . . . you look ready for summat.'

'I am,' Harper told her.

They were sitting in the bar, a few trusted locals scattered around the place, allowed in to drink on the Sabbath. She'd spent the last few minutes toying with a glass of gin while he'd drunk off a pint of beer.

It was almost dark. Instead of lighting candles, Dan the barman put a match to a taper and switched on the gas mantles. There was a small glow from each one, enough to bring a cheer from everyone in the room. It wasn't much, but it was a start. Leeds was coming back to life. Annabelle turned, smiling broadly.

'We've got gas!' she said, excited as a child at Christmas.

'You see that, Tom? The gas is back. I was starting to wonder if we'd ever have it again.'

He saw, but his mind was only half there. He was already thinking ahead to the next day, planning it all in his mind, where he'd place the constables, the dread of the things he might find at the house. Harper sensed her walk away and heard her chattering nineteen to the dozen with Dan. Tomorrow they'd find Martha. He was as certain of it as the fact that the sun would rise in the east. He just prayed that they'd find her alive.

In bed he held Annabelle close, feeling her breathing soften into sleep. But he couldn't rest. He couldn't let go of the thoughts. He lay still, not wanting to disturb her, his eyes closed, but the pictures wouldn't stop. You look ready, she'd said. He was.

TWENTY-TWO

He sat in Kendall's office, Reed standing behind him near the door. The super heard him out in silence, then took his pipe from his suit pocket, filled it and struck a match, puffing until he was satisfied with the draw.

It was a way to buy time, Harper knew, to think and put off a decision.

'You believe this chap Morgan?'

'I do. Maguire sent him over.' He saw Kendall grimace a little at the name.

'I do, too, sir,' the sergeant agreed.

'You've seen the house?'

'There's plenty of privacy. The shutters were closed, the drive is a good hundred yards long. Trees all around.'

The superintendent nodded slowly. 'Have you found out who the place belongs to? You said it wasn't on the list of Walker's properties.'

Harper smiled. He'd been at the Town Hall by eight, most of the swelling in his ankle gone and walking without the stick. The clerk had been reluctant to start digging into the records so early until the inspector had told him it was police business.

Magic words that had spurred the man into action. He opened his notebook.

'It belongs to a Mr Albert Walker. Bought two years ago.'

'Walker,' Kendall mused. 'And Tosh doesn't have a brother, you said?'

'No.'

'It couldn't be another Walker?'

'Having men beaten who ask for the bonus they'd been promised?' Harper asked doubtfully. 'I don't think so, sir. Do you?'

'How many constables do you need?' the superintendent asked after a while.

'Eight uniforms, and Ash among them. If Martha's there, he'll be a comforting face to her. I want to go in before noon.'

Kendall looked surprised at the number, then said, 'See Sergeant Tollman, he'll assign them to you.' Harper started to raise himself from the chair. 'And Tom, I hope to God you're right about this.'

'I am, sir.' He had no doubts at all.

They stood out on the Wetherby Road, hidden from the house in the shade of a tree. The sun shone down and the air felt dusty. In the last five minutes only one cart had passed, its load covered, the driver nodding a greeting. There was almost silence, the only sounds from the birds in the trees that lined that park across the street.

Another minute, Harper thought. He'd give the constables that long to position themselves around the house and make sure no one could escape. He pulled the watch from his waistcoat pocket, opened the lid, eyes on the second hand as it jerked slowly round.

'It's time,' he said finally, and set off briskly down the drive, Reed beside him. He brought his fist down on the door, then waited. Nothing. He tried again. Still no answer. He turned to the sergeant. 'Do it,' he ordered.

Reed brought the kit from his jacket and selected a pick, sliding it into the lock and holding it in place, then another, turning it around carefully, feeling it. He nodded. Harper turned the knob and the door swung open. It had taken less than half a minute.

They were standing in a broad hall, black and white tiles under their feet. To one side, a staircase rose to the upper floor. There were people here. He picked out the scent of cooked food.

'You look down here,' Harper ordered quietly. 'I'll go up there.'

Two of the treads creaked heavily under his boots. The landing was plain, dark boards, no rugs, no tables, no paintings on the walls. Nothing to give a sense of home. He tried the first handle, letting the door swing back to show a room that held a stripped double bed and a wardrobe.

The second bedroom had been slept in, the sheets rumpled, a bolster still showing the imprint of a head, the window raised to let in air.

There was a key in the lock of the third room. He turned it and pushed the door back, holding his breath.

They were there, three of them huddled together on the bed in their nightdresses. The shutters had been padlocked; there was just enough light to make out their faces, full of fear in their silence.

'Hello, Martha,' he said gently. 'Do you remember me? I was Constable Harper. It's going to be all right now. I've come to take you all away from here.'

The girls didn't move, they just clung closer together. He held out his hand, hoping one of them would take it. If they didn't he wasn't sure what he'd do; he couldn't drag them away. He looked around for clothes they could wear but spotted nothing.

There were sounds from downstairs, angry voices, but he ignored them. Instead he squatted down by the bed.

'I'm from the police,' he explained slowly. 'It's over now. Whatever happened, it's all over.' He looked from one face to the next and the next, seeing disbelief, terror and tears that trickled silently down their cheeks. Who could blame them? He didn't know what had happened here, but he could take a good guess. Whatever innocence they might have had was long gone, ripped away from them. He'd said it was all over, but it never would be for these lasses. They'd never be free of all this.

Finally he heard boots in the hall and the three small heads turned towards the shape in the doorway.

'Hello Martha, luv,' Ash said. 'I think we'll get you lot out of here now.'

And for the first time, the girl smiled.

*   *   *

They were holding a man and a woman in the kitchen, both standing, handcuffed. Reed was red-faced, barely containing his fury. But no one was battered or bleeding; he'd managed to keep himself in check.

'Who are they?' Harper asked.

'Robert and Barbara Sadler,' the sergeant answered. 'Did you find the girls?'

'They were upstairs. Door locked, shutters locked. Ash is looking after them. Search the rest of the house.' He waited until the door closed then turned to the pair. Robert Sadler looked afraid. He looked close to forty, mousy hair thinning, a skinny, pigeon-chested man in an ill-fitting brown suit, worn at the elbows and fraying at the cuffs, the short collar grubby and loose around the neck. He had the thin face of someone who'd never had enough to eat, and his eyes were wary.

His wife seemed little better, frizzy brown hair breaking out of a bun. Her skirt and white blouse were full of old creases, and all the colour had vanished from her round cheeks and lips.

'How long have you been here?'

She was the one to answer, not glancing at him. 'Six months. We're here to look after the girls.'

'And have them ready when men visit?' Harper said.

'It's not like that,' Robert Sadler began.

'No?' the inspector asked sharply. 'What is it like, then?'

But neither one answered. Six months, he thought. That meant there must have been other girls here. He rubbed his chin and asked, 'Who pays you? Who hired you on?'

'A man,' Sadler said. 'He comes out here every week.'

'What's his name?'

'He doesn't say.'

The inspector looked at Barbara Sadler. 'Who hired you?'

'Him as pays us,' she told him with a shrug.

'What does the name Tosh Walker mean to you?'

'Nowt,' Sadler replied, but he spoke too quickly, fast enough for Harper to recognize a lie. It didn't matter; they'd sweat it out of them at the station. One of the constables arrived to report.

'No one else in the house, sir.' He gazed in disgust at the Sadlers.

'Right,' Harper ordered. 'I want two of you to take this pair to Millgarth. And I want them to arrive in one piece,' he said pointedly. 'Not too many bruises, you understand?'

'Yes, sir.'

'The rest to search the house fully.' He paused, staring at Robert Sadler. 'Then start digging in the garden. Anywhere the earth looks disturbed.' He saw Sadler's mouth tighten.

'Yes, sir.'

The uniform marched the couple off and Harper strode away. He found Reed in a room that had been made over into an office, nothing more than a desk and two chairs sitting on the bare boards. This wasn't a home, he thought, it was a shell, a place to use, to make money.

The sergeant held up a book. 'Names and dates,' he said, his voice dark. 'And some of the names are important ones.'

'Anything to connect it to Tosh?'

'Not yet. There are beds in some of the rooms, and a sitting room for the Sadlers. That's about all I could find.'

'He's involved. We'll find it. Come on, Billy,' he said.

'Where? There's still plenty to do here.'

'We're going to arrest Tosh Walker. Let the constables take care of everything else. We'll put it all together later.'

First, though, they reported back to Millgarth station. Kendall listened in silence, anger growing on his face.

'How are the girls?' he asked when Harper had finished.

'Ash is looking after them. Martha knows him. I told him to take them to the Infirmary. Past that . . .' His words faded away. He didn't know the answer. Probably no one did.

'There are two girls missing from the workhouse and one from the orphanage. And Martha Parkinson,' Reed said. 'We only found three girls there.'

'You think there'll be bodies?' Kendall asked worriedly.

'I told the men to dig up the grounds, any likely places.'

It was enough to convince the superintendent. 'Take three constables,' he ordered. 'You said there's already a man on Walker.'

'Detective Constable Martin.'

The superintendent nodded. 'I want Walker here whole and unharmed,' he warned. 'Nothing for his lawyer to claim.' He stared at Reed. 'You understand?'

'Yes, sir.' The sergeant coloured.

'Walker will be at his office,' Harper said. 'Billy and I can take him. I need some people at his house, too. There'll be records there, and maybe other people.' He thought about the boxer's friend.

'I'll take care of that myself,' Kendall told him. It was rare for the superintendent to lead a raid. Running the station kept him at his desk. But Harper knew well enough that the man missed real policing.

'Yes, sir.'

'Go and get him, Tom. Just make sure it all sticks this time.'

'I will.' He grinned.

Detective Constable Martin looked like a copper. The large feet in their shiny black boots, the way he stood, trying to stay out of sight and inconspicuous, everything about him yelled police, Harper thought. He was a good enough detective, but he stood out on Park Row, where most of the men who passed looked sleek and groomed. It was a street of money, of banks, insurance offices and other, shadier businesses.

Walker had an office a few yards from the big new Post Office, an expensive address. But he could afford it. He'd have spotted Martin – he'd have been blind not to – and he'd be expecting a visit. They'd find nothing incriminating there – he'd already warned his accountant to run. But he wouldn't know they'd learned about the house on Wetherby Road and been out there.

'Who's in there with him?' Harper asked.

'Just a clerk as far as I can see.' A folded copy of the *Post* stuck out of Martin's pocket. 'You want me to go in with you, sir?'

'Stay here until we come out with him. If you see anyone running, stop them.'

It was a small office, just two rooms. One for the clerk who looked up, startled, as Harper and Reed entered, the other for Walker. But little business was done here. Tosh ran his empire from hotel bars and pubs. He liked to be seen, to remind people who he was and what he could do.

'I was wondering when you'd call, Inspector.' He nodded at the window. 'You've had your dog around me for a few days.'

'We're going down to Millgarth,' Harper said.

Walker smirked. He was a large, intimidating man, wearing a suit so perfectly cut it must have cost more than the inspector made in a month. His hair glistened with pomade, his moustache was carefully trimmed into a thin, razored line above his lip. A faded scar, the memory of an old knife cut, ran down the centre of his forehead to the bridge of his nose. But his eyes were dark and dead. There was nothing behind them.

'My lawyer will have me out in an hour.'

'We'll see. Stand up.' He nodded at Reed who produced a pair of handcuffs and snapped them on Walker's thick wrists. As they left, the man said to the clerk, 'Have Curtis come to the station.'

People stopped to stare as they passed. Harper led them up Park Row and through the shoppers on Commercial Street. Walker said nothing, walking with his head held high, as if this was nothing more than a morning stroll.

Tollman booked him in and came forward to escort him to a cell. Before he left, Harper leaned close to Walker's ear and whispered, 'Wetherby Road.'

It would give the man something to think about until they were ready to interview him.

TWENTY-THREE

A n hour. Harper kept pulling out his watch, seeing the second hand drag by and the minutes pass slowly. Someone brought him a cup of tea. He took a single sip then left it sitting on his desk to grow cold.

A packet of Woodbines sat in front of him. He lit one, blowing out smoke but barely tasting it, willing time to pass. Reed had taken one of the detective constables to question the Sadlers down in the cells. That was fine; he'd come back with answers. Harper needed silence. He needed to think.

Finally he was ready. He glanced at the dial one last time. An hour, right to the minute. He stood, pulled down his jacket, straightened his tie and ran a hand over his hair. At the door he gave a nod to Tollman as he passed.

There was a small deal table in the interview room, the wood scarred with dozens of names and dates and obscenities. Harper sat on one of the hard chairs, the one in shadow. Sunlight streamed in, and the window was closed and barred, leaving the room airless and stuffy.

Walker came readily, standing tall, still wearing the handcuffs. He smiled breezily as the constable escorted him to the empty, battered chair. It had one leg slightly shorter than the others, just enough to move awkwardly when someone shifted his weight. The sun through the window hit him full on the face.

'Wetherby Road,' Harper began.

'You said that earlier. What about it?' There was a gruff, hoarse quality to his voice.

'We were out there earlier. Found three girls in the place and a couple by the name of Sadler.'

Walker shrugged. The chair tilted and he slid a little, moving his feet to steady himself. 'So?'

'It belongs to a Mr Albert Walker.'

'Never heard of him.'

'Really?' The inspector gazed at him with interest. 'You're sure of that, Tosh?'

'Positive.' Walker's mouth was a firm, straight line.

'That's funny. According to the people who worked on that house last year, he's supposed to be your brother.'

'I don't have a brother.'

'I know that.' He let the sentence hang in the air for a fraction of a sentence. 'So who were the hard men you had there working for? The ones who beat the labourers up when they asked for what they'd been promised.'

'You done?' Walker began to rise. Harper reached across, put a hand on the man's shoulder and forced him back down. The chair teetered; Walker had to steady it again. 'I'm saying no more until my lawyer's here.'

Harper nodded at the constable. He opened the door and Laurence Curtis bustled in. He was a round, tidy man, in his sixties if he was a day. His white beard was neatly trimmed, eyes sharp and quizzical behind a pair of spectacles. He looked every inch the lawyer, from the worn leather of his bag to the black frock coat and neat tie under the wing collar.

'Fetch a chair for Mr Curtis,' Harper said and the constable dashed off to obey.

'What grounds do you have for dragging my client here through the streets, Inspector?' He sounded reasonable enough, almost friendly, with just the smallest hint of menace underneath the rich, educated tones.

Harper took his time replying, waiting until Curtis was seated, the tails of his jacket parted gracefully behind him. He let the silence build. Then:

'Child prostitution. Possibly rape. A murder or two, perhaps.'

He saw the colour flush through the lawyer's face. 'This isn't a time to be making jokes, Mr Harper.'

'The three little girls we rescued from a house this morning didn't find it funny either.'

'I want time with my client,' Curtis said.

'I'll give you a quarter of an hour.' He took out the watch. 'You have until half past.'

Harper and Reed sat in Kendall's office, waiting for him to start. He moved a pipe between his hands then set it down on his desk, next to his tobacco pouch.

'Just his wife and servants out at the house,' the superintendent said. 'You know what she's like, she's harder than Tosh. Nothing incriminating that I could find. I left a couple of uniforms to bring it all in.' He paused, picked up the empty pipe and sucked on it. 'Someone else had been there, though. An extra cup, tea still warm. And another bed that had been slept in. Whoever it was must have left just before we went in.'

'The boxer's friend,' said Harper. 'I'd put money on it.'

'Probably.' His voice was flat and dark. 'But how did he know we were coming?'

'Walker's clerk or his lawyer, possibly.'

'Maybe,' Kendall agreed doubtfully. 'Have you got anything from Tosh?'

'Not yet. Curtis is with him.'

The superintendent snorted. 'What about the couple from the house?' he asked.

'Still saying they don't know Tosh.'

'So we've got nothing at all,' Kendall said.

'Not yet,' Harper told him. 'If there are bodies up at that house, the Sadlers will talk. And we haven't talked to the girls we brought out of the house yet. They might be able to recognize Tosh.'

'That's if and might, Tom.'

'I know,' he admitted, slowly releasing out a long breath. 'Councillor Cromwell could have given us the link to Tosh and the killing at the Town Hall.'

'Cromwell killed himself,' Kendall reminded him coldly.

'Walker visited him before he shot himself.'

'That won't mean anything in court and you know it.'

Harper nodded reluctantly.

'I'm taking over the interview with Walker,' Kendall decided.

'Sir?' Harper could feel himself bristling. He'd discovered all this. He'd brought Tosh in, he wanted to draw the man's guilt from him.

The superintendent raised his hand to stop any protest. 'Think about it for a minute. You're the one who knows everything that's going on, Tom. I need you to put it all together, to look after the pieces.'

'Yes, sir.'

'Keep pushing that couple,' Kendall ordered Reed. 'They're the ones most likely to crack. But watch yourself.' He gathered up pipe and pouch, stuffing them into the pocket of his jacket, and stood. 'Right,' he said, 'we know they're guilty. Let's make them admit it.'

He didn't want to stay in the office, waiting for news, for anything that might finally send Walker to jail. He wanted to be questioning the man himself, cracking him open piece by piece. Kendall was good, he'd seen him work often enough. He was subtle and oblique. But he didn't know this case. He hadn't seen Martha Parkinson and the other girls in that house, he hadn't watched their eyes widen with terror as he opened that door, or the way they clutched each other.

He paced the room, smoking. He wanted to be doing something. Anything. Tollman brought him another cup of tea.

'Gas is back everywhere, sir,' he said, but the inspector barely heard him. He lit another Woodbine, not even able to remember when he'd put the last one out. A minute? An hour?

Finally Ash returned, coming into the office with his cap crushed under his arm.

'They're all still at the hospital, sir. They're keeping them in until tomorrow. Just for observation, they said.'

'And?' They both knew the question that lay behind the small word.

Ash cleared his throat. 'What we thought, sir. They've all been raped, over and over. The doctor was close to tears, poor lad. He said there might be some damage, he didn't know. Because they're all so small, you see. But he thought most of it would be here.' He tapped his head with a large, thick hand. 'Sir?' he asked.

'What?'

'Can I have five minutes with Bob Sadler? For Martha.' His face was hard, hands curled into fists.

'You know the answer to that,' Harper told him.

The constable nodded. 'Is Mr Reed with him?'

'Yes.'

'Happen he'll give him what he deserves, then.'

No, Harper thought. That was why there was another copper with him. The Sadlers would be safe enough. At least until they went to jail. Convicts hated anyone who used children.

'What are you going to do about those lasses, sir? I've heard about Betty Parkinson. They say she's in Menston.'

'She is.'

'I was thinking, sir.' He shifted awkwardly from one foot to the other. 'The other lasses, they can go back where they came from. But Martha's going to need someone to look after her. Me and the missus, we've never managed to have any children. She's always wanted a little girl.'

The inspector smiled. Ash was a good man. 'I'm sure it could be arranged,' he said.

'Aye, well, we'll see, eh, sir?'

Who'd care about girls who vanished from orphanages, the unwanted ones, or little Martha from Fidelity Court? She was nobody, nothing. If Ash hadn't been worried and come to him, no one would ever have known. And they'd never have found the blackleg's killer.

He was still making sense of it all when another constable entered, the dust and dirt roughly brushed from his uniform, brown smeared over dark blue. He was one of those who'd raided the house on Wetherby Road.

'What did you find?' the inspector asked.

'Two bodies, sir. Little 'uns, no bigger than them you brought out.' His voice was broken, gulping air between sentences. 'Surgeon's on his way there. Two of the lads are still digging.'

'Thank you,' Harper said quietly. He wasn't surprised, but that didn't make it easier to hear. Alone, he sat on the edge of his desk and lit another cigarette, smoking it down until the heat began to burn his fingers before striding briskly down the corridor, heels ringing on the tiles.

He walked into a room filled with silence. Reed and the detective constable sat on one side of a table, Sadler and his wife on the other. They all looked up as he entered.

'They've found the bodies of two children in the garden,' Harper announced. He stared at Mr and Mrs Sadler. 'You're going to hang for murder.'

'We don't know anything about that,' Bob Sadler protested, his eyes wide and wild. His wife kept her gaze on her lap.

'No?' the inspector asked.

'All we did is look after the girls. We'd only been there six months.' He looked at Reed. 'I told you already.'

'And what about the visitors?' Harper asked mildly. 'You wrote down all their names, didn't you?'

'Aye,' Sadler admitted reluctantly.

'How did you know who they were?'

'A gentleman takes his jacket off and there's time to look when he's occupied elsewhere,' Sadler told him, venom in his voice.

'How often was Tosh Walker there?'

'Never.' It was Barbara Sadler who answered, her voice so quiet that Harper had to watch her lips to make out the words. 'He had nowt to do with the place.'

'I don't believe you.'

'It's the truth,' she told him, looking the inspector in the eye. 'And we had nowt to do with dead girls, neither,' she continued. 'We looked after them like they was our own.'

'Your own daughters that you sold to strangers,' Reed said in disgust. She had no answer. Harper gave the sergeant a small nod and left. If they were going to get any information, it would come from the Sadlers. There was a crack there now; all they had to do was prise it open.

He sat in the office, taking the last Woodbine from the packet. He was still there when Kendall returned, bitter frustration on his face.

'Tosh isn't saying a bloody word. Claims he doesn't know who Albert Walker is. Just sits and bloody smirks at me. Curtis says that if we don't charge him soon, we'll have to release him. I hope you have something I can use.'

'Two bodies in the garden of the house. Children.' He saw the superintendent shudder. 'They're still digging. The Sadlers say they don't know anything about that. And they claim they don't know Tosh.'

'Do you think Reed can break them?'

'Maybe,' he said after consideration. 'We spent months looking into Tosh before and we never found this house. He's hidden it well. You know what he's like, he never lets the right hand know what the left's doing. He'll have had nothing to do with the Sadlers directly. Probably nothing we can ever prove in court.'

Kendall brought his fist down hard on the wood. 'I'm not going to have the bastard make a fool of us again.'

'You might not have to,' Harper said. 'I've been thinking . . .' He reached into his jacket pocket and brought out the small book they'd found at the house in Wetherby Road. While he waited he'd made a copy of all the names in it; it was hidden away in his desk.

TWENTY-FOUR

They released Tosh Walker four hours later. Harper was standing outside Millgarth as the man emerged, Curtis at his side, and squinted up at the clear sky.

The factory chimneys around Leeds were already pouring out smoke. He could taste it on his tongue and feel it in his lungs, enough to make a man hack and cough. People were back at their work. The town chattered and clanged with the music of industry. All around there was an undercurrent of sound. A city of empire once more.

'Mr Walker,' the inspector said.

Tosh turned, smiling and looking smug. 'You'll have to do better, lad. You're not going to get me.'

'I'm arresting you for supplying children for prostitution and living off immoral earnings. I'm going to have to ask you to come back into the station.'

Curtis stepped between them, holding his case close against his ample belly. 'Mr Harper, we've been through this. Superintendent Kendall was forced to release my client.'

'That was for murder.' He didn't take his eyes off Tosh. 'Some of Mr Walker's clients have decided to give evidence against him.'

It was the first time he'd seen panic on Tosh Walker's face.

'Now, sir, if you'd just come with me.'

The Sadlers had been exact in their note-taking. They'd written down not only the name of every visitor to the house, but the dates, the times and how long they'd stayed.

He watched Kendall leaf through the book, the horror rising on his face with each page. There were only twenty-three names in there. But there were councillors, including Charles Cromwell, businessmen, a clergyman and a judge. Harper didn't know why the couple had kept their record – blackmail or protection, perhaps? – but it had been complete.

'Dear God,' the superintendent said finally. 'If this gets out . . .'

'It doesn't need to, sir. Perhaps the Chief could have a word with one of two of the men in that list. In exchange for their willingness to write depositions against Tosh Walker, that book never sees the light of day.'

Kendall raised his eyebrows. 'That's blackmail, Tom.'

'That's justice, sir. And we'll be able to put Tosh away for a long time.'

The superintendent frowned, weighing the book in his hand as if it held all the heaviness of the world. Finally he nodded and went into his office, coming out with the top hat on his head.

'I'll be gone an hour or two,' he said.

'One last thing, sir.'

'What?'

'Twenty-three names, twenty-three resignations,' Harper said flatly. 'Or twenty-two. One of them's dead.'

After a moment, Kendall nodded.

The inspector went out, smelling the smoke which was taking over the air once more. He wandered around the market, buying another packet of cigarettes and smoking two of them as he walked. Given a choice, he'd have put every name on the list in jail. But that would never happen. Those men had too much power, too much influence. If he'd gone up against them, they'd have made certain everything was buried.

This way, using the chief constable, they wouldn't have that chance. He'd spent a long time sitting in the office and working it all out. And for those who baulked at losing their positions, he still had all the information. It could prove useful some day.

He passed by the café but he wasn't hungry. His stomach felt tight, every nerve taut, anger and anticipation tamped down tight. He crossed to Briggate, slipping between walls and houses through to Fidelity Court. The door to Col Parkinson's house was closed at the top of a small flight of worn stone steps, the windows blank and empty. A pair of children played, kicking a ball against a wall and paying him no attention. The night soil thrown out first thing had dried in the runnel, making the air stink of shit and piss. He passed through and out to the other side.

In a day or two he'd take Martha to see Betty Parkinson. Both mother and daughter deserved that. The girl would have a home with Ash and his wife. Somewhere to grow up safe and loved. And the other two girls? Just as the constable had said, back to the orphanage and Beckett Street. It wasn't much, but it would be better than Wetherby Road. Anything would be.

By the time he returned to the station, there was a report on his desk. They'd uncovered a total of four bodies from the garden. The police surgeon confirmed they were all girls, every one under the age of ten, in the ground for more than three months, probably closer to a year. Who had they been, Harper wondered? What were their names? Was anyone missing them and hoping they'd return? He'd find out. Sooner or later he'd be able to name the dead.

As Kendall returned, he gestured for the inspector to follow into his office.

'Close the door,' he ordered as he settled behind his desk.

'What did the chief say, sir?'

Kendall straightened his tie and took out the pipe, filling it with quick, deft movements, then struck a match, puffed and let it draw before he answered.

'What you'd expect. He talked to two of the men when I was in his office. They've both agreed that Walker offered them the girls, and they're willing to put that in writing as long as their names don't come out.'

'And resignations?'

'They agreed to that, too. Reluctantly. The chief's going to go around the others. You'll be able to read about them all going in the paper. There'll be speculation of a scandal, you know.'

'The papers can think what they want. They won't know the truth.'

'We'll let Tosh go. You can wait outside and arrest him again. I think you deserve the pleasure, Tom.'

He took Walker by the arm, his grip firm around the man's elbow. As they pushed through the doors, Walker leaned into him and spoke quietly.

'You think you've got the kingpin, Tommy boy. But you haven't. Not even bloody close. You just wait and see. It'll take time, but you'll find out.'

TWENTY-FIVE

He woke, and for a moment didn't know where he was. This wasn't the Victoria. He sat up in bed, mind clearing; he was in his old lodgings, for one final night.

Light poured through the thin curtains. He took the watch from the table at the side of the bed: almost seven. He couldn't recall when he'd slept so late. He glanced over to the new suit hanging on the front of the wardrobe, pale grey worsted, beautiful, light against his body, as perfect as a tailor could make.

'Stitched it myself,' Moses Cohen told him when he'd gone for a fitting on Tuesday. 'Take a little in here,' he said, fingers in the waistband, 'a good roll on the collar when we press it.' He smiled and nodded with satisfaction. 'For one day you look like a lord.'

He'd bought a new shirt from the Co-op on Albion Street, glistening white, the collar stiff and sharp enough to cut him, a new tie, even a pair of spats to set everything off. When he'd put everything on the night before he almost didn't recognize himself. The man in the mirror looked prosperous.

There was a jug of hot water outside the door, the way Mrs Gibson liked to organize it every morning. He stropped the blade and shaved carefully, running a hand over his chin to feel for any roughness, and trimmed his moustache with a pair of scissors.

By eight he'd eaten the eggs and bacon the landlady had bought. He was dressed and ready. The licence was in his jacket pocket. He had money, a handkerchief, everything he needed. He sat for a minute then was back on his feet, pacing around the room, eager for time to pass. He smoked a Woodbine, staring out at the buses and carts on Chapeltown Road. The day was already hot, not a cloud in the sky.

He couldn't see why Annabelle had made him sleep here the night before. It was no more than some ridiculous superstition. But she'd been adamant about it.

'Everyone knows it's bad luck to see the bride before the wedding,' she said when he complained. 'Anyway, I've taken care of it – I had a word with the landlady where you used to live. She'll put you up for the night. You just make sure you're at the register office for eleven.'

And he would be. He wound his watch for the third time that morning and slipped it back into his waistcoat pocket. Three more hours as a single man and there was nothing he wanted to do.

An hour later, still restless, he was ready to leave; all he was doing was pacing grooves into the floor. He presented himself at the landlady's door for her approval.

'You look a picture, luv,' she said, eyeing him up and down. 'More handsome than my Alan when we were wed. I hope that lass of yours knows how lucky she is.' She rose on tiptoe and kissed his cheek, leaving the smell of lavender water on his skin.

He walked into town, strolling, trying to stretch time. But three quarters of an hour later he was already at the market, buying a white rose to wear in his buttonhole. He'd considered stopping in at Millgarth to let them all see him in his best clothes. But in the last few days he'd spent too long there, preparing the case against Tosh Walker. Every night he'd worked long into the evening, checking then checking again that everything would be watertight, that the man wouldn't wriggle out of a long sentence in Armley.

Billy Reed was already in Park Square, sitting on a bench and reading the *Leeds Mercury*. Harper flopped down beside him. The sergeant glanced over quickly, then again.

'Bloody hell, Tom, what did you do, steal a rich man's suit?'

'Nice, isn't it?'

'Has Annabelle seen it?'

'Not yet.' He snapped open the watch. Barely ten o'clock. He lit another cigarette, watching the smoke rise and shimmer in the light.

'You'd better watch out. She might expect you to dress like that all the time.' He paused. 'Still, you'll look the part when they make you a superintendent.'

Harper laughed long and loud enough for people to turn and stare. 'Don't be so daft. I've got the wrong accent and the wrong politics. And the right enemies now. They're never going to promote me again.'

'You took down Tosh Walker.'

'Maybe. I'll wait until he's sentenced before I celebrate.'

The hackney arrived at eleven on the dot. Dan the barman climbed down, the first time Harper had even seen him in a suit and tie. He reached up to help Annabelle. Then she was there, in a pale cream dress that captured the sunlight, clutching a bouquet, a veil of lace covering the hair that had been combed up high on her head.

She smiled as she saw him and he reached out to take her hand.

'I always knew you'd scrub up well,' she said.

It seemed to be over almost before it had begun. The guests were all on time. His sisters brought their father, an old shell of a man who no longer recognized his own son or even his own name, helped by their husbands and children. Annabelle's brother and sister were there, spouses in tow, everyone gazing at the bride in astonishment. They stood and took their vows, a rush of words, he placed the ring on her finger, then she was Mrs Annabelle Harper and he was kissing her, feeling her lips cool against his. He heard one of his sisters crying quietly.

She'd taken care of everything, the photographer waiting outside, posing them into stillness for a picture, three cabs waiting at the kerb to take them all back to the Victoria. Weeks before, when he'd suggested luncheon at a hotel instead, she'd simply shaken her head.

'Tom, I own a pub and two bakeries. Why in God's name would we want to put good brass into someone else's pocket?'

By four, Harper's jacket was off, tie loosened, waistcoat unbuttoned. The bar was filled, more friends than family. Kendall and his wife sat off by themselves in a corner, a full schooner of sherry in front of each of them. Reed was talking earnestly to a regular from the Victoria who'd served in the army. The food was long gone and the men were intent on demolishing the fresh cask of beer, while their wives drank the gin.

He walked through the etched glass door into the tiny snug, astonished to see Tom Maguire there, holding court with two or three men listening to his every word.

'Surprised to see me, Inspector?' he asked with a grin.

'Very.' He looked around. At the mention of his rank, the others had vanished. He bent his head slightly to hear over the noise in the pub. 'How do you know Annabelle?'

'She was a friend of my older sister, God rest her soul. Grew up on the next street.' He raised his glass in a toast. 'I'd say you're a lucky man to have Mrs Harper.'

'I can't disagree with you there.'

'I ran into her during the week,' Maguire told him. 'That's when she invited me. She has some interesting ideas, that good wife of yours. Talking about lending money to those who need it.' He took a swallow of his beer.

'What did you say?'

'First I told her it was madness.' He smiled. 'Then I said that if a man thinks he's getting something for nothing, he'll value it that way. I let her know she'd need to charge a little interest for people to take her seriously.'

'What did she do?'

'Nodded and thought about it. She was like that when she was younger, too.' Someone began playing a piano in the saloon bar and voices joined in on *When You Wink The Other Eye*. 'That sounds like our signal to join the others, don't you think? And my congratulations again, Mr Harper. I envy you, truly I do.'

It was two hours later that his sisters took him aside, pushing small presents into his hand, telling him he'd married a lovely girl. He knew that. She was over by the bar, half-listening as her own sister's husband loudly set the world to rights. He caught her eye and nodded at the door. She smiled, made her excuses. He took her hand as they climbed the stairs.

'Happy, Mrs Harper?'

She pulled him close and kissed him.

'I am. And I'll be even happier when I take off this corset. It's killing me.'

AFTERWORD

There really was a gas strike in Leeds in 1890 and the workers did win. They had to make a few minor concessions, but it was essentially a total victory and a humiliation for the Gas Committee of Leeds Council.

Tom Maguire did work with the union and he was also a photographer's assistant. A relatively unsung Leeds radical and early socialist, he was also a published poet who died, too young, in 1895.

The character of Annabelle is based on a distant relative of mine – or at least on my father's stories of her, although the real person lived a good twenty-five years later. She did rise from servant to mistress at the Victoria in Sheepscar (which now sadly no longer exists) and owned several bakeries. My father wrote a novel about her that was never published, so this is my homage to them both.

Several people read an early version of this, and I'm grateful to Laura Woods, Rev David Messer, Nevine Henein and others for their thoughts and time. Thanks to everyone at Severn House/ Crème de la Crime for their faith, especially Kate Lyall Grant, Michelle Duff and Rachel Simpson who all work tirelessly for their authors. I truly appreciate it. Also much gratitude to my editor and friend, Lynne Patrick, and to my writing guru, Thom Atkinson. Perhaps he's finally starting to receive the credit for his work that's long overdue. Last, but not least, to Leeds Libraries, the Leeds Library and to Leeds Book Club for their ongoing support. And to Penny, of course.

Thanks also to you for reading this.